Long Walk
Home

BOOKS BY ELLYN OAKSMITH

Summer at Orchard House
Promises at Indigo Bay

ELLYN OAKSMITH

Long Walk Home

Bookouture

Published by Bookouture in 2021

An imprint of Storyfire Ltd.
Carmelite House
50 Victoria Embankment
London EC4Y 0DZ

www.bookouture.com

ISBN: 978-1-80019-316-1
eBook ISBN: 978-1-80019-315-4

To Mauri Oaksmith. Funny, genuine, and full of life. The real deal and my Dad.

CHAPTER ONE

The Promise

Two little words could change everything. Coming Soon. The moment she typed them, her open window banged slightly in a sudden wind. Lola remembered it later, thinking it was like something out of a movie. Two little words. They were the butterflies that set off a hurricane in the Alvarez family.

The Blue Hills Winery blog was Lola's vision of the winery and restaurant. The more colorful picture of her garden and her dog, her pizza recipes. Nobody in her family read the Blue Hills Winery blog. In their eyes, it was one more of Lola's fanciful ideas that, since it didn't cost a dime, Carmen, who let's face it, was the more like the empress than the directing manager, tolerated.

Which gave Lola a lot of freedom. Maybe too much. Enough to write a blog post featuring photos of tiny cabins that she'd found on Pinterest and become more than a little obsessed with. The kind of place you could hole up in and hide from the world. The outsides were charming, with peaked roofs, blue shutters, flower boxes at the window and front porches just large enough for two chairs and a table. Perfect for a couple to relax and share a bottle of wine after a long day of hiking, or swimming, or lazing at the beach. Later, Lola would wonder if the whole thing came about because she was the one who needed to escape.

Either way, it happened.

The butterfly flapped its tiny wings.

Lola distinctly remembered re-reading the post. Looking out the window before she hit publish. It was unseasonably warm. Her window was open, the smell of apples, sharp and sweet, drifting in from the orchard. A glass of wine at her elbow. The fortunate—or unfortunate—caption below the post about the tiny cabins (they always must be prefaced with a "tiny"; Lola instinctively knew this was part of their charm, the minute aspect) had been: "COMING SOON."

She'd hiked up to the top of the orchard, the place she alone called Daisy Hollow. She'd stood, with her dog, also named Daisy, at the idyllic spot where she'd last been one hundred percent utterly happy. She'd snapped a photo of the view.

To be fair, she'd known that anyone staying in this spot would be given a respite from ordinary life. Although it was on the winery estate, it was removed from the main buildings by a long steep slope. The rows of vines provided privacy and acted as a sound barrier. The hollow was a world unto itself. It was a community service, this blog post. She was willing to share Daisy Hollow with the world. Looking down from these heights would infuse even the weariest soul with a renewed appreciation for life. The vantage was from the highest spot in the orchard, snug against the striated cliff that was home to nesting owls and bats, who lived in the scrubby vegetation growing from the red soil, coming out to hunt in the orchard at night. Guarded by the cliffs, the orchards of Blue Hills spread like a lush velvet mantle down the hill, stopping at Orchard House, where the restaurant, built onto what used to be the master suite on the east side of the house, overlooked the lake. Below Orchard House was the old orchard, and across a narrow street, Lake Chelan.

From this lookout, the lake wound around a point until it vanished over the horizon into the North Cascades. The neighboring vineyard, Hollister Estate, was to the east. Lola's sister, Carmen, was marrying Evan Hollister this summer. Her wedding planning, combined with managing the Blue Hills Winery, was keeping her in a suspended state of stress that was three levels higher than her normal Type A frenetic behavior. She was unbearable to be around. Even more than usual.

Life at Orchard House had become a pressure cooker. The upside of Carmen being utterly consumed with her wedding plans was that it created a little more room for Lola to think. Maybe this was the perfect time to make her mark on the family business. Carmen's attention to detail had been split.

She'd hit publish on the blog post, sending her post out to her subscribers, thinking it was nothing more than a dream. The window banged. She'd wedged a ruler under it. Shut off the computer. Went to bed.

The next day she'd logged on and been shocked at the number of comments, rolling in even as she watched. People were really interested in the tiny cabins. They wanted in. When were they open? How could they book? Could they book all three for apple picking season? Were they heated?

Which was why, in the beginning, when Marcus had called, she'd listened.

She'd been at the beach across the lake from Blue Hills in Manson, throwing sticks for Daisy, when her phone had rung. Marcus was a PE teacher who'd stayed at Orchard House two summers ago as part of a grass roots effort to bring in the harvest at the winery when Lola's father, suffering from Alzheimer's, had nearly lost the business. In truth, it was a miracle Marcus had even stayed in touch. Carmen had framed the work party as a farm-to-table culinary vacation. In reality, it had been hard manual labor. Long days picking grapes in the hot sun. As Papi had said, why would people pay to do work that Mexicans like him had used to claw their way up the immigrant ladder?

But thanks to Carmen, it had worked. They'd brought in the harvest. Paid off the bank enough to keep going. Started the restaurant the following year. They were finally in the black.

"I think the cabins would be amazing. I'm dying to come back there. Staying at an actual winery was incredible! And that view!" Marcus enthused.

"They're not built yet," Lola admitted, wrestling the damp driftwood from the mouth of her mutt, an Australian Shepherd mix with one blue and one brown eye. Daisy cocked her head at Lola, body tense and coiled.

Lola couldn't very well tell Marcus that Carmen was dead set against any diversion of cash. That she felt she'd branched out enough with the restaurant. That was the part that stuck, like a thorn, in Lola's side. When Carmen spoke of the business end of the winery, it was always as if it was hers alone. There wasn't even a pretense that Lola had a say.

When Mami had died, Lola had been thirteen. Carmen, two years older, had been the one to wake up Lola and supervise homework while Papi had wandered around the house for six months like a man at sea. Carmen was the middle daughter, but while the eldest, Adella, was their leader when it came to comfort and nurturing, assuming household chores and bagging their lunches, Carmen's nature was to keep the ball rolling. Supervisor had suited Carmen's personality just as Lola's suited playing the rebel. Now Lola was a rebel with a cause.

"Take out a loan," Marcus said, with the enthusiasm of someone with no skin in the game.

Lola tossed the stick far out into the water. Daisy plunged fearlessly, bounding until she was paddling, zeroing in on the stick. Lola walked down the beach. "I can't." Not without Carmen's signature. "Not right now."

"Take reservations and use the money to build the cabins. They can be your first guests. Angel investors. People love to be on the ground floor of things like this. I can spread the word if you like. Post it on the blog."

Lola felt her heart leap at the thought of having ownership of something this unique. Of making her mark on the winery and not having her every contribution disappear down the throats of guests as a line chef at the winery restaurant. Cooking was her passion but working with Neil had tainted the kitchen. Tiny cabins would allow her whole self to shine. She could see them already. Why else had she been haunting Pinterest, poring over photos of tiny cabins like a pregnant woman gazing at babies? She could make them her own. Show her family that she could create something of value on their land. Take ownership. She needed this.

"Thank you, Marcus. That's a great—" Lola felt a tap on her leg. She looked down to see a little girl in a damp bathing suit. Puzzled, she followed the girl's pointing finger toward the blue lake. Daisy had bypassed the stick and was swimming, paws churning ferociously, towards the middle of the lake. She was almost out of the protected waters of Manson Bay. "Marcus, I'll call you back!"

Lola thanked the little girl and sprinted to a man in a speedboat pulling up to the city dock, waving her arms frantically. "My dog is in the middle of the lake! She just took off!" She was breathless with fear. How many high school kids towing wakeboarders were out there on the water?

"Get in!" the man said.

The rescue wasn't without its struggles. Like her owner, Daisy didn't give up easily. The man was kind. He turned off the motor and held Lola awkwardly off the side of the boat as they drifted close to the dog. It took three passes until Lola could reach around the dog's front legs, pull her to the side of the boat and, with help, lift her aboard. Daisy promptly vomited lake water onto both her rescuers, collapsing into Lola's arms with relief.

"What was she doing out there, anyway?" the man asked.

Lola explained: Daisy, a rescue dog who'd shown up at the winery and adopted her, was like a homing pigeon. If she knew that home was across the lake, she'd go there. Daisy, like her owner, had a finely tuned sense of belonging. Home, no matter how long it took to get there, was a place worth the struggle.

She couldn't help it, Lola realized. Any more than Lola could help the need to create something of her own. It was in her nature.

*

A month and half later, after a long shift in the kitchen, putting up with Horrible Neil, Lola tracked Carmen down in the winery office, high up in the vineyard above the house. The hike up to the winery should have calmed her down. The damp smell of soil mixed with ripening grapes usually gave her a sense of peace, but she was sick of having the same old conversation with Carmen.

Carmen glanced up from the computer. Before Lola could say anything, she glanced at Daisy, who stood at Lola's feet, unwilling to separate herself from her owner. "Um, can the dog stay outside?"

Her tone was so snarky. Why not say *Daisy*?

"Sure," Lola said, simply pointing to the door. *The dog* reluctantly got it. She didn't want to be around Carmen any more than Carmen wanted her around. Daisy wasn't one of those dogs who needed everyone to love her. She was an independent soul.

Carmen gave Lola a tight smile. "If it's about Neil, the answer is no. We've been over this a thousand times. He's good for business."

"His Instagram followers alone have doubled our business," they both said at the same time.

It was Carmen's favorite line. Her self-proclaimed stroke of genius: a summer "artist in residence" program, offering famous chefs a summer in Chelan, cooking at their winery. Driven as she was, Lola had to hand it to Carmen. She was a marketing whiz. Prior to quitting to save Blue Hills Winery, Carmen had been on the fast track to Senior Director at a big deal Seattle tech marketing firm. At first Lola had wondered why a chef would want to come to sleepy Chelan until she she'd made it sound like heaven on a plate. And if Neil hadn't been so busy berating the staff for not meeting his big city standards, he could have left early and come in late, availing himself of the blue skies and turquoise water as Carmen had suggested. Carmen didn't have to deal with a chef who wouldn't adjust.

"It's not about Neil," Lola said, although Felicia and she had been planting their iPhones around the kitchen, trying to catch him in the act of being a colossal creep.

Carmen rubbed her eyes, grimacing. "It's about the cabins."

They'd had the same argument approximately a thousand times. Or so it felt. Lola argued that five tiny cabins would bring in business. She laid out the whole thing, again, promising that all she needed was a little money to start. She'd buy a golf cart and ferry fresh baked goods to their guests before starting her shift in the restaurant. She'd manage the cleaning staff, the reservations, the whole thing. The cabins would be heated, so guests could stay in the winter—cross-country skiers, and families whose children could sled in the orchard or hike in the snowy hills. They could build a fire pit and leave kits for s'mores. Bridal parties could stay in the cabins, and they'd ferry the bride by golf cart down to the winery for the ceremony. There were so many wonderful possibilities, not to mention Instagram-worthy moments. By the time she finished her pitch, Lola could see the tiny cabins as if they already existed in their minute perfection. Shrines to her vision. Her tenacity. Her ability to talk Carmen into something. Anything.

"All you'd have to do is sign the checks."

"Lola, Lola, Lola," Carmen said, taking off her computer glasses and leaning back in her office chair. Her tone was so condescending,

Lola wanted to scream. "'All you'd have to do is sign the checks.' Like it's so simple. We just paid off the bank and we're in the black. The restaurant is doing really well, thanks to Neil. Why would we add an expense at this point? When we're finally in the clear?"

When she'd first conceived of the idea, Lola had made a PowerPoint presentation for Carmen with spreadsheets on how long it would take to recoup the cost of the cabin construction. She'd included photos and statistics from similar businesses. Granted, none of them were on an actual, large scale vineyard, but she'd done her homework. The first time she'd asked Carmen if she'd gotten the email, Carmen had just mumbled something as she was signing a grocery order. The second time, Lola had gotten an, "Oh yeah." The third time, Carmen had snapped something about how many emails she got per day. Lola didn't think Carmen had ever opened the PowerPoint.

It hurt. Made her double down on her desire, her resentment, and her fervent need to prove to the family that her projects were worthy. That her contribution to the family business meant something. There wasn't any point, Lola decided, in asking Carmen again about the presentation. It would hurt more to know she'd clicked on the slides, and still decided it wasn't sustainable.

To Carmen, Lola would always be the little sister. The flaky one who'd dropped out of art school. Never mind that Lola had worked backbreaking hours in the kitchen ever since it had opened, and continued to do so even though Carmen had hired an egotistical drama queen who liked to corner female subordinates in the walk-in refrigerator. Who had a way of brushing up against female staff in an accidentally-on-purpose way. Who called Felicia and Lola "his girls," which made Lola bite her lip so hard that sometimes it bled.

The bottom line was that Carmen always thought she knew better. Would always think she knew better. Lola would always be her little sister. Second.

Which was why, when the email from Marcus's friend had arrived, asking how to get involved, Lola hadn't hit delete. Hadn't responded that no, they weren't taking reservations because the tiny cabins didn't exist. Instead, she'd made a file called "Tiny Cabins Investors." It was strangely satisfying, having that file. Today, when Neil was particularly horrible, it had comforted Lola. As if keeping a secret from Carmen, knowing what she was going to do, was her private little revolt.

It felt delicious.

A hint of her old, rebellious self.

Marcus had unknowingly pried opened a little crack. A tiny bit of daylight, which opened the possibility of doing this without Carmen. One part revenge for Horrible Neil, and two parts sheer, exhilarating freedom. Lola had hemmed herself into Carmen's ideas of what Blue Hills should look like—which was a clone of every successful winery in Washington. Weddings, wine tastings and a restaurant, if you were lucky enough to live in a tourist destination. That was it. It was a formula, Carmen had often reminded Lola, that worked. A winning formula.

And Lola had twisted herself into Carmen's vision like a pretzel. Worked herself to the bone in the kitchen, only to have Carmen hire Neil, sight unseen, without saying a word to her except, "Oh yeah, I hired this amazing chef. He starts in two weeks. Check out his Insta."

Lola had continued to write about the beauty of the tiny cabin experience. The simplicity. How the cabins put you in nature without you having to actually sleep on the ground.

Like the original plan to save Blue Hills Winery, Lola planned on inviting people to become part of the winery experience. Invest in the cabins and have first dibs when the summer reservations opened. Enjoy free breakfasts their first morning. Vote on the artwork to go on the cabin walls. The ideas wouldn't stop coming.

One day, on a whim, when she was in Chelan, Lola stopped at a bank and opened her own business account. She came out onto the hot sidewalk of Woodin Avenue, blinking in the daylight, shocked at how easy it had been. The account sat there until she linked a Square online business account, gathering courage as she sat at the hard blue-coated tables outside the Lakeside Drive-thru, eating French fries. She came home and opened her Tiny Cabin file. There were forty-five people who wanted to make a reservation. Forty-five people who were willing to buy into a business that she'd created.

The rest had been shockingly easy.

Once she had other people buying into the idea, Lola didn't look back. Daisy Hollow was so much more than a beautiful spot on the Blue Hills vineyard. Something in Lola wanted to build more memories on the place where she'd fallen in love and shared so many secrets.

The last carefree night they'd had, without sneaking around, it had been summer. Gus's old truck had rumbled up the driveway to Orchard House, bouncing them both like marbles. Earlier, there had been a beach bonfire. They'd laughed and sung, howling at the moon with the sheer pleasure of being alive. Lola had dragged Gus to the edge of the water, handed him a flat stone and challenged him to a rock skipping contest. Their rocks had tripped along the smooth surface of water, lit by a moon that seemed to hang in the sky for their enjoyment alone. It had been one of those summer nights when their future had seemed to unfurl before them like a ribbon with smooth, silky promise.

At Orchard House, Gus had spilled out of the driver's seat, racing around to the passenger side to open the door.

"My lady." He'd bowed, nearly toppling over, laughing too loudly.

Lola had tumbled out, but Gus had caught her, wrapping an arm around her waist, holding her upright.

She'd known something was wrong by the look on his face.

Papi, who'd been waiting on the patio, stepped out of the shadows telling Lola to go to her room, saying he'd talk to her later. She'd been afraid of him, but still she'd refused, knowing what was coming. She'd stayed and seen the whole ugly thing, knowing it would stay in her brain like a dark stain, a blot. Papi, yelling at Gus, saying he could have killed Lola, driving drunk. Gus, insisting he wasn't drunk. Lola had known he'd only had one beer, but had he smoked weed too? How many times had she glimpsed him slipping out a side door at a party, returning loose-limbed and smiley? She'd hated it.

"Don't lie to me!" Papi had yelled.

"We were drinking beer."

Papi had pointed his finger at Gus. "I know where you come from, Gus. That you haven't seen how a man honors his family. Protects his family. And for that, I am truly sorry. But I am that kind of man, and I will go to hell before I let you take my daughter down the road you're traveling." He'd pointed at Lola. "My girls are all I have, Gus, and you are putting my daughter's life in danger. Too many kids die on these roads."

"I would never put her life in danger, sir." But then Gus had done a dumb thing. He'd smiled. That's when she knew he'd smoked. Stupid. Stupid. It cost them so much. She didn't know it then, but it was the beginning of the end. Gus was unraveling.

"You are drunk right now. If I ever see you again with Lola, or on my property, I will kill you. Don't come near her, or so help me God, I'll tear you apart. And nobody would think twice."

Gus Weaver pulled the truck over near a sign that said, "WELCOME TO CHELAN." Apples, the lake, and a girl waving while water skiing. Dated, but charming. Like his hometown. He took a deep breath as the old truck coughed a little, as if the drive from Seattle had taken the wind out her. After a few long moments gazing at the farm-flanked corridor that led to the faux winery housing developments and then the lake, Gus pressed down on the accelerator, giving the old girl a shot of fuel. She was a gas-guzzling hunk of iron held together by rust and prayer. Somehow or another, he'd been nursing her along since high school. His cousin had brought her to Seattle for him a few years back. He was glad to be in the familiar truck now, because driving her back to Chelan felt like the end of the longest journey of his life.

His family, and all those hard complications. Of wanting to belong, but not wanting to assume the mantle of Weaver, which meant being one of a hard-scrabble clan that you spent your life running from, not to. That was, if you wanted to live past middle age and not live at the bottom of a bottle. Gus had had to have so many normal life things explained to him over the years: the concept of taking a car into the garage before it fell apart, of cooking vegetables, of going to a dentist regularly. All the things that other people took for granted. The first time he'd seen someone take off their shoes before entering a house, he'd thought the man had gone mad. Feral. A good word for the Weaver clan. One they'd embrace.

This approach to Chelan there was nothing but a few scrubby bushes, but Gus knew that when he continued down the slope, he'd see the lake. Ten long years had passed since he'd last seen the lake. He'd grown from a headstrong, angry teen to a steady, strong man. Still, coming back here brought up so many memories. The only good ones were with Lola. As always, the thought of her calmed him, like taking a deep breath. If he was honest with himself, Lola was the reason he'd come back—but Gus couldn't admit that to anyone, least of all to himself. It had been ten long years. Too long to hope for anything. Besides, he'd left Chelan in true Weaver style. In the back of a police van. Nobody in town would have forgotten it.

Gus put the truck in gear, checking his rear-view mirror and pulling into traffic. The old truck and the young man made their descent into the valley. His first glimpse of the lake caught in his throat. The shimmering aquamarine water danced in the long rays of the late day sun. The closer he got, the prettier the scenery became, with vineyards and orchards flanking the lake shores. Gus reached lake level and passed Pat and Mike's gas station. He drove to the right, down the lake, until he'd reached the stone bridge that led into the town of Chelan, with its old brick storefronts and quaint awnings. Gus's throat tightened with a multitude of warring emotions.

For better or worse, he was almost home.

CHAPTER TWO

The Magic Word

Chef Neil sailed into the Blue Hills restaurant kitchen holding a white plate of six scallops aloft, heading straight for Lola.

Perfect, Lola thought. Carmen was there. At last, she'd see what kind of monster she'd hired for her head chef. Carmen, who'd come in to check on a food order for a wine tasting, was tucked into the little kitchen desk typically used by the head chef in a corner behind the door, out of Neil's view. Lola faced Neil with barely suppressed glee. It was a #MeToo moment in the making, and for once her older sister, who thought Chef Neil was the best thing to happen to Blue Hills Vineyard since grapes, would witness what everyone in the Blue Hills kitchen already knew.

Lola gave Felicia, at her elbow at the salad station, a smug look. The truth would out. She'd heard enough drama students rehearsing Shakespeare to know a thing or two about exposing a villain.

Lola straightened her shoulders, looking up from the sauté station. Time vanished when working her station in a busy kitchen humming with life, producing dishes that elicited smiles and compliments from customers. Even Neil's pretentious menu, with fussy foams and overly complicated dishes (a quail's egg salad constructed in a nest of fried glass noodles), was an interesting challenge.

After having flailed for most of her early twenties, jumping from hospitality, to art, to a brief fling at a sandwich stand (it was a disaster but flirting with local farmers at open air markets had been a definite upside), Lola finally found a place for her pent-up creative energy in the kitchen. It wasn't perfect but the feeling of floating dissipated, somewhat. She loved the pressure, the heat, the camaraderie, and the creativity. She adored the pungent smell of spices, the bite of fresh herbs, the sizzle of butter as she dropped plump scallops into a hot pan. Days flew by, lost in a haze of hard, rewarding work. But under it all was loathsome Neil, her horror show of a boss.

As Neil came closer, her toes curled with excitement.

Neil had no idea that Carmen was in the kitchen. As he approached, Lola grew increasingly optimistic. Today could be the day.

Who knew, maybe Carmen would even give Lola a shot at head chef—at least temporarily, while she looked for someone else. Lola wasn't nearly experienced enough, but she had a knack for learning on the fly. Her gadfly existence had brought transferable skills.

Neil slid up to Lola now, his beefy face tight with tension. He shoved the plate of scallops under her nose, so roughly that one of them slid down beneath her white apron, making a wet spot on her T-shirt. Neil pretended not to notice, drilling his dark eyes into hers as he leaned over the stainless counter, all towering six feet of him, sandy gray hair a carefully styled mess. "What do you call this?"

Lola pulled the slippery scallop out of her apron, studying it, knowing, with a sinking heart, what this was about. Last week, Neil had insisted that the scallops be seared at the same time the pasta went into the boiling water. Which meant the scallops would be overcooked, or cold from sitting. She'd questioned it, and Neil had insisted they could be left in the cooling pan.

"A scallop," Lola said, staring at the plate slammed down so hard it was amazing it didn't crack.

Neil reached over the counter, grabbed her hand, and squished it on top of the remaining five white scallops on the appetizer plate. The plate was slick and greasy. Cold.

Lola could feel the tension ratchet upwards in the kitchen. They'd all witnessed the argument last week. Neil had told Lola that he knew scallops, and that they weren't timing the pasta correctly. Ruelle, the dishwasher, was humming, a habit of his when he was nervous or upset. Mike, the busboy, sailed into the kitchen with a load of dishes, just in time to see Neil clamping Lola's hand onto the plate of food. He recoiled backwards, bumping into Carmen's chair, apologizing profusely.

Neil's eyes went narrow as he lowered his voice, spitting saliva into her face. His breath smelled of last night's wine, acrid and sharp. "They are stone cold. Clammy and inedible." Neil took his hand off hers, shaking his head. He grabbed a cloth to wipe his hands. "It's my name on this food, kiddo. Not yours. Stop sending crap out of my kitchen. They are seared. They are hot. They go out. Time it right or get out. Stop thinking about yourself as a cook. Start thinking about yourself as *my* cook. You're on a pirate ship and I'm the captain." He waved at Felicia. "You can make salads and listen, sweetheart." He picked up the plate, sliding its contents onto Lola's workstation, making a mess. In a commercial kitchen, a line chef's workstation was their real estate, their fiefdom. Everything about a cook could be read by their workstation. Neil had just crapped all over Lola's world.

He wasn't done.

"You've been pampered. I get it. But it's time to grow a pair. You're with me. You're in the big leagues now." Neil patted his chest. Lola opened her mouth to argue, saw his eyes narrow and gave up. "It's my food. Do it my way. Seared and hot." He nodded, moving as if to leave her station, but came back, shaking his head, placing his meaty hand over his heart—although she seriously doubted if there was anything other than a shallow cave under his rib bones. "You know I love you. I love all of you. That's why I push. If I didn't care, I would just fire you. You are amazing. I'm trying to train you the best I know how, but whoever started your education was a loser. Work on your timing, listen to what I teach you and you're going to be a sexy beast in the kitchen. You're going to be a hot chef someday. I feel it. I really do. I'm feeling your energy. So, let's do this." He clapped his hands around the kitchen, yelling. "You guys are amazing. I love you. Keep up the great work."

Lola glanced over to see if Carmen was listening. Her sister was hunched over the desk, with her typical concentration, writing something down as if her life depended on it. Probably one of her precious lists.

Neil ignored Carmen as he stalked out to the back patio where Rodolfo was working the huge stone wood-burning pizza oven that Neil had insisted they build. The pizzas were, Lola hated to admit, a huge success.

While Lola fumed, Felicia pointedly ignored her, studying an order on her iPad, taking out a salad bowl, sprinkling it with microgreens.

"Don't bother," she said, nodding towards Carmen as she briskly mixed ingredients for the chopped salad.

Lola wiped the sticky scallop residue off her hand, throwing down the towel. "She had to have heard that."

Felicia clucked her tongue, shaking her head. "You know she didn't. Neil knows exactly who is in the room and who can hear what. He's worked in kitchens his whole life." She pointed to the exhaust hood over their heads. "He knows that one fan can suck your words up like a vacuum cleaner. Carmen didn't hear anything he said, except when he raised his voice and said, 'You guys are amazing.' Don't waste your breath. We need to record him in action. Show your dad."

Lola fumed as though a black cloud hung over her head. After she'd compulsively cleaned up her workspace, eliminating every trace of Neil, wiping down the stainless counter to a spotless sheen, she marched over to Carmen.

Carmen looked up, looking pleased. Lola was right. Under Carmen's pen was one of her endless lists. "Hey. How's it going?"

Lola could feel her face flushing as she pointed back to her station. "Did you not hear any of that?"

Carmen smiled. "Oh, yeah. Neil is a team builder, right? I don't know why you and Felicia have such a hard time with him. All I hear is him trying to coach you. I know things have really heated up in here, but Lola, we are on track to having our best year ever."

Lola crossed her arms. "He's harassing us." She pointed back to the workstations. "He told me to cook the scallops too early and then got mad when he got the results I predicted."

Carmen stood up, placing her hands on Lola's shoulders. "Look, sometimes you learn the most from the toughest teachers."

Her tone was so condescending that Lola had to grit her teeth. She felt like screaming but forced herself to speak calmly. "You're not listening to me."

Carmen lifted a finger. "I do. I do. I do. But Lola, you're asking me to get rid of a guy who's not only bringing massive amounts of tourists to the winery, he's bringing us wedding business." Carmen waved her hand around the busy kitchen. "We're catering our own weddings. We're in the black for the first time in years. And no matter how much he bugs you, Neil's part of it. I'm going to ask him if he'll stay beyond the summer. Make it permanent."

Lola slapped her hand over her face. "Shoot me now."

Carmen crossed her arms. "Don't be melodramatic."

"What part of the word 'harassment' don't you believe?"

"What I see is a somewhat rough-around-the-edges team builder."

Lola waved her arms around the kitchen. She could tell that the staff, although they were all busily working, hung onto their every word. If you weren't eavesdropping in a commercial kitchen, you'd be next on the chopping block. "You're not here, in the kitchen."

Carmen's Apple Watch dinged. "I've got a meeting at the winery office. Have tried on your bridesmaid dress yet?"

"Yes," Lola fibbed as Carmen headed out the kitchen door onto the patio. Lola didn't even know if she wanted to be in Carmen's wedding. Yes, it was passive aggressive, refusing to try on the dumb dress, but she didn't care. Carmen's whole life was running the winery and planning her wedding to Evan Hollister, the guy next door who knew he was marrying a Type A high maintenance workaholic and adored her anyway. Her life was set. How hard would it be for her to stop for one second and really listen?

Carmen turned back, grabbing her hand. "Look, I know it's hard to work for someone with a big personality. I get it. But hang on. Good things will happen, Lola. I know they will."

Lola gritted her teeth to stop the torrent of angry words she felt building up. What a bunch of trite baloney. Exactly the kind of thing people say when they want to keep the status quo. Yes, the ship might be sinking, but good things are coming your way. Yes, the Great Depression is really a bummer, but happy days are right around the corner.

"Lola, he might be hard to work for but he's doing exactly what he promised," Carmen continued. "Bringing in tons of customers and running a catering business on top of that. I can't say no to that kind of income. Anyway, even if I did want to get rid of him, which I don't, he's catering my wedding."

Lola sighed, her shoulders drooping in defeat. "*I* should be catering your wedding."

Carmen squeezed her arm. "Lola, some day you will be an amazing head chef. Give it time. Listen to Neil. You might learn something."

Half an hour later, Lola was still fuming, hissing to herself, "You might learn something," as she scraped a lemon with a zester, sprinkling the pungent peel over a plate of rainbow trout before adding some crispy sweet potato fries. She sprinkled the entire plate with a shower of Maldon salt and paused to enjoy the bright colors, textures and tantalizing aroma of the food before it was swooped up by the wait staff and carried into the restaurant.

Felicia kept up the steady work of making salad and appetizers, listening to Lola grumble. Felicia had worked in five commercial kitchens since high school. Neil wasn't anything new for her. The difference was that Lola believed that she could actually do something about him.

Lola was still muttering under her breath when Papi strode through the restaurant door. "Come on. In here." He beckoned a reluctant visitor into the kitchen.

"Hola, Señor Alvarez!"

"Señor, hola!"

"Cómo estás?"

Papi was always greeted like a visiting celebrity. Her father, a smiling, congenial man in his early seventies with a thick head of salt and pepper hair, was universally adored. Papi had time for everyone and treated everyone with the same respect. A man who ran a large winery was treated the same as the migrant pickers who worked his fields. Mike, the busboy, passed Papi as he hurried towards the dining room. Papi patted his back with congenial enthusiasm. He waved to everyone else with his customary graciousness.

His visitor, a handsome man in his early thirties, shifted uncomfortably in his flip-flops, pushing back his thick black hair from his forehead. He shoved his hand in his cargo shorts pockets, looking confused as to why the friendly old man had dragged him here.

Lola wished for the second time that day that she could sink into the kitchen tiles. Why, oh why, oh why did she have to work in a family business? Was there anything worse than her father trying to fix her up in front of her colleagues? She'd never hear the end of it. The reason she knew Papi was fixing her up now was because he did this. All. The. Damn. Time.

"Lola, come here. I have someone for you to meet." Papi beckoned as if he were the foreman on the factory floor with some important matter that needed attending to. It didn't occur to him that this was Lola's place of work. To Papi, it was his home. His kitchen.

Lola ducked her head, fuming. She chopped away furiously, making sure her knuckles were pulled back so she didn't cut a finger. Papi wouldn't dream of poking his head into the winery office to pester Carmen. But Lola was right here. Available, in every sense of the word. Which was why Papi was standing in the middle of Lola's workplace, trying to set her up. Like the rest of her family, Papi thought he could manage her life better than she could. Going so far as to try to find Lola a boyfriend.

Again.

Lola's family was driving her nuts.

While Papi patiently waited, Lola mixed the bowls of pasta with herby olive oil and cheese.

"One second, Papi," Lola shouted above the kitchen din.

"Hola, Señor Alvarez." Felicia was busy plating an appetizer of labneh, garlic roasted cauliflower, fried saffron squash blossoms and some of her famous home baked seed crackers.

"Buenos noches, mi belleza." Out of the corner of her eye, Lola saw Papi tip an imaginary hat from his thick salt and pepper hair.

Zoey, a waitress, pushed open the swinging door from the wine bar with her butt, balancing a tray clattering with dishes, nearly bumping into Papi and his companion.

Zoey grabbed the tray with both hands, covering some of the dishes with her body so they wouldn't fall. "Oh. Sorry, Mr. Alvarez."

Papi looked momentarily bewildered by the commotion in the kitchen. As if he'd forgotten the transformation of his once quiet home. Which, given his slowly progressing Alzheimer's, was entirely possible. He was sometimes unprepared for the military efficiency of flashing knives, clattering pans, the steamy whoosh of the dish sanitizer and his youngest daughter, right in the thick of it, cheeks flushed, curly hair pulled into a tangled bun.

Five kitchen staff were crammed into the small kitchen. Felicia was Lola's partner in crime, maker of salads and insanely decadent desserts and baked goods. Ruelle and Mike spent most of their time over the sinks facing the window. When they had a free second to breathe, they'd glance up into the vineyard, spreading in all its midsummer verdant glory into the hills.

Felicia, Mike and Ruelle had a running bet on how many prey Papi would drag back in any given week. Mike, who kept a closer eye on the front of the house, was winning this week. He'd bet three. Lola didn't remember who'd come up with the term "prey." Probably Felicia. The prey were the poor souls who'd come into the wine bar for an innocent drink or dinner, unaware that Papi, mostly retired from the winemaking business, had decided upon a second, late-life career. Matchmaking. Sadly, his only client wasn't interested in his services. But no matter how many ways Lola politely asked, then begged—and finally demanded, in no uncertain terms, that he cease and desist—he'd raise his hands and repeat the same thing:

"Lola, mi amor. You will thank me one day. I know best. You will see."

Three or four nights a week, Papi sat in a quiet corner of the wine bar, nursing a glass of Pinot Noir, scouting for an eligible man for his youngest. His criteria, as far as Lola could tell, were simple: Hispanic and employed. Although they'd never discussed it, Lola was sure that Papi's most important criterion was Hispanic. Her oldest sister Adella had married a gringo, and Carmen was engaged to another. Although Papi admired both his son-in-law and soon-to-be son-in-law, Lola was Papi's last hope for having another man in the family who spoke Spanish. Someone raised in the same culture, who might appreciate Papi's old world ways.

In the year since Lola had been working as a line cook, the men Papi had lured into the kitchen included: Domingo, a high school teacher who Papi had enticed from his best friend's birthday party; Tito, a stunningly handsome chef from Wapato Resort across the lake, who'd taken Lola dancing at a house party, whispering in her ear that it was shame he was gay but her dad was so nice he hadn't been able to resist making him happy; and Rojilio, an electrical engineer who'd turned sheet white and begun stuttering after Papi's pitch as the kitchen staff watched, enrapt. By the time poor Rojilio had been dragged into the kitchen, the staff had grown to love Papi's performances. They'd turn off the burners, leave the dishes, stop the sanitizer mid-cycle and savor Papi's increasingly flowery speeches. And the scarlet hue of Lola's cheeks.

"This is my Lola. My youngest. The light of my life. She is a very passionate cook. Very interested in the street food of Mexico City and the recipes of my dear departed Mercedes, her mother." This was the part where Papi would cross himself before inhaling like an opera star, sucking in enough oxygen to complete his sales pitch. "She has a dog named Daisy that she spoils like a child, which means, of course, that she would make a wonderful mother. Her Spanish is rusty but, with practice, she can become fluent again. Isn't she beautiful? Why don't you ask her out on a date?" All this said with a flourish of his hands towards Lola, as if he was a game show host displaying the ultimate prize.

After each prospective Mr. Lola had stumbled out, the kitchen work resumed with a delighted critique of Papi's sales method. "I think he should include your bra size," Felicia had once said.

Ruelle snickered, adding in Spanish, "And the fact that you have all your own teeth. But you cannot understand what I'm saying, because you are losing your native tongue." He pulled a rack of clean wine glasses out of the sanitizer. And added in English, "So sad. Tragic, really."

"I was born here," Lola would snipe, but it didn't matter. It was all systems go in Operation Find Lola A Man. And thanks to Alzheimer's, Papi's never very firm filter was long gone.

On the menu today: Hidalgo Ruiz. The poor man stood blinking and bewildered, looking eagerly between the door and Papi, clearly torn between not wanting to be rude and his desire to beat a hasty escape back to his quiet drink.

"Hidalgo, this is Lola, my youngest daughter. She is a chef here," Juan pronounced proudly.

Hidalgo, despite being obviously well mannered, had been shooting covert glances in her direction—although Lola got the distinct feeling he was actually checking out Felicia.

He grinned in an adorably bashful way as if to say, yes, this is horribly embarrassing but I'm a good sport and I'm going to make the best of it. He raised his hand in greeting. "Hola."

"Hola," Lola said, wishing the tiles beneath her feet led to a secret tunnel, preferably to another country where she could assume a fake identity.

Papi glanced between the two potential lovebirds, rubbing his hands as if the ball was now in their court and they should immediately launch into conversation, flirting, or, best of all, break into song as if this were one of his beloved musicals from another era.

After a long, awkward silence, during which Ruelle theatrically coughed, making a bad situation a thousand times more awkward (*note to self,* Lola thought: *strangle that man*), intrepid Felicia jumped into the breach. "Hidalgo, did you have a chance to try an appetizer? Lola does a mean seared scallop."

God bless Felicia, Lola sighed.

Hidalgo shook his head. "No. I just got here." He nodded, looking around the kitchen with desperation in his eyes. "It smells good. The food."

"Thanks," Lola said, bending her head over the chopping board, concentrating on her blade work.

"Okay, well, I should let all of you get back to work," Hidalgo said, clearly ill at ease.

Papi cleared his throat, clamping his hand on Hidalgo's shoulder. Hidalgo glanced at the hand uncomfortably, but was too polite to move. "Hidalgo has his own construction company."

"Construction?" Lola's head shot up, giving Hidalgo a second look.

Hidalgo nodded, visibly relieved to be on solid conversational ground. "Yeah. We do vacation homes. Boat houses, renovations. That kind of thing."

Horrible Neil swanned into the kitchen, zeroing in on the scallops, his face a map of irritation. He was about to launch a tirade when he was brought up short. "Mr. Alvarez." Even Horrible Neil loved Papi. How he justified tormenting Lola and gushing over her father, she'd never know. But then again, Neil wasn't the most logical person. "How nice to see you." Without waiting for a reply, he turned to Lola. "How are those scallops coming along?"

Sliding the scallops on the waiting plates, Lola drizzled them artfully with the reduction, sprinkling them with thyme just as Connie, another waitress, arrived from the swinging restaurant door. Nimbly stacking the plates up her arm, she carried them to the door, bumping it open with an elbow before spinning into the dining room.

Lola couldn't resist giving Neil a saccharine-sweet smile. "Out the door in record time, jefe."

Neil's eyebrows crinkled in irritation. He demanded that his staff called him Chef. El Jefe drove him nuts. Driving Neil crazy was Lola's absolute favorite pastime.

"Bit heavy on the thyme," was Neil's parting shot. He stalked out to the back patio, muttering about checking the temperature of the wood-burning pizza oven, which was his code for having a smoke.

Lola nodded her head toward the back door through which Neil had just exited. "That is Neil. We hate Neil."

Hidalgo suppressed a smile. "Do we?"

Felicia raised her eyebrows. "Some of us can't afford to be honest."

Papi, who clearly didn't like the way this was headed, cleared his throat. "Neil is a famous chef." He raised his finger authoritatively. "Muy importante."

"Con un ego a juego," Lola said. "With an ego to match," she translated, for Felicia's benefit.

"Lo siento." Hidalgo grinned. "I'm sorry," he translated, also glancing at Felicia.

Papi shifted uncomfortably. "Lola, maybe you shouldn't talk about family business in front of other people."

Lola grinned. "Says the man who brings single men back to the kitchen to meet me."

Papi jutted his chin out. "Single Hispanic men. Because I know what's best for you."

Maybe she'd reached her tipping point for the day, because she didn't hold back. "Oh, you know what's best for me? Siding with Carmen over every single thing. Is that what's best for me?"

Papi frowned, not liking this latest turn. "Carmen is a very good businesswoman."

Lola raised her knife to gesture. "So am I. But you never give me a chance, do you?"

It was as though someone had rung a bell. They both stepped into the ring and began the familiar arguments, shouting over one another in rapid Spanish. Lola was vaguely aware of Hidalgo watching with growing discomfort as they argued. She waved her knife to emphasize a point. Felicia, a seasoned pro, stepped away.

"You always take Carmen's side!" Lola insisted.

"You're impatient. Your ideas are too radical for the winery!"

"If my ideas came out of Carmen's mouth, you'd love them!" Slash went the knife. Felicia took another step closer to the kitchen door.

Hidalgo's head swiveled between Papi and Lola as they argued, switching between Spanish and English with mindboggling rapidity, leading to a Spanglish mash-up that nobody but father and daughter could completely follow.

The whole thing hit a crescendo with Lola shouting, in Spanish, "You don't even trust to me to find my own boyfriend!"

Papi replied, in Spanish, "Of course I don't. Look at your past!" His face flushed as he turned to Hidalgo. "May God bless you with sons."

Felicia smiled warmly at Hidalgo. "Just wait."

Hidalgo glanced longingly at the dining room door, clearly wishing he could finish his beer in quiet instead of being thrust into the middle of a family argument. But Felicia was right. They'd reached a stubborn impasse.

Hidalgo swallowed, as if unable to think of an appropriate response. He nodded his head at Lola. "Uh, well, it was nice to meet you."

Before he could retreat, Papi, unable to let an eligible Hispanic man slip away, blurted, "Lola is done with work at eight o'clock."

Hidalgo's face flushed. There was only one way out of this kitchen, back to the safety of the dining room. "Uh, Lola. Do you want to, um…" He looked at Papi, who nodded encouragingly. "Do you want to, uh, grab a beer after work sometime?"

Lola could tell that she shocked the hell out of him by grinning widely. "Thank you, Hidalgo, I'd love to."

CHAPTER THREE

Daisy Hollow

Gus had changed his shirt five times in the last half hour. His trusty Levi's 501s, which he'd owned since high school, stayed put, of course, but the shirts all looked wrong in the narrow mirror on the back of the bathroom door in his tiny new apartment. His favorite flannel, washed to silky softness, was too hot for summer. He'd sweat like a pig. The white polo made him feel like a preppy poser, despite his neatly trimmed beard. The vintage rock band T-shirts, collected from Seattle thrift shops and his travels over the years, seemed too casual for a job interview.

A job interview. Just the thought of it made his palms slick with sweat. He'd practiced answering the toughest questions with Jeremy, his therapist in Seattle, a few hundred times. At first, seeing Jeremy had been part of the terms of his parole, a new program for young offenders that had got him out six months early. Then, Gus had gone beyond the required meetings. He'd recognized, before he'd even set foot in his first therapy session at seventeen, that his life was out of control. It didn't take a genius to figure out that if you were in a State of Washington Corrections Department van with a bunch of gang members with tattooed skulls, headed for a two-year stint, while your girlfriend was at home, waiting for you to ask her to prom, maybe you weren't living your best life.

Maybe you were an asshole. Maybe you had some issues and it was time to stop blaming other people. Like your parents. Or Mr. Alvarez.

Gus's first therapy meeting had been in Chelan County Regional Justice Center in Wenatchee, Washington. He'd sat in a barren room with cinder block walls, in a circle of other offenders on folding metal chairs. A social worker had led the meeting. She'd looked soft and too young and by the end of the meeting, during which Gus had listened intently, he'd felt like a pre-schooler. The young social worker counseled men so rough, so lost, that Gus felt filled with shame at how relatively easy he'd had it. Maybe he hadn't had a great family, but he'd had a teacher who'd cared. Had a girlfriend. Because he'd blamed everything on everyone else. Now, looking out the window of his second-floor apartment across the street towards the old First Methodist Church, its first floor built of solid logs, the stocky spire shooting up towards the green mountains framing Lake Chelan, he cringed at the memory of opening his mouth at the first group therapy meeting: "I'm here because I come from the wrong kind of family."

To her credit, the social worker hadn't laughed. She'd nodded her head, taken a moment and then replied, "Okay. I get it. But Gus, if you pee in the wind, is it your parents' fault that you get drenched? The question that we're all here to ask ourselves is, what are you going to do with that? It's your life, Gus. And every step that you personally have taken has led you to this room and this moment."

That had been a rude awakening.

Blaming other people had been super convenient.

Yes, he'd been in jail. His life had been off the rails. He'd committed a crime while thoroughly drunk. True, his cousin had been the one to actually rob the convenience store. Gus had walked into the place thinking his cousin was bragging. He wouldn't actually do what he'd been shooting his mouth off about all night. But nobody had put a funnel in his throat or forced him to hold the gun (in direct line with the security camera) while his cousin emptied the till, so yes, maybe it was him.

After he'd served his time, he'd gone home with his journal, which sat accusingly on his kitchen table with everything he'd planned on doing. Keep up with therapy. Talk to his brother. Find his brother and apologize for not coming back and getting him out of a bad situation. Avoid drinking too much.

His journal seemed to be mocking him. *Why don't you do it? I'm just going to sit here and wait, but the clock is ticking. You ain't gonna be free until you face your past. You know it. I know it. The whole damn world knows it, but no, you go on and play Minecraft or watch another documentary where the cute little antelope gets offed by the cheetah, dude. You got your priorities. I get it.*

Finally, one night, in his attic rental room, after a day spent installing cabinets in a six-million-dollar Lake Washington waterfront mansion, when all he'd wanted to do was zone out on TV and crash, he'd gotten out his therapy notebook and sat on the couch. The white lined notebook with his lists of plans that sat un-checked, while he mentally flipped through ugly scenes from his past.

Once he'd started writing, though, it went fast. As though all those ugly moments had been waiting under his skin.

It had been painful, recognizing that his actions had harmed people. People he loved. People who'd tried to help him. Who'd even written him in prison, like his shop teacher, telling him to write back.

His little brother.

Lola.

Lola's dad.

Every single one of them lived in Chelan.

Jeremy, his therapist, had warned Gus that returning to the place where he'd been at his worst could be dangerous. Some of his friends would still be doing drugs and drinking heavily. Lola might be nothing but a high school fantasy. She could have married, Jeremy pointed out. (Gus knew from friends that she hadn't.) She would have certainly moved on. His family might not like the new Gus. They might find his mainstream life, his job, his desire for stability, threatening.

Gus tried to remember back to those interview practice sessions in the Department of Social and Health Services offices when he'd first been looking for work. His back aching against the hard folding metal chair.

Jeremy had nodded patiently, making him repeat his story. "Okay, now say it again. Keep your eyes on me. You have nothing to be ashamed of, man. If you're interviewing with someone who can't see the man you are today, then you don't want that job. You got it?"

Gus glanced at his phone again now. He had thirty minutes to get up to Manson. What was it that Izzy had said? Dress like his boss? Well, his boss was a construction company owner, and they usually wore polo shirts with the company name on it when they went to a job site. Gus studied his discards lying on the bed of his tiny apartment above Twig hair salon. He could hear the hairdryers humming below, a comforting sound. Throwing on a yellow polo and grabbing his car keys, Gus left the spartan apartment, taking the narrow stairs two at a time.

He hit the already hot pavement, glancing into the salon window as he passed on the way to his truck. Izzy, his mom's friend from high school, peered out of the little salon. She was one of the few people who had come by the Weavers' double wide mobile home, back when she'd been a drinker. Her past was much like Gus's mother's, except Izzy had gotten divorced and stopped drinking. The other two women working in the salon—Stella, who Gus knew from high school, and Rachel, who must have been a kid when he'd left town—didn't notice him. Izzy gave him a thumbs up. Gus waved, inhaling sharply. Izzy was constantly reminding him to breathe.

Izzy had approached Gus on the first night he'd arrived back in town two weeks ago. Rather than deal with his brother, who didn't know he was here yet, he'd checked into a cheap motel and crossed the street, walking down to Señor Frog's. Drinking the filthy coffee (even worse than the stuff Seattle had to offer) he'd kept his eye on the shimmering bottles, wondering if he should have a drink. The place, as usual, was lousy with tourists, but he recognized some people. With his beard, they didn't recognize him.

Izzy, wiry in middle age, with piercing blue eyes and a smattering of tattoos on her thin arms, had sat down beside him without asking. She favored black clothes, and had the sharp directness of a woman who'd been to the edge and come back to tell her story. She'd ordered her own coffee. Later, Gus would wonder what a reformed alcoholic had been doing in a bar—but he suspected it was just Izzy being Izzy. Even before she'd gotten sober, she'd been the herder of lost sheep. She, of course, couldn't be fooled by facial hair.

"Do you remember me?" she'd asked, saying he'd been "knee high to a grasshopper" when she'd been out to their trailer home.

Gus's ears had colored at the thought of anyone having seen that old wreck. The duct-taped windows, the patchy carpet, the yard littered with old truck parts and random junk his father was always going to fix up but never did. Her silver bangles had jangled as they shook hands. "Of course," he'd said, looking into his drink as though it could blot out the past.

"I remember you went out with the Alvarez girl, right?"

He nodded. "Right." Could it have been much worse? He was sure his face was turning fifteen shades of red. Thankfully she'd started talking about his current situation.

"Who you staying with?" she asked.

He liked that she assumed he'd be with someone. "I'm at a motel down by the river." He'd tried to keep it vague but anything on the road to the river wasn't the kind of place anyone with another place to be would stay. A disreputable place inhabited by migrant workers and less savory sorts.

She'd played with her plastic straw, her lips pursed, thinking. "Hey." She brightened. "I think the place above our salon is renting. If you don't mind small. It's a studio."

"I can do a studio," he said, feeling a flicker of hope. Izzy had that effect on him.

They'd talked about the changes around town. The big houses and insane prices. Chelan's trendy vibe. The good old places that were still around, like the bakery, the theatre and Campbell's.

"What are you doing back in town?" Izzy had asked in a disarming manner.

He'd made X's on the condensation of his water glass. "That is an excellent question. I suppose, you know, I left in a hurry and it wasn't to go accept any awards. I left my brother alone to deal with…everything. I had people who cared about me. Lola. I guess I dropped the ball and I want to say I'm sorry. I always wanted people to care about me and then when they did, I split."

Izzy nodded as though he'd told her it was a nice sunset. "I know all about that." She took a sip of her soda. "Take it easy. Don't rush things. Talk to people when the time's right. Take care of yourself first." She'd lifted her phone. "I'm going to call about that apartment, alright?"

"Thank you," he'd said. She was already dialing.

As Gus slid into the overheated cab of his old Ford truck now, his phone pinged with a message from Izzy. *You got this.* Gus grinned to himself, checked his rear-view mirror and pulled out into the traffic. He drove down Main Street, marveling again at how little the town of Chelan had changed in the ten years he'd been gone. He took a right at Campbell's waterfront resort, crowded with tourists on the wide wooden front porch. Tourists ate brunch in the bright summer sun. The blue lake beyond was busy with paddleboarders, sailboats and tourists slung up in parachutes, being dragged at the end of a string by speedboats. Gus had never understood why people paid good money to be towed around on a string.

Gus found Ruiz Construction on the main drag in Manson, a town a few miles up the east side of the lake. Manson hadn't changed much, either. A couple restaurants, a couple stores, a hardware store, and a beach. Gus pushed open the small storefront office of the construction company. It was nothing more than an old desk facing two chairs. A small fan droned against the growing heat. A losing battle. Hidalgo Ruiz was at the desk, hunched over his computer. He stood up to shake Gus's hand. They were about the same height, and probably the same age, Gus thought. Hidalgo was a good-looking, clean-cut guy. Prosperous-looking. A businessman.

"Hey man, thanks for coming in." Hidalgo motioned for Gus to sit down in one of the two chairs facing him, offering him coffee or water, both of which Gus politely declined.

Gus perched on the edge of his chair, unable to get comfortable, knowing what was coming. "Looks like you've got a neat little operation here."

Hidalgo shook his head. "It's just me. I hire by the job, and Chelan's booming, you know. I, uh, called your references and they all had great things to say about you and your work. I don't have to tell you that your furniture is impressive. Really cool stuff. I'm looking for someone to do custom cabinetry work for higher-end homes. Some fancy custom cabins with some built-in benches, and maybe even tables and chairs for the smaller places. Kitchen nooks. Shelving. That kind of stuff."

Gus nodded eagerly. "Awesome. I grew up in Chelan, so I know the area. I saw some amazing houses on my way up here." Gus had been struck by how many luxury homes now crowded the waterfront, sprawling across double lots. Empty lots, bulldozed of their old homes, were like missing teeth up and down the lake. The old cabins and middle-class family homes were quickly disappearing. Chelan, Gus realized, had become a two-tiered system: those who owned vacation property and those who lived here year-round and worked for the wealthy vacationers, served their food, cleaned their houses and made sure their lives ran smoothly.

Hidalgo nodded briskly. "Yeah. The thing is, Gus, I looked into your background and I'm going to need more information about your incarceration. I don't have to tell you that it's a red flag for an employer. If I hire you, you'll be going into people's homes. Working on their property. I need to be clear on what exactly happened before I make up my mind. Clearly, you're qualified, but this is something I need to dig into. Is that going to be a problem?"

Gus nodded, taking a deep breath. "No, not a problem at all. I understand why you're asking. I'd do the same thing." He swallowed, remembering what Jeremy had told him. That whenever he felt nervous or unsure, he could ground himself by thinking of a happy memory. Lola's laughing face. Or her smile when she crested the trail at the vineyard, spotting him. Maybe that wasn't the healthiest memory, but it was happy. His nervousness abated. "Yeah. So, I was seventeen. In high school. I was with my cousin at a convenience store. He had a gun and decided to rob the convenience store. While he was emptying the till, I held the gun, which was why I served time. My cousin shot the guy and took off. I stayed behind to help the guy and ended up in prison. I was tried as an adult because it was armed robbery. I was nineteen when I got out for good behavior. I lived in a halfway house in Seattle for one year, and apprenticed myself to a builder. I'd worked in the prison shop and the shop steward had let me build some of my own stuff. I found out I liked building stuff. Working with my hands."

It felt better getting it all out. As he spoke, Gus realized that Lola had never heard his side of the story. The one where he stayed and helped the guy. There was no version where he wasn't guilty but he'd like to tell her how every day since he'd tried to make up for it.

Gus stretched his legs. Leaned back into his chair. "The rest of it's on my résumé. I had a lot of teachers. I kind of traveled the world, learning how to build."

Hidalgo tapped his fingers on the desk. "You know, if I hire you, I need to know that all that stuff is behind you."

Gus exhaled. "One hundred percent." He felt his body relaxing. "One thousand, actually."

Hidalgo nodded. "Do you still have family in the area?"

Was this a trick question? Gus's brother was still here. His cousins were still around. Scamming tourists in the casinos. In and out of jail, like his father. How much did Hidalgo know about the Weaver clan? Hopefully not much.

"I do." Gus chewed his lip, trying to balance how much to tell this guy, who was, hopefully, going to be his employer. It was possible that he'd heard about Gus's cousins. Some of them worked, off and on, in construction. "Look, I'm not here to pick up where I left off. I'm here to work. Make a little money. Keep making furniture. That's it." And to do some apologizing, but this guy didn't need to know that.

Hidalgo's face relaxed into a smile. He stood up from the desk and offered his hand. "Cool. You're hired. Can you start tomorrow?"

Gus's face split into a broad grin. "Absolutely. Thanks, man."

On the drive home, Gus felt himself grinning without even thinking about it. How much easier it would be to face Lola when he was employed. For once in his life, Gus Weaver felt like things were actually going his way. All he needed was a break.

Hidalgo sat on the patio of 18 Brix, the restaurant of Karma Cellars, wondering if he should have picked someplace else. Maybe Lola didn't want to hang out at another winery, since she already worked at one. Lived on one. But the setting was perfect for a first date. Really good food and a casual, outdoor atmosphere, surrounded by the lovely flowering gardens of Karma Cellars. The patio, sheltered from the sun with a white sailcloth cover, was crowded with tourists and couples. Hidalgo sipped his wine, curious as to how this evening would play out.

He'd been surprised to get Lola's phone call confirming the date. He'd thought she was just being polite, saying she'd like to have a beer with him after her father had made it so awkward to refuse. But here she was, weaving her way around the patio tables, looking lovely in a floaty summer dress, her curly hair down around her shoulders. Clearly more relaxed than when they'd met.

"Hey," she said, sitting down before Hidalgo could get out of his chair and pull her chair out for her.

He'd been half out of his chair, so he had to slide back into his seat without commenting on why he'd gotten up. Hopefully, he looked polite. Hidalgo found dating unbearably awkward. First dates felt like being shoved onto the stage in a play without any direction or script. It was easier just to bury himself in work.

"Hi," he said. "Thanks for calling me."

Lola shook out her napkin, putting it on her lap. "It's the least I could do after the trauma my father and I inflicted upon you."

"He seems like a really nice guy."

Lola took a long sip of her ice water. Even though it was eight thirty in the evening, it was still ninety degrees. "He is a really nice guy. Unless you happen to be his youngest daughter."

Hidalgo suppressed a grin. "I noticed a slight bit of tension between you two."

"Wow, you think so? Very perceptive."

"He seems a little protective."

Lola nodded. "I was the last one left at home and he threw everything he had into me. I was his chance at a do-over." She shook her curls. "Needless to say, it didn't take."

The waitress arrived to take Lola's order. Without looking at the menu, she ordered a beer. When Hidalgo raised his eyebrows, she laughed. "I know. The winemaker's daughter drinking beer. My little rebellion. I like cooking with wine, but I'm not a huge wine aficionado." She pulled a face. "If you tell anyone, I'll have to kill you."

He lifted his hands. "I don't know much about the stuff, either."

Her beer arrived, fresh and foamy. She lifted her glass, clinking it to his. "Here's to little rebellions."

The meal had gone surprisingly well, Lola thought. She'd only called Hidalgo because, hello, he was a builder. Ever since Papi had dragged him into the kitchen, she'd thought about the perfect symmetry of hiring someone clean-cut and Papi-approved. He'd literally been thrown at her.

Besides, if she wanted the cabins built by the wedding, they needed to have been started yesterday.

Who was she to ignore fate?

Plus, Hidalgo was a gentleman. She hadn't yet found a way to talk about his work because, shockingly, unlike every man she'd dated since high school, he seemed to be genuinely interested in her. He asked questions about her tense relationship with Carmen at the winery. All the ideas she'd put forth that had been summarily shot down. He listened to her unfiltered, unedited feelings about Horrible Neil. How Felicia and she dodged him around the counter and had a system for the walk-in. If either one of them saw Neil follow the other into the refrigerator, they immediately began a rescue mission.

Hidalgo listened; he didn't fidget or look miserable. Either he was a really good actor, or rarest of all, a really good guy.

Lola counted out all the excuses she'd made. "I've said Felicia's car alarm was going off. She doesn't have a car alarm. I've said there is a customer that Neil needs to deal with, who always leaves before he gets out. What else? I've said I slipped and might have sprained my ankle."

"Let me guess. You didn't."

Lola lifted an eyebrow. "Commercial kitchens are dangerous places." She had the burns and scars to show it, running up both her arms. There was no avoiding splattered sauces, slipping knives and hot ovens. It was part of the job.

They were splitting a dessert. Lola liked how Hidalgo let her scoop the fudge sauce off the ice cream, pushing it to her side of the plate.

She licked the homemade fudge sauce off her spoon, enjoying the bite of the bitter dark chocolate, the cold spoon on her tongue. If Horrible Neil let her have any say on the dessert menu, she'd add a Mexican frozen hot chocolate to it, with warm mini churros, but of course, he wouldn't. She'd have to focus on her own project.

Seemingly apropos of nothing, she said, "So, you build things."

"I do." She liked the way he leaned back expansively, as if enjoying himself. As if talking about his work interested him.

"Do you know anything about building tiny cabins?" Weirdly, she felt something spark, as if the money sitting in her business bank account was going to catch fire if she didn't invest it in timber to fuel her vision. As if the cabins were out there in the universe, waiting to be realized.

Hidalgo pinched his thumb and his index finger together, leaving an inch to spare. "How tiny?"

"Not that tiny. You know, like little cabins. Super cute little things that make you want to move in and have the coziest vacation in human history. It's a thing on the Internet. They have a small footprint. Some wineries around here have added some for guests. There is something about the smallness, you know. It's irresistible. Humans seem to love tiny things."

"Yes. That was my attempt at humor. We have done some. Not many. I just hired a guy that I hope can help with more. He's a master carpenter, so he can build out most of the interiors. Those tiny cabins look really simple on the outside, but people usually want them built out with beds and shelves and closets. Takes a lot of work for a small space."

Lola nodded with her whole body, practically levitating with enthusiasm. "Cool. So that's something your company can build?"

Hidalgo nodded, although he didn't seem too happy about this turning into something of a job interview. "Yes."

But she couldn't stop. How could she? She had a builder right in front of her. "So what if I wanted to, say, build five of them on the vineyard, how much would that cost?"

"It depends on what kind of buildouts you want in them. Are they for winery guests?"

Lola nodded, scraping the last bit of chocolate from the dish, hoping her eyes weren't glittering in a fanatical way, but suspecting they were. "Yes. I have the perfect place for them. High up on the hill, right by the canyon wall. They'd have a view of the vineyard, Orchard House, the orchard, the lake." She could see it as she spoke. "It's so beautiful. I'll have to show you."

"I'd love to see it."

She raised her eyebrows, not so secretly thrilled. "Seriously?"

"Yes. It sounds amazing."

"Do you have time now?"

Hidalgo nodded, looking around for their waitress to get the check. "Absolutely."

As she drove past the turn off for Blue Hills Vineyards, with its distinctive gold and blue sign, Lola glanced into her rear-view mirror, making sure Hidalgo was still following. His truck slowed momentarily at the Blue Hills driveway. Three deer grazed in orchard near the road, raising their heads to gaze at the cars. She knew Daisy would be on her hind legs at the living room window, whining at the deer. Hopefully, she wasn't barking.

To the right of the road, the satin waters of Lake Chelan reflected the last pastel washes of the sunset. This was her favorite stretch of road. Lake to the right, home to the left. The mingling of the orchard with the mineral scent of the lake. Her favorite smell in the world. Home.

She turned on her indicator and took a left at the unmarked dirt road. Her old Toyota shook as she dodged the holes and grooves in the packed dirt formed by spring run-off. She'd have to pay someone to have the road graded. Once she'd convinced Carmen that the cabins were a good idea, they could add it to the maintenance of Blue Hills. After all, they paid someone every year to regrade the Blue Hills driveway before the tourist season, shortly after the snow melted.

It was slow-going on the rutted road. They passed the Blue Hills orchard on their left and Papi's old broken dark barn where he kept his ancient truck, then wound their way up to the edge of the vineyard, driving along the side of the cliff until they'd reached the clearing. There was a natural parking spot to the left, where the land flattened before it sloped down to rows of vines.

Hidalgo jumped from his truck and joined Lola in the hollow. They stood side by side, watching sunset colors leach from the pale violet sky. Mineral-rich soil scented the air as the irrigation pipes dripped water into the vine roots, feeding the clusters of grapes growing fat on the vines. The fruit was green, deepening into purple, on track for harvesting in September. The long summer nights would coax their sugar levels upward until they were ready to pick.

Bats flitted from the cliff walls, darting into the vineyard to swoop for bugs. Crickets sang into the soft air. Far below, fairy lights twinkled from the trees on the Orchard House patio. The upstairs windows peered from their gables, their wobbly panes shining in the night. A light hum of conversation floated up from the wine bar patio on the opposite side of Orchard House, facing the lake.

Hidalgo whistled long and low. "You weren't kidding. This is one of the most beautiful places on the lake."

"*The* most beautiful," she insisted with a grin.

"And this is where you want to build?" Hidalgo asked.

"Don't you think this is the perfect place?"

What Lola liked about Hidalgo was that he considered things. He didn't answer right away, or parrot what he thought she wanted to hear. He was steady and thoughtful. He turned his back on the view, giving the hollow careful consideration. Stepping away from her, he paced the small curve of the cliff wall, crunching across the dry grass. He went over to the other side the hollow, measuring the distance with his long strides.

"I think we can fit five in here," she said.

"Oh, you do, do you?" Hidalgo kept measuring until he was at the far end of the hollow. He walked back to her, kicking the soil in a few places. "It's weird. This place seems soundproofed. Nothing carries, does it?"

Lola shook her head. "I'm not sure if it's the cliff or the vines or both but it makes it even more private."

He nodded, shoving his hands in his pockets. "Very cool. This could be really sweet."

She pointed to the back of the hollow, where the meadow sloped into the cliff wall. "They'd be in a semi-circle, with some kind of barrier. Maybe I'd plant some vines on trellises, maybe some hops, because they grow really fast and they're pretty. In the center, I'd have a couple fire pits."

"What about plumbing?" Hidalgo asked.

She tilted her head. "We can't very well have people hike down to the house. It's quite a hike."

"Okay. I can probably plumb this from the irrigation pipes if I get very creative, and if we agree to make the water usage minimal. We can probably even run electrical up here from the house or the road. It's not that far."

Her eyes went wide. "Wait, are you saying you can do it?"

"Do you mean me personally, or in general?"

This date was turning out so much better than she'd thought. Was it fair to take advantage of his attraction to her? Probably not. But if these cabins didn't get built, people would be arriving and find... what? Half built shelters? Or worse, nothing. What had started as a Pinterest infatuation had turned into a full-blown obsession.

Hidalgo looked a little bashful. "Are you saying you want to hire my company to build them?"

"Yes."

He smiled and nodded. "Yeah. I can do it."

She jumped up and down, clapping her hands like an overexcited little kid. Daisy shot out of the vineyard, nearly knocking her down with happiness, spinning in delirious, crazy circles.

After she had given Daisy a thorough back scratch, the satisfied pup shot over to inspect Hidalgo. Hidalgo bent down to pet the dog, who sniffed thoroughly.

"This is Miss Daisy," Lola explained. "She adopted me right after I started working in the kitchen. She always knows when I'm on the property, and howls by the back door to be let out. Someone must have taken pity on her."

Hidalgo looked up at Lola as he held his hand out for the dog, who slid her snout neatly under his fingers for a good head rub. "Not to be a buzzkill, but don't you have to talk to your family about all this first?"

Lola cleared her throat awkwardly, kicking at the dirt. "No. This is my project. I'll get Carmen to sign off on it, of course. Technically, she's the winery manager, but I'm managing the cabins."

"Okay, that simplifies things."

"When can you start?"

Hidalgo stood up, following her to her car. Venus had come out over the horizon, glittering in the deep navy sky. "I can drop off the paperwork tomorrow. I'm going to need a down payment before we start."

Lola opened the creaky car door. Daisy hopped in, settling into the front passenger seat. Lola nodded. "No problem. I'll come get the paperwork tomorrow morning."

Hidalgo rested his hand on her car door. "Great. See you tomorrow. I'll text you my office address."

"Great. Thanks for dinner. I had a really good time."

He was close enough to kiss her, and she got the feeling he was considering it. "Me too."

They both shifted uneasily in uncertainty, neither sure of what was going to happen in the next moment. First dates were shaky things to begin with, but this had to be the worst moment. Luckily, Lola remembered something. "There's just one more thing, but it's kind of important."

"Yeah?"

"I need the cabins built in time for Carmen's wedding. Just over a month."

Hidalgo raised his eyebrows. "They'd have to be pre-fab. Assembled on site."

"Do they look nice?"

Hidalgo nodded. "They look great."

"That's perfect. I want the bridal party to stay here."

Before Hidalgo could object, or tell her that five cabins in that time frame was an insane deadline, or that he'd have to put his new guy on the job 24/7, Lola slipped into her little Toyota, executed a five-point turn, and slowly made her way down the rutted road. Daisy's head poked out the window, ears flattened, thoroughly enjoying the ride.

In her rear-view mirror, Lola could see Hidalgo growing smaller as he watched the dust settling on the road on the dark. The look on his face was that of a man realizing he'd just been had.

CHAPTER FOUR

Tricks

Neil snapped his fingers inches from Lola's face. "Hello? Hello? Is anybody home?" It was a particularly frantic lunch hour. The dishwashers, waitresses, Felicia, and Lola were all struggling to keep up with a large group composed of vacationing families who'd all placed their lunch orders at the same time. The waitresses clustered anxiously by the door for the salads as Felicia rushed through her orders.

Lola looked up from the lamb burgers she was frying. Neil's face was inches from hers. "You put Gouda on the last four lamb burgers. There's no cheese on a lamb burger. Just the sauce, the onion confit and the tomato jam." He counted off the condiments on his stubby fingers. "You know better. Don't mess those up." He pointed at the burgers sizzling in the pan.

"The customers asked for Gouda." A complete and total lie, but she'd been moving so fast and it was such a dumb mistake, she couldn't possibly admit that she'd confused them with regular burgers and slapped cheese on without thinking.

Neil turned around to Connie, who was tapping her foot impatiently. "Did four people order lamb burgers with cheese?"

Connie raised her dark eyebrows. All the waitresses had, at some point, received Neil's unwanted attention. Any chance to get back at him was a delight.

"Yes," Connie lied. Her customers hadn't noticed the Gouda, but of course, Neil had.

The kitchen staff had become a shell, closing in around whomever Neil was badgering. Lola clasped her hands in gratitude, mouthing a quick thank you to Connie before Neil turned around. "Doesn't the customer always come first?" Lola asked with wide eyes.

Neil glared at Connie before turning back to Lola. "You're just lucky that I can't fire you. All I can do is make your life so miserable that you'll quit."

She stuck out her chin. "And miss seeing you every day?"

Neil's piggy eyes flashed. "Don't push it."

It wasn't like Lola to make a mistake like that. As boring as lamb burgers were, they were easy. Today, she was distracted. The check for the cabins was tucked beneath a produce order on a clipboard in the kitchen. Only the signature line showed. On cursory glance it would seem as though she was signing the weekly produce order. Once the check was signed, she'd rush it to Hidalgo, and she'd be in business. She'd withdrawn all the money in her business account and transferred it to Hidalgo's company. The rest would have to be withdrawn from the Blue Hills account. Lola knew that if she got Carmen to sign a check, she could keep the expenditure hidden until Carmen returned from her honeymoon.

Lola hoped.

*

All day long, Lola waited for Carmen to come down from the winery office and sign what she'd think was the orders from their suppliers. Naturally, she took her time. Finally, at six o'clock, Carmen wandered into the kitchen from the wine bar, picking up the clipboard while chatting with Ruelle about some stemware that seemed to be highly breakable in the dishwasher. Lola's heart thumped in her rib cage as though she was facing a bear. Her mouth felt dry and ashy. This was ridiculous. Maybe she wasn't going about this the right way, but Carmen had literally given her no choice. A rebellion was afoot, and it felt glorious.

But first, she had six duck breasts on the burners. "Keep an eye on these, would you?" she asked Felicia, without waiting for an answer.

"I added more cheddar and took off some of the greens because my garden is producing a lot," she said to Carmen, waiting anxiously for her to sign the first stack of orders on the clipboard.

Carmen bent down, signing each page while looking at Lola with raised brows. "Would you have one cake with three different layers, or just three different cakes?"

"For what?"

Carmen stood up, rubbing her lower back. Under her eyes were pale purple crescents. "Did you really just ask me that question?"

"Oh right, the wedding." Lola was having a hard time thinking about anything other than the cabins.

Carmen pursed her lips, annoyed. "Honestly. What else would I be talking about? Anyway, the baker said she can do three layers of three different cakes and stack them, or three separate cakes."

Lola took a deep breath. "You don't want my opinion."

Carmen rubbed the bridge of her nose. "If I didn't want your opinion, I wouldn't ask."

"Here's the thing…"

Carmen lowered the clipboard. "Okay, tell me the thing."

"The thing is, you'll ask my opinion, but you won't take it. You never do."

"That's presumptuous."

Lola shook her head. "Based on a lifetime of research."

Carmen put the clipboard down. "I'm listening."

Lola crossed her arms, trying desperately to keep her eyes off the clipboard. "Three flavors is too much. People like simplicity. Plus, it makes it too hard to serve. Some people will want a certain combination of flavors and it will slow the service way down. That's the kind of stuff you have to think about. You're having a big wedding, Car."

Carmen snorted. "You're telling me. Half of Chelan is coming. Not to mention half of Seattle. Evan's parents are still inviting people."

"Rude," Felicia interjected from the sauté station.

"Right?" Carmen said. "They keep sending me texts. *Please send an invitation to Mr. and Mrs. Beaverton Cartwright the third. We forgot Millicent Carter and Reginald Waxworthy, please invite post haste.* Who says post haste in a text? I keep screenshotting them and sending them to Evan and he's like, whatever. Tell the caterer. We're up to two hundred and sixty."

Lola knew she should hold her tongue, but she was sick of Neil's stupid overblown menus. He was needlessly racking up costs and the prep of the wedding, insisting that the baker do three different flavors of cake. He'd keep the kitchen staff exhausted, and for what? A bunch of overly fussy food. "Keep the cake and the meal simple. The cake should reflect your heritage. One gorgeous tres leches cake with flowers decorating it. It can be made ahead and kept in the fridge. It's the one cake that actually gets better with age. The flavors mellow out and get richer while they're in the refrigerator."

"I'm sure the baker Neil uses doesn't do a tres leches cake. That's really specific."

Felicia waved her hand like a school kid. "Oh! Oh! Oh! Pick me. Pick me! I do! I do! I do!"

Carmen sighed. "Felicia, that's really nice, but we've already hired this baker and she's the one Neil likes. It's part of the contract."

"Carmen, why would you make your wedding just like everybody else's wedding? Why not make it something more authentic? Something that really reflects you? Mami's tres leches cake was famous in Chelan. Felicia can do it."

Carmen's eyes flashed. She opened her mouth, then snapped it shut again. "Because, Lola, I've got a plan and a business to run. And I know you think my wedding is going to be boring and conventional and you've got a vendetta against Neil, but do me a favor and give it a break. Don't make my wedding about how much you hate Neil."

She snatched up the clipboard and scribbled her signature on all the documents before thrusting it at Lola and storming out of the kitchen.

"Shocking. She didn't take my advice."

"Did she sign it?" Felicia asked.

Lola beamed. "She did."

"Ooooh, girl, you are asking for so much trouble."

Lola turned up the flame on her sauté pan of duck, checking the burner to gauge the steady ring of blue flame. "I'm the youngest child. It's expected."

Sometimes they were lucky and Neil stayed in the bar. This made it easy to clean up and get out of the kitchen. Lola was itching to run the paperwork to Hidalgo's office and slip it under the door. But tonight, Felicia and she were still cleaning up when Neil pushed his way into the kitchen from the restaurant. Lola took one look at his wobbling gait and knew the night was unraveling. Disaster. Felicia was in the walk-in, storing butter and checking supplies. Lola was prying open boxes of vegetables that Neil had ordered from his suppliers. One of her many arguments with Carmen was about buying produce locally. Two months ago, before Neil arrived on the scene, Lola had grown most of the greens, tomatoes, chilis and herbs used in Blue Hills recipes. The rest had been sourced by local growers. Neil had changed all that, using the same supply chain he'd used in Seattle. Produce trucked in from larger growers in California, Wenatchee, and Oregon. It was cheaper, but the flavors, in Lola's not so humble opinion, weakened the further they traveled. A red pepper that might have been crunchy and flavorful when it was picked, was rubbery and bland by the time it reached Chelan. As usual, her arguments fell on deaf ears, even though she already had her own locally sourced suppliers.

"I saw some water on the garlic lemon pasta, okay?" Neil said, coming over to her now. "Reduce it down in the pan more. We want it a little sticky. And watch that thyme on the scallops. It's a big flavor for a delicate bivalve, okay?"

"Yes, but—"

Neil's eyes narrowed. "There is no *but*, Lola." The way he said her name was like an insult. "There is only 'yes, chef.' That is the response. Now try it again."

"Yes, but the pasta water is what makes it sticky. It just needed another stir. And the thyme is a nice contrast to the salty scallops." She bet he hadn't even tried the scallops. Or the nicely sauced pasta.

He held up a finger, closing his eyes, making a buzzer noise. "Wrong answer. Try again. And this time get it right, or you'll be in here mucking out the reefer. Got it?" When she didn't respond, he crossed his arms. "I'm waiting."

They were at the point where a sane person would recognize the futility of her situation, say "Yes, chef," and move on with their life. Instead, Lola took a deep breath and crooked her finger. "Come here." She marched outside and around to the gravel path at the side of the house, where her kitchen garden, covered in netting to keep out the deer, was planted in neat rows. Just looking at it made her happy. Fresh herbs sprung from the earth in pungent green clumps. Plump red tomatoes in all shapes and sizes crowded the dusty green plants. Shining red, purple, yellow and green chilis hung from squat plants. Furry beans clung to vines that climbed the stakes she'd buried in the dirt. It never ceased to amaze her that such abundance came from soil and a handful of seeds. It was life in its simplest and most generous form.

Surprisingly, Neil had followed her, his Crocs crunching on the gravel. He stood in the shadows behind her, his arms crossed, his bloated face unreadable in the dark.

Lola waved her hand across the garden. "This is mine. We have all these fresh herbs, chilis and tomatoes just sitting here. I don't know why we can't use them in your recipes."

"Do you know why people come to the Blue Hills winery restaurant?"

"Because they're hungry?"

"Don't be a smart-ass."

"To eat your food."

He nodded, glaring at her garden. "Exactly." He pounded his chest in way that made Lola queasy. "My recipes. You garden isn't the draw. So as much as you love your trendy little garden, we can buy triple-washed herbs and not have to worry about people finding bugs in their food." He pointed at the garden. "Give it away. Sell it. Do whatever you want, but if you put this stuff on the food, I'll bust you down to dishwasher. Don't think I won't."

As soon as they stepped back inside, Neil's beady eyes scanned the kitchen.

"Where's Felicia?"

"I um, don't know," Lola lied, shutting the screen door behind her. It was a very small kitchen. They both knew she was lying. Hopefully, he was too drunk to put two and two together.

Neil nodded, his cheeks flushed with wine. He headed for the walk-in. "You hungry?"

"Uh, no thanks. I'm leaving."

Neil rested his hand on the reefer door. "I'm making saltimbocca."

He disappeared into the walk-in, leaving the door slightly ajar. Lola counted to three, waiting for Felicia to dart out. When she didn't appear, Lola went in after her.

An instant chill brought goosebumps to her skin. The walk-in was a narrow space lined with shelves. Barely large enough for two, let alone three. Neil's eyes glittered in the dim light. He was uncomfortably close to Felicia, who was contorting her body to avoid him. He willfully stood between them, blocking Lola. "Oh, it's a party with my two favorite line cooks."

"Come on, Felicia, I'll give you a ride home," Lola said.

"Nobody wants saltimbocca?" Neil fake pouted.

Felicia pressed her body against the shelving, scraping past Neil, who leaned down to sniff her hair. "Mmmmm. Lemons."

As Neil turned to forage in the shelves for ham and chicken, Felicia's face twisted into disgust. "Uh, excuse me."

In the bright light of the kitchen, Felicia slammed the reefer door a bit too hard. "Maybe he'll get locked in. There is a way to arrange it."

"A girl can dream."

Felicia grabbed her purse off the hook, nodding at the reefer. "It's darker in there than it used to be. Do you think he took out a bulb?"

Lola shrugged. "I wouldn't put it past him. Mood lighting."

Felicia walked to the back door. "He probably did it so we can't record him."

"Probably." Who would have thought it would be so hard to capture someone so aggressively and frequently horrible? But it was always in corners, away from staff when he pressed into them a bit too closely. Or outside, like the time he'd smashed six glasses on the patio because Rodolfo had burned two pizzas in a row. His tantrums were unpredictable and sudden. His sexual innuendos were whispered and hard to record. If they set it up in the kitchen, he called them into the dining room. Often it was simply the way he said something.

If Lola told Carmen that Neil had leaned into Felicia's hair and said "Mmmmm. Lemons," she wouldn't get it. Still, they kept trying to catch him out. Lola's phone battery had died eight times in the reefer. Once, just when they'd thought they'd caught him pressing into Felicia in the walk-in, Felicia had stumbled against the shelving and her phone had fallen into an open vat of sour cream she'd been measuring.

"Okay, see you tomorrow," Felicia said, slipping off her bandana, releasing her glorious dreadlocks.

"Hasta mañana."

A few moments later, she poked her head back in. "Look, I know you're mad at Carmen, but maybe you should give it one more shot."

"We both know what she's going to say."

Felicia shook her head. "True that. Maybe we could take him water skiing and cut the line."

The reefer opened. Neil appeared, chewing on a chunk of Brie. "Ah, my two kitchen serfs." He whipped out his phone and took a photo of them. "This one is going on my Insta." He pecked at his phone. "What should be the caption be? 'How do I ever get any work done'?"

"How about 'A day in the life of harassing my female employees'?" Lola snapped.

Neil's lips twisted as he tapped away on his phone. "So feisty. I love it. BTW, if you've never had my saltimbocca, you're really missing out."

"Don't drive, Neil," was Felicia's parting comment.

Lola followed Felicia out onto the patio. Getting away from Neil was its own kind of sweet release. The irrigation system hissed in the vineyard as the balmy summer air enveloped them with the smell of tiny bitter apples from the orchard. They turned to watch Neil through the kitchen window. He unwrapped a chicken cutlet, pounding it in a neat series of staccato beats with a mallet. Even drunk, the man could work with admirable speed and efficiency.

"The worst thing about him is that sometimes he's a really good cook," Lola sighed.

"About those cabins." Felicity hiked her purse over her shoulder, jingling her car keys. She didn't need a ride.

"The tiny cabins," Lola said, watching the vineyards for signs of Daisy. A hawk circled lazily in the purple sky. Somewhere on the lake, a speedboat buzzed. Daisy shot out of the vine rows, barreling into Lola with full force. She crouched down, pressing her face into Daisy's sweet woolly fur. This was always the best part of her day.

Felicia nodded toward the kitchen window. "I get that Carmen brought that horror show into our lives, but I don't know, Lola. Are you sure the cabins aren't just your way of getting back at your sister?"

Felicia bent down to give Daisy a rub on the head. Her stump tail twitched with delight before she shot back up into the hills, looking back at Lola with anticipation with her one pale blue eye and the other cocoa brown.

Lola stretched her arms above her head, happy to be outside. She considered her answer to Felicia's question as they walked across the patio, bordered with the glorious profusion of roses Lola's mother had planted, glowing orange, hot pink, and bright white. Their scent mixed with rich earth and the sweet tang of the ripening grapes. "No, they're not," Lola said, eventually. "Carmen is built for business. She moves like the Terminator. Her entire world is making this winery successful. If Evan hadn't been trying to buy the vineyard from Papi, I doubt she would have even noticed him, but even her marriage is business-related. If the cabins are going to happen, they'll happen because I out-Carmen Carmen. I bulldoze ahead."

Felicia hunted for her car keys in her cavernous backpack. "And you really think there's no way to get her to see the light?"

Daisy woofed a gentle reminder.

"No. Consider the messenger. To Carmen, I will always be the little sister," Lola said.

"What does that even mean?"

"It means that unless I do my own thing, I am never going to make my mark on the family business."

CHAPTER FIVE

New Job

Gus had been fast asleep when someone knocked on the door. The pale, early morning northern light squeezed through the blinds, illuminating the brick walls of his bare studio apartment. He looked at his phone. It was five in the morning. Who in the hell visits someone at five in the morning? He grabbed his jeans off the floor and hopped into them as he stumbled to the front door, opening it without thinking. His brain simply didn't function at this hour.

A bright-eyed Izzy thrust a take-out coffee cup at him. She pushed into the apartment, all excited smiles and bustling energy. "It's your first day of work! I was so excited I couldn't sleep. I woke up before my alarm went off and thought, 'Today's the day!' My goodness, were you asleep? How can you sleep? You've got a new job. Don't construction jobs start early? I got you an Egg McMuffin. Do you like those? I was going to get you a breakfast sandwich from Starbucks, but the line was too long. Is this okay? Lord, kid, you need some furniture. There's no place to sit but a bed."

Gus did have one chair by the window. After he opened the blind, he dragged it over so she had a place to sit while he took the bed. She was the only person who'd been here since he'd moved in. Somehow, Gus thought, that felt right. "I don't know which question to tackle first."

Izzy plopped her purse onto the ground and sat down on the hard chair, leaning into Gus with fierce concentration. Clearly, she was a morning person. On steroids. "It doesn't matter. I'm just so happy for you. My baby bird is leaving the nest."

Gus sipped the coffee gratefully, sitting down on the bed across from Izzy. Since moving out of the motel, he had quickly grown both fond of and uncharacteristically reliant on the ebullient woman, but he wished she'd turn it down a notch. It was an ungodly hour. "Uh, did I miss something? Isn't the nest when people actually live together?"

Izzy waved her hand, flashing with silver rings. "I don't know. It just feels that way. When I stopped drinking, I decided that helping people was my new mission, and now I just think of the people I, you know, not so much help as give a little push, as my children. God knows, I messed up a lot with my own children, so I'm trying to get it right. Your first job back here as an adult feels like a big step. I'm really proud of you, kid."

Gus took another sip of coffee, feeling the caffeine entering his system, doing its job. "Thanks, Izzy."

"Don't you thank me. You deserve this."

Gus raised one eyebrow. "Okay."

"Yes. Okay. Be proud of yourself. I know how you're thinking. You're saying to yourself, I don't deserve this. I'm going to mess it up. She doesn't know what a bad person I've been. I messed up before and I'll do it again."

Gus scratched his beard, looking down at his bare feet. "Am I that predictable?"

Izzy nodded her head, before reaching across to pat Gus's knee. "It's something I learned when I got sober. I got really good at telling myself that my mistakes defined me. Which is a really good tool to excuse me, or you, from trying anything that's too hard. The story we tell ourselves is that, oh, I failed at these things so I'm going to fail at everything else. Which is true. Yes, we will fail, because we're human. Mistakes are the human condition. And the only thing we can do is try to learn from them. You could have gotten out of that correction facility and come back here and hung out with the same crowd. Gotten in trouble again. But you didn't. That was all you, at a very young age, saying no, I want something different, even though you didn't have one adult role model. You went out and found those people. When a therapist asked you hard questions, you didn't get up and leave. You turned yourself inside out to become a better version of yourself. You and I know what kind of determination and grit that takes. Don't you ever forget that you got yourself here. Nobody else." She crossed her legs. "So tell me. How are you feeling?"

Gus wasn't used to checking his emotions, let alone sharing them. As a kid, Gus had imagined himself a shark. Keep moving or you'll die. Don't dwell on any feeling for too long or it might drag you to the bottom of the ocean. Lola was the one person he'd ever opened up to, before Jeremy. Normally, he would have simply lied. Not a whopper, but a lie in the way most people say, "Oh, I'm fine," when their guts were ripped out by something. Better to lie than to be vulnerable.

But Izzy wasn't the kind of person he could lie to. Not even a white lie. Her bright blue eyes, framed with a lifetime's worth of crows' feet, had a way of pulling the truth right out of him. He warmed his hands on the paper coffee cup. The old brick building cooled down at night, despite the July heat. "I'm nervous, I guess."

"So, what are your fears?" When he stared at her blankly, she pushed. "Come on, Gus. Your nerves are telling you that something is wrong. That's fear speaking. Sometimes it's healthy and sometimes it's self-sabotage. What are you afraid of?"

Seriously? Izzy was a one-woman machete who cut through the BS. He had nowhere to hide. Which was annoying, particularly at this hour of the day. But she'd showed up for him in so many ways, he owed her honesty. Besides, he had nothing else to give but the truth. Might as well honor that.

"Last night I walked down the street, and you know how Chelan is on a summer night. People are sitting outside, having drinks, laughing, and all the summer people are kind of, you know, sunburned and happy, and I felt like, you know, lonely. I thought, would the world end if I called up my cousin and we had a few drinks? And I felt so close to slipping back into that world. Not the drinking, just the sense that nothing matters, you know? That your life isn't of consequence. It just made me think that being here has made a very thin line between who I used to be and who I am right now. Like I am one phone call away from being the old Gus. Like what difference would it make to anyone if I just got hammered and let loose? I just kind of panicked. I thought, what the hell am I doing here, putting myself in this situation?"

And Lola. What would happen when he saw Lola?

Izzy's grin was two parts shared pain and one part sheer love. "My darling boy." She lifted her index finger, pointing at Gus. "Unlike all those people sitting out enjoying their drinks, you are here for a fresh start. Which sounds fun but it's hard work. Trust me on that one. I've had several." She smiled at herself. "The tough thing is, that makes you vulnerable. Because you want something. Life matters to you because you see possibility, a future. You have skin in the game and all you've got is your honor and your intention, but I'll tell you what, it's enough. Being afraid of falling back into old patterns means that you care. You want something different. That's why you're here. Now eat your Egg McMuffin and go kick some ass on your first day of work."

Gus unwrapped the sandwich, feeling strange about eating in front of Izzy, who had nothing but coffee, until she said, "Go on. I'm a mom. Nothing makes me happier than seeing a kid eat."

"I hate to burst your bubble, but I'm twenty-seven, Izzy."

She waved him away. "An infant."

Gus chewed on his sandwich, swallowing a bite. "Thank you, by the way."

"You're very welcome."

"You're not going to do this every day, are you? Because I don't start work until seven."

Morning sunlight flooded the storefront office of Ruiz Construction, illuminating the dust motes flickering lazily in the air. Gus had a mug of coffee at his elbow as he completed the paperwork for his employment: tax forms, social security forms, insurance forms. It had taken him the better part of an hour to work his way through them, and he was nearly done.

Hidalgo was outside talking to his crews in the parking lot, each headed out to different sites around Chelan. They gathered in front of their trucks, smoking and nodding, eager to be off to their work sites before the sun began to beat down mercilessly.

By the time Hidalgo entered the tiny office, Gus was finished.

Hidalgo took up the paperwork, placing it in a file. "Thanks, man. Hey, um, I've got a job I'm going to need you on today that's kind of a weird one. This gal wants five cabins done in lightning speed. She calls them tiny cabins. They're pre-fab exteriors, and I need you to do the interiors. Shelves, cabinets, molding. I don't have the manpower right now to have anyone supervise this, but are you up for it? It's a great location, but I need someone who can work on their own. I can't afford to pull anyone off another job. I know I'm kind of throwing you into the deep end, but it seems like you've done lots of stuff like this. You okay with that?"

Gus perked up. The idea of working on his own was ideal. There was nothing he loved more than the solitude of allowing himself to fall into a steady rhythm without outside chatter or distractions. Also, he was a bit of a perfectionist, so calling the shots would make his life much easier. "Sure, where is it?"

"Blue Hills Vineyard," Hidalgo said.

Gus, who'd just taken a sip of coffee, coughed convulsively, splattering it all over the desk.

Hidalgo waited for him to stop coughing, clearly wondering if he should hit the man's back, tense with concern. "You okay?"

Gus swallowed, wiping the coffee off the desk with a paper towel. "Yeah. Fine."

"Yeah, so Lola Alvarez is your contact."

This kept getting stranger and stranger. He must be hearing things. "Lola?"

"Yeah."

"Lola Alvarez?"

Hidalgo was giving him a weird look. "Do you know her?"

Gus nodded. "I went to high school with her." That was all Hidalgo needed to know.

Hidalgo gave him a piercing look. "You okay with working for her?"

Gus took a deep breath. "Sure." Her old man might run him off the place with a shotgun; there was that. Maybe he'd get a chance to work on his therapeutic apology while staring down the barrel. It would sure as hell keep him honest.

"It's on the Blue Hills property, but it's at the top of the orchard. Near the cliffs. You take the second left after the winery. I've had someone grade it and the cabins will be delivered tomorrow. Why don't you go up and stake out the property? We don't have much time and I want them in the right place. Once they're in, you take whatever equipment you need out of the shed. I'll order whatever you need from our suppliers."

Gus nodded, standing, eager to be outside. "I'll head over there now." Lola was building cabins in the hollow. Their hollow.

"Yeah, I might stop by later." A faint smile touched Hidalgo's lips. "Lola's quite a character. I uh, well, never mind. Call me if you have any problems finding the place."

Gus nodded. Finding the place was not going to be a problem. Not getting his ass handed to him by Lola's father was another situation altogether.

Gus slowed as he drove past the Blue Hills Winery and Orchard House. The old place looked good. Hell, it looked great. The sign for Blue Hills was freshly painted, glinting gold and deep blue in the morning sun, surrounded by a bed of petunias, blooming in a riot of color. Faint mists came off the grass in the old orchard. The gnarled old trees hung thick with ripening apples. Up the long driveway, he got a glimpse of Orchard House, looking as majestic and welcoming as ever with its familiar gables. Between the trees, he saw the expansive living room front window overlooking the lake, and the river rock chimney above the house like a sentinel.

In high school, he'd always felt awed by the fact that he was dating a girl who lived in a such a beautiful old house. Gus's home was a double-wide trailer way up in the hills across the lake. It sat on a scrubby patch of land, surrounded by cars that hadn't run in decades, rusting bike frames and boats that his father always said he was going to fix up and sell for a profit, but never did. Gus had never had anyone over but his cousins. They'd hunker in front of the TV and play video games for hours, making themselves scarce when Gus's dad was drunk.

Lola had always taken her home for granted. She'd spent a lot of time complaining about her old man. All his rules. When her sisters had left for college, her dad had doubled down on the discipline.

Lola had to come home right after school. If friends wanted to see her, it had to be at the Alvarez home. Even before Gus came onto the scene, Lola had been chafing under her papi's restrictions. Maybe all Gus had been to her was a rebellion. It wasn't the first time the thought had crossed his mind.

As much as Gus had wanted to date a girl who didn't have curfew, he knew what it meant. A curfew meant that someone cared about you enough to want you home, safely tucked into bed. Safe. What was the saying? Nothing good happens after two a.m.? Gus had driven drunk enough times in this very truck to testify to the truth of that statement. He clearly remembered gripping this steering wheel, squinting drunkenly at the road, wondering where the lake started and the road ended, thinking that that keeping the truck on the wavering road was like playing a video game. It hadn't occurred to him at the time that this was a game that could end in death.

As Gus flicked the truck's turn indicator to turn left, he remembered the hundreds of times he'd driven up this road with his headlights turned off. He wondered why Lola had chosen this place to build her cabins. Was it because they'd been happy there, sneaking stolen moments, making promises that they'd never keep? Or was it because she wanted to build over her memories? Blot them out to make something new? Surely on a winery this size, she could have chosen another place for the cabins. He refused to believe Daisy Hollow didn't mean something to Lola. That wasn't possible.

He remembered leaning on the hood of his truck, watching a hawk soar overhead, listening for the sound of Lola crunching through the snow-dusted dirt. His breath a white fog in front of him as he waited, hoping she'd been able to get away. There was usually a case of beer stashed behind the driver's seat. If she didn't make it, he'd drink it with his cousin. If Lola couldn't get away, he'd blot the world out with booze.

Winter it was quiet, easy to slip off and meet. Dusk fell early this far north. Mr. Alvarez would be inside, dealing with paperwork from the sales of their wine. Lola would make sure he was busy in the cave and slip away. Text Gus to meet her. He always dropped whatever he was doing when she texted and drove up the lake with his heart beating a mile a minute, thinking about seeing her, remembering what it was like the first time he'd kissed her. How he'd thought that this was what he'd wanted his entire life without knowing it. Everything in his scattered life had clicked into place when their lips met. It was the first time he'd felt that he belonged to someone. It had been the best feeling in the world. She had been his anchor. Their relationship had been outside his rough friendships with boys. Outside of his family life, where there had never been enough of anything. With Lola, life had felt bountiful.

From the first minute he'd kissed her, and she'd looked back at him with those beautiful brown eyes, Gus had felt the universe expand, wrapping itself around the two of them. He'd felt safe. Life with Lola was different. He didn't have to be tough or scrappy or any of the things he'd learned to be from a very young age, just to get along in life. Lola had met him head on and accepted him. Even the worst part of him—until she had realized that it was destroying him. Then she'd done her damnedest to stop his partying. She'd tried. God knows, she'd tried.

Gus would never forget waiting in the hollow with the vineyard and orchard below, frozen in crystals, feeling like a speck and yet vast with possibilities. They'd loved each other, and it had been the single most important fact in the world. Lola would show up, glowing from the hike, cheeks pink from the cold. Telling him how she'd waited until her dad was busy in the cave or on the phone with his winery manager. She'd tell the story of how she'd made herself scarce for a while before slipping out the side door of Orchard House. Then she'd throw her arms around him, lift herself up on her toes and kiss him. Gus had thought he'd explode with happiness.

That was the miracle of Lola. She'd wanted him. Risked getting in trouble for him. Gus had felt singled out. Touched by fate. A miracle.

The plans they'd made, Gus thought now, as his truck bounced up the rutted road, its ancient suspension groaning in complaint. They were going to build their own home, someplace high up like this hollow. Somewhere with a view of the lake. Lola would cook big dinners, have her own garden. Maybe some goats. She'd make cheese from their milk. They'd have flowers in the summer and fires in their river rock fireplace in winter. Gus would build on what he'd learned in wood shop in school. Create things. Make a life for them with his hands.

By the time Gus reached the hollow, he half expected to see his younger self sitting in the trampled grass with Lola, weaving crowns of daisies, placing them on her head and laughing.

He sat in the old truck for a moment, tapping the steering wheel. He was back on Alvarez land after ten years. Nothing from this vantage had changed. Daisies pressed their faces to the sun. The brilliant green of the vineyard stretched down the hill toward the turquoise lake. He got out of truck, facing the water, gulping the fresh morning air. The trucks would be here tomorrow, bringing the disassembled cabins. He'd looked up the manufacturing company on his phone. He knew the dimensions. It would take a hell of a lot of work to get all of them up and running, but he could do it, even if he had to bring a sleeping bag and spend the night.

He turned back to the hollow, glad that his workspace was well away from Orchard House. He rolled up his sleeves and assessed the land with a keen eye for where the cabins would naturally fit. He went to his truck to get some stakes and rope, falling into the rhythm of work, hammering in the first stake with neat precision. After an hour, he was completely absorbed in the task of fitting five cabins into a relatively small area, making sure the land was level, staking and re-staking. He stood back and gazed at his work with a critical eye. If these five cabins were going to be done in time, he'd be working some long hours. Which made him happy. This was as good a place as any to hide out and focus on building some credentials in the Chelan construction community. Hidalgo Ruiz had given him a chance. He wasn't going to let the man down. These cabins would be on time and perfect.

One day at a time.

Gus Weaver was ready to work hard, but he sure as hell wasn't ready to face old man Alvarez or his daughter.

CHAPTER SIX

Spotted

"You're mighty cheery," Felicia said as she plated some salads, sprinkling them with slivered pistachios and a fan of freshly cut pears, and dotting the mound of greens with blue cheese.

Connie snatched the plate with an annoyed glare. She had little patience with Felicia's dramatic plating technique.

"I am." Lola did a little tap dance as she fetched some butter from the opposite counter, twirling like a ballerina, executing a curtsy as she plopped the dish on the counter. She glanced around to make sure the coast was clear. "Today is the day!"

"What day?" Felicia asked.

"You did not just say that," Lola snapped, slicing off a chunk of butter and plopping it into a hot sauté pan. Was there anything better than watching a pale-yellow slice of butter melt into bubbling liquid? Her panko-encrusted chicken cutlets waited like plump pillows nearby.

Felicia nodded, looking at her iPad orders without missing a beat. "Your nefarious plan has begun."

"Ooooh. I like it. Tell me." Ruelle popped in between their heads. The man was a ferret.

"Don't you have some dishes to wash?" Lola asked.

Ruelle gathered a dirty sauté pan off the countertop. "There are no secrets in this kitchen. Well, let's be honest. There are no secrets in any kitchen."

A rattling sound came from the silver walk-in refrigerator door. Sometimes the door latch didn't connect, and the door had to be opened from the outside. It was dangerous, but by the end of each day, nobody ever remembered to have it fixed. Probably because Neil was the only one who constantly got locked inside. Which the rest of the kitchen staff enjoyed with unadulterated delight.

Ruelle looked around the kitchen with purposefully vacant eyes. "Did anyone hear that?"

"Hear what?" Felicia asked.

A steady thump, followed by another, echoed from inside the refrigerator. Neil had been in there for a while. They all knew his arms would be loaded with the ingredients for his evening specials. He'd be kicking the door with his Crocs, trying not to drop his precious cargo. The best part was imagining him inside, kicking away, his cheeks puffing with anger as he deliberated whether or not to go through the process of unloading his arms. It would put him in a foul mood, but the light mood in the kitchen was always worth it.

"How long do you think he can survive in there?" asked Connie.

"Who?" asked Ruelle, with innocent eyes.

"Oh, come on, I know you guys do this," Connie snapped as she gathered dishes of butter off the counter for her tables.

"It gives us a little peace," Mike said, loading a tray with clean water glasses.

"What gives you a little peace?" asked Zoey, who'd just come in the back door and was tying on a clean apron.

Neil's muffled swearing came from inside the reefer. He kicked three more times before screaming, "Ow!"

Zoey tied her luxuriant brown tresses back into a ponytail. "You locked Neil in the reefer again? Well done."

Felicia chopped some red peppers with neat efficiency. "We didn't lock him in. The lock's a bit fussy."

Zoey shook her head. "No, it's not. Someone has to set it up. Luke showed me once. If you want it to lock shut for the next person, you lift up the handle as you leave, and it has nothing to catch on." She looked at her watch. "I'd give him fifteen minutes before hypothermia sets in. He's insulated."

Felicia waggled her eyebrows with a devilish grin, glancing at her watch. "Hmmmmm. I wonder how that happened."

Five minutes later, Carmen poked her head into the kitchen. "Lola, can I have a word?" She paused, cocking her head, listening to the banging noises. "What's that?"

Well, this was awkward.

"Is anyone going to answer me?" Carmen raised her eyebrows.

For a second, Lola was terrified that she'd start giggling, but she managed a nonchalant shrug. "Mice?"

"Mice?!" Annoyed, Carmen marched through the kitchen and swung the walk-in refrigerator door wide open.

Neil stumbled out, his arms overflowing with packages of meat, vegetables, and containers of broth.

"You look cold, Neil. Go outside and warm up," Carmen said briskly, as if Neil had been goofing off in the reefer on purpose.

Everyone waited for Neil to explode, but he stood shivering, gripping his food, glaring at his staff, who'd all suddenly made themselves terrifically busy, washing dishes, tearing lettuce, sautéing chicken.

"Why didn't anyone hear me?"

Ruelle shrugged. "Hear you what?"

"You all heard me!" Neil thundered. Dumping his packages on the counter, he stalked outside, muttering to himself that someone would pay.

Shaking her head at the odd scene, Carmen turned to Lola. "Can I see you upstairs? It will only take a second."

The only thing weirder than working with family, Lola always thought, having them constantly barge into her workplace, was that the restaurant was carved out of a chunk of their house. Her commute was walking down a flight of stairs. The reason Lola went for a hike every night was to put some separation between her work and home life. But today, like most days, her family blurred the lines. She dutifully followed Carmen up the creaking stairs, hoping that whatever this was, they could indeed be done in time for Lola to stay ahead of the lunch rush. Once Neil defrosted, he would be on the war path.

Once upstairs, Carmen ushered Lola inside her bedroom. Its gabled window overlooked the vineyard. Lola glanced out the window, idly wondering how far up into the vineyard Carmen could see. Much to her horror, at the top of the vineyard, far off, was a crane, presumably off the side of a truck, lifting building supplies. Carmen would really have to be looking to see it at this distance, but Lola thought with her luck, Carmen could potentially spot it and shut things down before they'd even started. Lola's heart clutched in a tight knot as she ran from the window, focusing on the clothing rack in the center of the room, at the foot of the bed.

"Oh my god, Car, your dress!" she shouted, hoping to distract Carmen from the window.

"Yeah, you've seen it." Carmen gave her a closer look, as if wondering why on earth Lola was so excited about a rather conventional wedding dress. Lola's previous reaction had been tepid at best. Never terribly good at concealing her opinion, she couldn't get excited about a wedding dress. Food, yes, but the whole white wedding thing left her cold. If she got married, it would probably be in a field, or on the beach, barefoot, with Daisy as the ring bearer.

"I forgot how incredible it is. Let's get a better look at in the light." She grabbed the dress off the rack and darted into the hallway to her own room.

Carmen followed, a puzzled look on her face. She glanced around Lola's room. "I forgot how pretty your room is. Remember when we used to shop online and pretend to be rich society ladies? Fill our carts with tens of thousands of dollars of gowns and jewels just for the fun of it? I was Felicity Farthington and you were—"

"Clarissa Conklemore. We shared a penthouse with four poodles and ten servants." Lola felt herself softening at the memory. "No husbands. Just dogs."

Carmen squinted at her dress, hanging from a hanger in Lola's hand. "The light's not better in here. Anyway, I just wanted you to try on your bridesmaid dress." She turned around to cross the hall to her bedroom, but Lola darted in front of her.

"I'll get it."

"Why can't you try it on in my room?"

"Because..." Lola stretched the word out, giving herself time to think. "I feel more comfortable here."

"Okay. That's a little weird."

Lola nodded. "Yes, it is." She dashed into Carmen's room, glancing out of the window. The crane stuck out at the top of the hill, far enough away not to be noticeable but trust Carmen to pick out an anomaly. She'd have to keep Carmen away from the window for a good long time. Back in her own room, she held the dress out in front of her. It wasn't a bad dress, as far as bridesmaid dresses went. A floor-length slip dress made of silvery satin. "This looks different."

Carmen closed her eyes, clearly exasperated. "It isn't."

"Are you sure?"

"Just. Try. It. On."

Sighing heavily, Lola made a big production out of taking off each item of clothing until Carmen practically had steam coming out of her ears.

"Lola, I was hoping this could be a nice little moment in our day. But we both have to get back to work."

Finally, Lola slipped the dress over her head. It fit perfectly. She turned to look in the mirror. "It's so pretty."

Carmen placed her hands on her sister's shoulders, kissing her hair. "You look amazing. Thank you." She turned. "Hang it up, please," Carmen said on her way out.

"But wait!"

Carmen popped her head back in from the hall.

"Are you going back into your room?" Lola asked, stalling for time.

"No. I have to get back to the office. Because I have a job."

Lola grinned with relief. "Okay."

"What?"

"Nothing. It's just... Thank you."

Carmen's face softened, as if she'd been expecting something much worse. "You're welcome, Lola."

Lola waited until her sister's footsteps had receded before dashing across the hallway into Carmen's bedroom. The crane was still there.

"Hey!"

Lola nearly jumped out of her skin at the sound of Carmen's voice at the door. She stood on her tiptoes to block as much of the view as possible. "Hey?" Lola's voice twisted into a wavering, choked cough.

"I just wanted to say that I'm really glad we're getting along." Carmen left. Came back. "And that you like the dress." She disappeared again. Popped back into the door frame. "It means a lot to me." Disappeared and reappeared yet one more time. "I'm sorry if I'm, well, a little rough on you sometimes. I know things aren't perfect in the kitchen. I'm aware. It's just, I feel like you can handle it. And you'll learn things. I'm really glad you're going to be in the wedding."

Lola swallowed. "Me, too."

Carmen's hand went to her chest. Was that a glimmer of a tear in her eye? "I feel like we're really getting along."

Except that, Lola thought, *you'd strangle me in my sleep if you knew what was happening in the vineyard.* Lola grinned. "We are. We absolutely are, Carmen."

Carmen raised her eyebrows. "Hidalgo seems nice…"

"We've had one date."

"But you like him?"

"Maybe."

"Nice guys aren't the worst, Lola."

"You know what's fun? Having Papi reel them into the kitchen so I can get grief about it from my co-workers for three days. That's super fun."

"Maybe give this one a chance."

"We'll see."

Her phone rang while she was outside delivering prosciutto to Rodolfo on the patio. He worked in the summer heat at the mouth of a roaring hot brick oven. Turning to Lola with a grateful smile, sweat streaming from his face, he took the platter of meat, sprinkling it liberally onto the waiting pizza dough before sliding them gently into the oven on his wooden paddle. He was clearly slammed with orders, rolling out dough as fast as he could, but he still found time to thank her. They didn't have a reefer outside, so Felicia and Lola took turns bringing Rodolfo ingredients, trying to anticipate his needs. The poor man barely had time to breathe, let alone run into the kitchen. He made fifteen pizzas an hour during the lunch rush, a victim of his own success.

Lola glanced into the kitchen window to make sure that Neil wasn't around, before slipping her phone out of her back pocket and answering it as she slid into a corner of the patio hidden from the kitchen windows. "Hey, Hidalgo."

"Hi. I just wanted you to know that my guy is busy supervising the installation of the cabins. They arrived today. He'll be there most of the time now, but I'll try to stop by whenever I can. He's a really good guy, though. He just started with me, but I've seen his work, or photos anyway. Says he went to high school with you. You don't have to worry. It's all going to be great."

Lola pretty much knew who he was talking about. Robbie Bright had gone into his family's construction business and, she'd heard in the bar, just left. He was a good guy. "Thanks so much. I'm really excited."

"I knew you would be. Anyway, I just wanted to let you know."

"Thanks, Hidalgo. I appreciate it."

"Sure."

Slipping the phone into her back pocket, she floated back into the kitchen, not even bothered by Neil, who snapped, "Well, Lola. Nice of you to show up."

"You're welcome," Lola said with a beaming smile, which, gratifyingly, seemed to really piss him off.

"Come on, girl." Daisy bounded ahead of Lola up the vineyard like a rabbit as she crossed the patio. After obsessing about it all day, she could finally visit the building site. Maybe build a fire. She took a bottle of wine and some paper cups. It had been a long time since she'd done this, and she deserved to gloat a little. Her tiny cabins were actually going up. Was there something wrong with her that she didn't feel guilty doing this? Wouldn't most people feel a twinge of regret at taking such a drastic tack? And what if it didn't work?

It would work.

Carmen had left her no choice.

And why should she feel guilty about finally having a chance to make her mark on the family business? She'd spent the last two years putting everything into Blue Hills vineyards. Carmen would never willingly relinquish control. If Lola didn't break out of the mold, she'd be slaving away in the kitchen under some version of Horrible Neil until her teeth fell out.

It was late, around eight thirty. Getting out of kitchen had been one thing after another. Last-minute orders. A supplier who couldn't deliver an order the next day, so she'd had to track down some trout because Neil was nowhere to be found. A glass had broken on the counter and they'd had to decide if all the food in the area had to be tossed. (Yes. Because: glass shards.) Mice had gotten into the flour. Again.

All those thoughts drifted from her mind as she climbed into the hills, feeling the familiar ache in her thighs as her muscles warmed. The sun had disappeared behind the cliffs, leaving the sky a wash of tangerine and pink. Boats hummed across the lake, and the winery bar, by the sound of it, was doing brisk business on the patio. Lola's feet sank into the reddish soil on the path between the vines. The fruity smell of ripening grapes, hanging thick and promising on the vines, competed with the loamy irrigated soil. This particular smell, the intersection of earth, vegetation, and water, was the smell of home. She breathed it in, trying to release the tension of the day.

It was a steep incline, and she had to stop for a moment to catch her breath. Daisy gave a light woof, as if wondering what was taking her so long. Her small furry form rushed back to prod Lola on. She sat on her stumpy tail, as if ready to fly back up the trail, impatient for their walk to continue.

"I'm coming, girl. Some of us were on our feet all day." Daisy dashed down one of the rows as Lola continued her ascent, popping up much further ahead of her on the trail. For every step Lola took, Daisy took about twenty-five.

As they grew close to the hollow, her heart surged in anticipation of seeing the building site with the tiny homes becoming a reality. Her contribution. This was it. Her dream was coming together.

CHAPTER SEVEN

New Same Guy

Late in the day, probably night by then, a little dog appeared at the edge of the hollow. It was a cute little thing, about the size of a small coyote. Some kind of herding dog. She cocked her head and looked at Gus with highly intelligent eyes. Although the sun had dipped behind the hill, Gus could still see that she had one brown eye and one pale blue. It gave her an other-worldly look that appealed to him.

After a day spent alone, she was the perfect company. He called to her with something inane like, "Here, puppy," positioning his hand outstretched, as if he'd pet her, but she gave him a doubtful look and didn't budge. She was completely self-contained, sending the message, "Not a chance buddy," which made him think that she was even smarter than she looked. An exceptional dog.

She kept glancing down one of the stony paths between the vines, as if waiting for someone. Her ears attuned to something Gus couldn't hear. Her nose gently sniffing the wind.

Gus put down his hammer and stretched his back. He hadn't realized how long he'd been working. The prefab cabin company had delivered the cabins in pieces the day after he'd started. He'd had to figure out how to prop the pieces together before he joined them. It was a two, if not three-person job, but he'd just managed. It was exhausting work that had required a lot of heavy lifting. He'd called Hidalgo. Told him that the cabin pieces were very heavy and hard to move. After a long talk, they'd both decided that Hidalgo would stop by when he could to help. They were on such a short deadline.

"You sure you're up for this? That's a lot more work. I can send someone from another site," Hidalgo had said.

Gus didn't have to think about it long. He loved being up here by himself. The two days he'd been here had unraveled a lot of tension in his body. Convinced him that he'd made the right decision, coming back to Chelan. Not just because it reminded him of one of the best times in his life, when he was young and in love with Lola. It was the solitude. The chance to work without the chatter and distraction of other people. No radio. No boss looking over his shoulder. Just the work. The sky. The birds. And the view of this incredible lake. In a way, it was the perfect introduction back into Chelan. He could enjoy the best part of Chelan—its beauty—at a distance. He wasn't yet entangled in the messy side of it. It was like easing himself inch by inch into the place with new parameters. Ones that he set.

Provided he didn't run into Lola or old man Alvarez.

Lola decided whoever had been working here had left. There was the one cabin, framed in the dark. Large pieces, which had to be the other cabins, were on the ground, lying on tarps or still on pallets. She didn't have anything other than her phone for light, and contented herself with walking around the perimeter. She'd left the kitchen a little too late and wasn't used to being up here at night alone. She'd have a much better look in the daylight when she could linger. But for now, a fire, a quick glass of wine and back down the hill to bed.

Lola took her time making the fire. She crumpled up each layer of newspaper as if she was the survivor of an Arctic plane crash and her life depended on the warmth, layering each chip of wood like a tepee, the way Papi taught her. When they were little, Papi used to take them to the beach for barbecues. Mami stayed home, waving from the patio, telling everyone to wear their sunscreen and not swim alone. Mami used to make a big deal about how much she'd miss them, when in fact, often the whole point of the barbecue was to get the little girls out of the house. Papi would show them how to build the fire, wrapping the newspaper into spiraled cones, layering them with wood. He'd send the girls off to find kindling, traipsing gingerly under the ponderosa pines, coming back with sticky feet and stories. When they'd give him their wood chips, he'd exclaim as if they'd offered him gold instead of broken branches. They'd roast hot dogs and squeeze condiments from baggies. Papi prided himself on packing the perfect picnic. He wrapped individual s'more kits for each girl, presenting them like gifts. "Sweets for my sweeties."

A tiny flame finally caught in the center of the kindling. Daisy lay in the dirt at the edge of the circle of chairs, watching Lola with eyes that gradually grew sleepy. Occasionally her eyes would flick shut, but a noise in the distance, a coyote or hawk, would make her open them and lift her head. She'd settle down and start the whole sequence again moments later.

"Have you been hanging around here keeping an eye on things?" Lola asked her dog.

Daisy perked up, eyes bright now, listening carefully. Lola loved the way she tilted her head, like a cartoon dog.

Daisy lifted her head, whining.

There was a noise behind one of the cabins. A scraping. Something crashed onto the ground. It sounded like a ladder being knocked down. Now she felt a creeping fear.

Chelan sat at the foot of the Cascade Range, home to black bears, cougars, lynx and bobcats. Further to the north were grizzlies and wolves, but they were rarely found this far south. The big cats tended to be more elusive and shy. Black bears, on the other hand, frequently ventured into cabins for food. Some of them had to be relocated when they became pests. Had someone left some open food?

Lola tried to calm down by telling herself that it was probably raccoons. They tended to use the vineyard as a freeway down to the lake, waddling down to the orchard to forage before heading to the lake for a splash and a drink.

Daisy growled, making Lola even more uneasy. Lola stealthily crept towards the dog, grabbing her collar in a sudden move.

"Come on, girl," she whispered.

Daisy refused to budge.

"Come on, Daisy," Lola pleaded.

Daisy's growl became more intense while Lola wrapped her arms carefully around the wriggling dog. Every summer, the Chelan newspaper featured a bandaged dog being held by a smiling owner after the dog had held off a bear or cougar. Lola had no intention of letting Daisy get herself into that position. After a few tries, Lola managed to lift Daisy into her arms, embracing her firmly despite the dog struggling to get free.

"Stop it, Daisy. No!" she whispered vehemently. Carefully, keeping an eye on the shadows, she made her way towards the framed cabin. It occurred to her before she reached the cabin that she'd have to lower the dog to push aside the temporary plastic sheeting that was hung over the door. She reached the steps and carefully positioned Daisy on the middle step. Holding Daisy's collar with one hand, she reached with the other for the plastic.

Daisy exploded into a chorus of barking and snarling. Lola ripped away the heavy plastic sheet, and was trying to drag the dog up the last step when Daisy slipped her collar, scampering down the steps, disappearing into the dark. Lola dropped the plastic and ran after Daisy. A large figure loomed in front of her.

Lola screamed, smashing her fist into something large and dark. A hand reached out and stopped her fist.

"Lola, it's me. Gus." He dropped her fist. "Weaver."

Lola panted with fear, clutching her heart. Gus Weaver? It was hard to tell in the dark but it sure sounded like him. She willed her heart to steady but the idea of Gus in front of her and at Daisy Hollow was more than she could believe. Ten years. It had been ten years. What was he doing here? But instead of the thousands of questions running through her brain, all she could blurt out was, "I thought you were a bear."

"You were punching a bear?"

Gus stepped into the light. It was Gus. He had a beard but she'd know that face anywhere. He was solid and real and her mind hadn't quite caught up to it yet. Gus Weaver was really here. How could she have ever thought he was anything but a man? She felt stupid, relieved, and angry all at the same time. How dare he show up after all these years? "I would if he had my dog."

Gus bent down to pet Daisy. "I'm pretty sure she'd run circles around a bear."

"Well, you scared me." Gus. Did she hate him? Love him?

He lifted both hands. "I'm really sorry. This really isn't how I wanted to say hello."

What the actual hell? Hello?

Gus Weaver. Nothing for ten years then, bam. Leave her messed up beyond belief and now this? Her dad had scraped her off the chair in the sheriff's office where she'd begged to see him. She barely remembered that night or the weeks afterwards. He had no idea.

Hello.

His lean frame had filled out, but there was something about the slope of his strong shoulders, the way his shaggy hair hit them. He was more muscular, but the way he put away his tools now, placing each one carefully in a lock box, was all Gus. He talked as he stashed them. "I thought you'd come up and, I don't know, check things out. Guess I thought you came up here more than you do. Funny, I guess I've thought more about this place than any place in Chelan. Now I'm working here." Despite being raised in chaotic house, or perhaps because of it, Gus was a tidy person. His truck had never been dirty. His glove box had always contained the essentials for running an old vehicle.

She nodded, not trusting herself to talk.

How could this be? Her fingers itched to call Hidalgo and ask him. Had he hired Gus Weaver? What was Gus doing back in town? How many times had she wished for exactly this? How many hours in high school had she spent lying on her bed, crying? How many sleepless nights? How could he have just left her and then never tried to call? In an instant she could feel the pain, like an animal thing, ripping her apart. She remembered her dad walking into the sheriff's overlit waiting room. The fear in his eyes at seeing his daughter like this. All she was thinking about was when she could see Gus. She didn't know it would be ten years.

Her heart was going a million miles an hour. Gus. Was. Here. His beard, unfairly, made him look even better. He had that whole mountain man thing going for him. As usual, the man wore a pair of Levi's better than anyone had a right to. Her brain raced to place all the facts in some semblance of order. Half of her wanted to jump up and run to him. To wrap her arms around him, ask what had taken him so long, and to kiss him. Those kisses. Never in her life had Lola been kissed like that, before or since. Gus kissed every time as if it were their last.

The other half of her wanted to slap his face, yell at him for never, ever calling her. Saying he was okay. She didn't need to get back together back then. Just to know that she'd meant enough that he'd thought enough to call. Say something. Not leave her hanging. It was a death of sorts. She wanted to dash back down to the safety of Orchard House, to give herself time to think. To compose herself, and remember that she wasn't a callous kid. This was a job. Could he really be working here?

"Yeah. Small world." Brilliant, Lola. Got any more banal cliches? Toughen the hell up.

Gus Weaver was here, on their land, building her cabins.

OMG.

She needed a plan. She couldn't just fall apart. She wouldn't give him that. She wasn't that kid waiting in a lobby for a guy who was never coming home. She was a grown-ass woman. This was her project. Hers.

Should she actually let him work here? Was it a good idea? Hidalgo had said he'd gotten someone really good. Someone he was very happy about. And it was Gus. All along, it had been Gus. She could feel the vein in her temple that pulsed when she was anxious. She absentmindedly felt it with her fingers. She needed to make sure nobody in her family saw him. But first, she needed to let this information sink in. She felt like a cartoon character, running in six different directions at once in her brain, while her body was trapped in the hollow.

It had been ten long years since she'd last seen Gus in the high school parking lot, shivering in that truck, keeping an eye out for her dad. It had been the last day of school, the beginning of Christmas break. She'd sat next to him trying to think of ways she could sneak out and meet him over the holidays. Her father had declared Gus off-limits the summer before, and winter was making it hard to see each other outside of school. Then her father had pulled in, parking by the front school entrance. Knowing he'd be looking in the other direction, she'd leaped out, working her way across the icy lot in case Papi noticed Gus's truck. Papi was smiling when she got in, handing her a hot cocoa, asking if she'd help bake cookies. He'd just bought baking supplies. Gus had gone home to a trailer where the electricity had been cut off—not because his mother didn't have the low-income subsidy payment. But because she didn't have stamps to mail it in.

Her father had driven her off the high school parking lot and Lola hadn't seen Gus since. Ten years of trying to forget about him. Trying to wipe from her mind that last look at his narrow face, his hand up in the cold cab of that truck with the heater that didn't work. Of trying to forget the worst night of her life when a group chat said Gus Weaver was in jail. Headed for prison. Ten years of worrying about what had happened to him in that prison, thinking that it couldn't be as bad as the movies—but what if it was? Of worrying about what had happened to him after he got out of prison. Where had he gone? Of looking at every guy who was the right age and size from far away, and being disappointed, but maybe a little relieved, when they turned out not to be him.

Ten years of thinking that maybe he hadn't really loved her, because he vanished, didn't care enough to dial a number he'd memorized. But seeing him now as he stretched his arms up into the sky, bending backwards so his Nirvana T-shirt rode up, showing a slice of abs that would have meant a lesser mortal spent hours at the gym—but oh no, Gus Weaver, in addition to his height, his shaggy good looks, his piercing dark eyes, was just built that way—all the same feelings came rushing back. Lust mixed with need, a desire to be physically close. It was embarrassing how everything rushed back. Her mind never stood a chance. Her body remembered everything about Gus Weaver. So many emotions, it was impossible to string them all out and examine them. Anger, too, because he'd never reached out to her. She'd kept the same cell number. He could have called any time. Part of her didn't want to hear what she feared most. That he'd never cared. Not as much as she had. Even now that would be awful.

She needed lots of time to think. This had been a long ten years, but when she saw him, time seemed to compact itself into a world that contained just the two of them. It was vibrant, intimate, and hyper charged. The only thing she knew for certain hadn't changed was that when Gus Weaver was present, her brain wasn't running the show.

Lola let her heart settle, looking up at the moon, breathing deeply. Wisps of cloud floated across its crescent face. Her anger had morphed into something manageable.

"How did you want to say hello?" she said, finally.

Gus tilted his head in the same way Daisy did. As much as Lola hated herself for it, she remembered that he'd done that in high school and yes, it was still cute. "Sort of like, hello. You might have noticed that I'm working here."

"I see."

He scratched his beard. Lola hated beards on most men, but Gus was the kind of man who could get away with it. "How could you not?"

"You're very cocky for someone impersonating a bear."

He nodded, grinning. "Nice fire you got going there."

"It is. Very cozy. Gus Weaver, are you fishing for an invitation?" Oh lord, she sounded flirty. *Stop it, Lola. Just. Stop. This isn't high school and you're not seventeen. This isn't your freaking do-over.*

Her body wasn't listening.

Gus's grin broadened into a smile. "Well, I thought I'd do the neighborly thing and say hello. So, hello and I'm sorry I scared you."

"Where's your truck? Are you still driving that old thing?" Weird, how she assumed he was driving the old truck. Gus without his truck would be like Han Solo without the *Millennium Falcon*.

He nodded down the road. "I am driving that beautiful old thing, but I went swimming during lunch and left it down there. I also left the lights that I use at night in the truck. That's why I was fumbling around in the dark. Okay. So now that I've scared you to death, I'll say goodnight." He nodded and turned around.

"Wait." She hated how fast it came out of her mouth.

He stopped, but didn't turn around. "Yeah?"

"Why don't you stay?"

He kept facing the opposite direction. "I can tell you about twenty reasons why it's not a good idea, Lola."

"Okay," she said. "I get it." She wanted him to turn around. She hadn't wanted anything so badly in such a long time, her longing nearly knocked her over. Her breathing had just been settling down, but now she found she was holding her breath, hoping he'd stay. She knew they couldn't pick up where they'd left off, but she wanted to drink him in. Just a moment more. Maybe two.

Slowly, he twisted around in the dirt until he was facing her. "Number one, your father wants me dead. Number two, from what I hear in town, you were out with Hidalgo and I'm guessing he doesn't know about us. Number three through seventeen, I don't even want to get into."

Us, Lola thought.

They faced one another across the few feet of meadow where they used to meet. Night noises grew around them, filling the air with crickets, rustling grape leaves, distant music floating across the water from Wapato Point. It was all so familiar. So enticing.

"Stay anyway," Lola said, surprising herself with the words as they came out of her mouth. Gus had always been able to get her to do and say things that surprised her.

He looked at her for a very long time, shifting uneasily. Finally, he nodded. "Okay, Lola. Okay."

She nodded, suddenly eager to do something with all the crazy emotions flooding her body. Something besides closing the distance between them. Reducing the space between their bodies to nothing but heat. It would be both like they used to be and brand new. What would he feel like now? She shook her head, as if to clear it. *Stop it. Stop it.* "I've got wine in my backpack."

He shook his head. "No, thank you."

"I brought one beer. I don't think it's cold."

He made a point of approaching the fire from the other side, avoiding her. "Nope, I'm good. Why don't I work on the fire and you get yourself something to drink?"

Lola could not stop staring at him across the fire pit. The way the firelight made his cheekbones look cut from marble. Or the way he could look dead serious one second and lit from inside the next. Oh, this was bad. She could not be thinking this way. "Okay." She fished around in her backpack. Took out the paper cups, balanced them on a rock, finding herself looking at him more than she should.

"Got any water in there?" Gus asked.

"I do." Her hands shook as she pushed aside the junk crowding her backpack. She used it as an all-purpose summer and work bag. Left bottles and wrappers lying in the bottom. She probably had half her life in this thing.

She moved away, shining her phone light in the backpack, feeling the jittery beats of her heart, whispering to herself, "Come on, Lola. Get a grip. You are a fully functioning adult. Act like one."

She poured herself a cup of wine and took a sip, watching Gus crouched by fire, thinking of all the times she'd dreamed of their reunion. She was bringing him a cup of water. Ten years later. She balanced both cups, staring at them, thinking that when she looked up, she'd find she'd imagined him—but no, he was sprawled out in one of the folding chairs he'd brought from the work site, as if he lived here. He was clearly deep in thought, but jumped up when she came near, taking the water and thanking her.

He lifted his paper cup. "To new beginnings."

She lifted her wine, not sure if she wanted to drink to this toast. New beginnings could mean so many things. It could mean everything, or nothing at all. Regardless, Lola lifted her cup, touched his and drank.

"New beginnings," she said.

Lola hiked down the path toward Orchard House slowly, watching for rocks and roots. Daisy followed reluctantly. The dog seemed transfixed by Gus. Normally she was the first one down the hill, wagging her tail like a beckoning flag, but tonight, until Lola called her, she'd stayed there at the top of the vineyard right at the edge of the hollow, unmoving.

Lola thought about Hidalgo. What would he think if he knew he'd hired her ex-boyfriend? It had been a long time ago, true, but it would bother most people at least a little. Then there was her family. Gus would certainly get fired if they found out he was here, and she'd be in even more trouble. Of all the people Hidalgo could have hired, it had to be the one person her father wouldn't welcome with open arms. If there was ever a small-town moment, this was it. Nothing like seeing someone (sort of) and finding out that he'd just hired your ex. The only one that mattered.

Lord.

Lola would have to think this one through. Maybe she and Gus should just have a normal employee-employer relationship. Pretend they didn't know each other. Not talk, unless it related to the cabins. That would work, wouldn't it? Lola was a grown woman. She could handle complicated situations. She didn't need to respond to ancient signals leftover from another time.

Her dog, however, had other ideas. Daisy wanted nothing more than to linger at the fire with Gus. She'd stopped walking, turning her head to gaze longingly up the trail. Lola hissed at her, not wanting to call out in the night. Daisy dragged herself slowly down the hill, making sure Lola knew that this was against her wishes and that they'd both be better off by the fire. Naturally, Lola had adopted the most stubborn dog in Chelan.

*

No. No. No. No. This wasn't happening.

Couldn't be.

And yet.

Shit.

Gus hiked down the dusty road towards the lake to get his truck, thinking about the encounter. How when her dog first appeared, he knew it was hers. Lola's dog was exactly the type of dog Gus would adopt. Scrappy and lively, gazing back with intelligent, almost mischievous eyes. He ticked off all the things he could have predicted about Lola. That she'd be up at Daisy Hollow, looking more gorgeous than anyone had a right to.

Stop.

Stop it right now.

Had she been flirtatious? The thought sent electricity through his limbs. His brain filled with earlier visions of them in the spot, young and desperately in love. Kissing with an urgency that had blocked out the entire world. His problems. Her father. This place had been their escape hatch.

The path was dark, but Gus was able to orient himself by the lights shining off the lake. The orchard smelled sweet with ripening apples. The deer that seemed to visit twice a day were reaching for the lower apples. One of them had her hooves on the trunk of a tree, stretching her neck. It had been surprisingly comfortable, talking to Lola, after the initial scare. He'd walked right past people on Woodin Avenue that he'd been to high school with in Chelan without them giving him a second look. He'd braced himself for the inevitable awkwardness of trying to pretend that they were going to catch up, meet for a beer, when they'd never been close in the first place—and then, surprisingly, nothing. But with Lola, it was as though they'd never been apart.

The thing with being back here was a fresh start. Not something old. He and Jeremy had come up with the plan. Apologize for leaving people hanging. His brother, Lola, Mr. Alvarez and if he could find him, his old shop teacher who'd begged him to keep in touch. If they didn't respond well, too bad. Either way it was a way to close that chapter in his life. To stop those nights when he did what Jeremy called catastrophizing. He clung to the past as if being a Weaver was a leaky boat and he was surrounded by sharks. But he was a fully formed man who, Jeremy convinced him, could move forward if he put a full stop to the past by apologizing.

Easy.

Until he held Lola's arm and looked into those gorgeous brown eyes.

That moment? Not part of the plan.

Gus took inventory of his feelings, something therapy had taught him to do. It was a way of managing difficult emotions. Coping skills he used every single day. Today there was more need than ever. Lola. If anything, she'd had gotten more beautiful. Her cheekbones were high under those beautiful brown eyes, the long lashes, the mischievous smile. The way one side of her lip turned up when she smirked. Her appearance shook him to the bone. Brought back everything. He wanted her.

Which was a terrible idea.

Wasn't it?

A better man would step down. Let her find someone easier. Someone who came with a family and less baggage. Someone like Hidalgo, who seemed like such a solid guy. But then again, he could hear Jeremy in his head asking if this was his insecurity. Was he trying to stop feeling something because it was easier that way? He'd lived a life of relative anonymity, working on his craft, building furniture as a way of reaching out to the world. There was a slight numbness, living that way, but maybe that was better than risking searing pain. He could never have predicted how one moment could change everything.

Gus came out on the road, checking the road for traffic although there wasn't a car for miles. Chelan shut down after dark once you left the town. All the tourists stayed on their patios, drinking wine or in their hot tubs or watching movies in the air-conditioned homes. Meanwhile locals went about making it possible for them to relax, serving their drinks, stocking their groceries, building their vacation homes. The lake glistened invitingly, a smooth gleaming black swath winding its way to the Cascade foothills. It was magical out here. Gus was happy he'd moved back. Seattle couldn't offer anything like this, despite the stark class distinctions. This lake was a balm to his soul.

Gus's mind was in turmoil. He was supposed to see her, speak his piece and move on. As soon as he'd seen her face, he knew that was impossible. You didn't move on from a woman like Lola.

How was he going to deal with this? Did he even have a choice? Could they just be friends? Could he do that? What did it mean with Hidalgo in the mix?

He couldn't take his mind off Lola. He could smell her hair. The minty shampoo she used. He could feel the velvet of her skin, remember how brown she got in the summer. How her hair went wild with curls after she swam, something she didn't like. How she didn't know she was beautiful and brightened when he complimented her. What if he put himself out, confessed his feelings, and the most likely scenario happened: she wasn't interested? He'd be okay. Wouldn't he?

It had taken him ten years to work up the courage to come back here. He could wait.

But Lola was the person he most wanted to get it right for. The person he'd failed the most. She was the single person who'd loved him with all his flaws. Who'd put herself out there for him and tried to prevent him from even more reckless behavior. All the parties she'd insisted they leave. If he was honest, she'd probably saved his life. Given him something to live for when the future was so bleak. When all he had been able to see down the road was a broken-down trailer and a yard filled with junk, she'd shown him the possibility of building a life on a foundation of love. Trust. Things that had been in scarce supply in Gus's childhood. When he'd had to be the adult, driving to the Department of Public Utilities with a check, walking through the snow to the nearest neighbor when his brother spiked a fever and there wasn't a single bottle of children's medicine in the house. Lola had allowed him to be a teenager. To laugh and hold hands. To see silly movies and throw popcorn at the screen. Lola had taught him to ride a bike. Bought him presents. Made him laugh.

She'd put so much trust into him, and if as he'd learned tonight, he was still deeply in love with her, what if tomorrow she nodded at him, said hello, and moved on? Turned into someone who said, "Yeah, friend me on Facebook"? What if he'd kept a love alive that had died for her long ago? What would he do then?

CHAPTER EIGHT

Off Went the Gloves

"Lola, I have someone for you to meet!" Lola looked up from her Gus-induced daze. She should be paying attention to the burning flame and food in front of her. Not obsessing over last night. It was the middle of the first wave of the happy hour rush, when everyone piled into the restaurant, starving from their long day at the beach and buzzed from their first glass of wine. The kitchen fans couldn't keep up with the summer heat. Everyone was dripping with sweat. And once again, Papi had shown up, back to his old tricks.

Oh, dear lord. He'd dragged in a tall, thin guy with a bashful smile who kept pushing his owlish glasses up his nose in a nervous gesture. Instead of having her usual public showdown, Lola calmly put down her wooden spoon, asked Felicia to keep an eye on the onions she was caramelizing, and hurried over to Papi.

"Hi, nice to meet you," she said to the poor guy, watching as the light bulb went off over his head. He was being dragged back here to meet the old dude's daughter. He didn't seem too upset about it, though, brightening visibly as the pieces clicked together.

"Hi, nice to meet you," Glasses Guy said, a little too happily, as if his life had suddenly turned around and Lola was his new future.

She turned to Papi. "Can we talk?"

"Excuse us," Papi said to Glasses Guy in his most cordial manner.

Glasses Guy seemed content to wait. Lola suspected there weren't many things competing for his attention. Poor guy looked like he didn't spend much time around women and appeared very happy to be in close proximity to one.

She slid her arm into Papi's, escorting him unceremoniously over to the kitchen desk. "Papi, I'm kind of dating Hidalgo." She felt a bit weird about saying this, given her reaction to Gus and that it was a slight exaggeration of her status with Hidalgo (okay, a big exaggeration) but if it got Papi off her back and out of her kitchen, why not? Hidalgo was the kind of guy she should be dating, not the super-hot, troubled, super-hot (it was worth repeating) guy currently working in the upper vineyard. Who she should not be thinking about. Ever.

Papi's face blossomed into a smile. "Es verdad?"

Lola nodded. "Sí, es verdad."

"Well, this is very awkward," he said, as if she were the one dragging men into the kitchen under false pretenses.

"What did you say to him?" she hissed.

Papi grimaced. "I don't remember. Only maybe that I had a single daughter and she was the cook and maybe he should meet you and go out sometime."

"You have to stop doing this!"

He wrung his hands. "He seemed so happy."

"Of course he was," she hissed angrily. "He probably thought you were going to buy his meal." She took a deep breath and went back to Glasses Guy. "I'm really sorry about this. My dad just wanted us to meet but I'm at work, and…" She pushed him towards the door. He was as malleable as clay, shuffling to the door, his eyes huge under the round glasses. "It's been very nice meeting you. Enjoy the rest of your meal."

After the door swung shut, Lola turned to Papi, who was grinning and rubbing his hands together. "So, Hidalgo. Maybe we have a double wedding?"

Lola rolled her eyes as Felicia choked with laughter. "Papi, we have been on exactly one date."

"Next summer?" Papi asked.

Felicia was doubled over.

"Papi, here's the thing. Thank you so much for bringing random people in here and setting me up with them"—she waved her hand across the kitchen—"in front of all my co-workers. It's been a lot of fun for everyone. However, I can run my personal life from now. I know you think that at twenty-seven I still need your help in just about every aspect of my life, but seriously, I've got it."

Papi looked dubious. "You would be happy with a man from the same culture."

"Duly noted. But while I've got you here, let me ask you something. Remember when I asked you about building the tiny cabins up above the orchard in that little hollow?"

Papi nodded. "Hidalgo is a very nice young man."

"I'm talking about the cabins, Papi?" This was her way of very slowly and carefully preparing him for the fact that if he saw Gus on their property, he shouldn't grab his shotgun. She was trying to be responsible. Carmen would be furious if she found out, but Papi could potentially go ballistic.

Papi shook his head. "Talk to your sister." He patted her arm. "I'm very happy that you are going out with Hidalgo, Lola. You're making your old man muy contento." He lifted his finger. "You see, I do know what's best for you." He raised his eyebrows suggestively. "And next summer, who knows?"

If Lola could have chosen one house for herself on all of Lake Chelan, it would have to be Indigo Bay. Unfortunately for her, it was off the market. Carmen's best friend Stella had received it from her new husband as a wedding present last summer. Indigo Bay was a 1950s ranch house with a lovingly refinished interior, overlooking a neat square of grass, an oval patio and a long dock into the lake facing west. The entire cottage was the perfect vantage point to enjoy spectacular sunsets over the Cascade Range—with a glass of perfectly chilled wine in hand, of course, because Paolo, Stella's husband, was a consultant at Hollister Estate.

It would be easy to hate Stella, what with her dreamy Italian husband who gazed upon her with adoring eyes, humoring her every whim, and the massive Lombardy wine estate where she lived most of the year, returning to her perfect lakeside cottage for summers. But Stella was impossible to dislike. Not only was she hilarious and charming, she'd overcome losing her twin sister as a child and had finally found happiness with Paolo. Lola had grown up with Stella, who had sometimes lived at their house for long stretches when her own parents were falling apart after her sister's death. She was like another older sister, except nicer. While Carmen bossed Lola around like she was more sheep than human, Stella always listened.

Now Stella's own twins were a little over two months old. It was hard to believe that two tiny, nearly hairless creatures could demand the complete and utter attention of three adults. Carmen, Stella, and Lola were in the living room of Indigo Bay where the plate glass windows looked out on the placid water. Under a nearly cloudless azure sky, the sun glinted off the lake. They were utterly surrounded by beauty, but they hardly noticed. Ostensibly they were there to paste the special wine labels for Carmen's wedding on the bottles of wine. It was a gorgeous label that Stella had designed. A photo of Carmen and Evan at the vineyard on a chalkboard-black background with faux-chalk doodles around it; the date and the Blue Hills logo on one side and the Hollister Estate logo on the other. This was supposed to be a festive, girly time to chat and drink wine, but they'd hardly been able to talk and had gotten exactly six wine bottles done. The shockingly loud twins kept erupting into frantic tears any time they put them down. Thanks to jet lag and Stella trying to get them on some kind of west coast routine, their nap time was long overdue, and apparently when darling little babies didn't get their naps, they morphed into wailing banshees. Now the overtired darlings were too hysterical to sleep. Which made zero sense to Lola.

Ugh.

Lola was jiggling Rosie, who was a red-faced, snotty mess. Since she didn't know much about babies, she was approximating a hopefully soothing jostle that she'd seen in countless movies. It didn't seem to be doing any good. Rosie, far from calming down, was giving her an alarmed, overwrought side-eye that said, *I don't know you. I don't trust you. One false move and I'll take out your eardrum.* She seemed to have two modes: desperately sad and furious. Lola walked her over to look at the lake, pointing due west. "See, over there? That's the winery. When you're older, I'll take you into the bar and we can hang out. But for now, what about if you just went to sleep? You have jet lag, which is pretty cool for you since you're so young, but not so cool for your mother. I'd question why she's holding her little party now, but since she answers everything with 'Mommy Brain' and pretends to shoot herself in the head, I'm not saying anything, because that would be just plain mean."

Stella was patting Carlo, the dark-haired cherub named for Paolo's father. They were stunning babies, but oh lord, could they scream. One of them was loud enough, but when the two of them got going it was enough to make Lola want to jump into the lake.

Stella paced the room, the dark circles under her eyes so pronounced, it looked like her mascara had run. (Lola had make the mistake of telling her.) "If I don't get some sleep tonight, I'm going to do to something really stupid. Like agree to have more children."

"Then don't you want to keep them up during the day?" Lola asked.

Stella shook her head. "No. That's the weird thing. You want them well rested. It's weird. If they miss their naps, they go berserk during the night." She pulled her head back to look at Carlo. "Please baby. For mama. Just sleep."

"What if we give them some wine?" Lola asked brightly.

Carmen and Stella exchanged alarmed glances.

"Just a little," Lola said.

"Don't think I haven't considered it." Stella smiled weakly.

Carlo, peering over Stella's shoulder, was briefly still for a millisecond as he tracked, with enrapt fascination, a seagull hopping around on the patio. Lola had an idea. "Okay, let me try something." She dashed outside and found Daisy in the shade. She'd brought her along so she wouldn't disappear onto the construction site. "Come on, girl. Want to play nanny?"

Half an hour later, the babies were drifting off contentedly in their portable cribs, staring at Daisy, who sat between them, looking from child to child with a preternatural calm. The twins were utterly entranced by the dog, who took her responsibilities very seriously. When either child uttered a sound, she'd press herself against the netting of their crib. Tiny fingers explored her thick fur, soothing themselves with the lush texture. Daisy was utterly content.

"That dog is a freaking miracle," Stella said when Lola crept down the hall.

"I know, right?" Lola sat down at the dining room table, where Carmen and Stella were now happily pasting labels.

"How much does she charge for babysitting?" Stella asked.

"She's very reasonable," Lola said. "She works for peanuts. Actually, peanut butter, if I'm being specific."

A short while later, blissful silence still ruling, Stella, Carmen and Lola were idly gossiping about the upcoming wedding: who would get drunk (the entire kitchen staff and two of Mami's friends who always ended weddings crying in each other's arms), who would hook up (Connie, Izzy and Ruelle with random strangers), and who would make the worst speech (hands-down Evan's parents, who were a wee bit racist and tended to say things like they knew lots of Mexicans: their cleaning lady, gardeners and waiters).

They were all laughing, sipping wine, and finally having a good time, when Stella idly asked, "How's things in the kitchen?"

Lola's eyebrows shot up and Stella glanced between the sisters, knowing she'd hit a sore spot. "Oh? That good?"

"Carmen hired a chef who makes Gordon Ramsay look like the Dalai Lama," Lola said, taking a sip of her wine, raising her eyebrows at Carmen.

"Ohhh, sounds like a gem," Stella said. At heart, Stella was still a girl who loved a good story. Before she'd married Paolo, she'd run and owned Twig, the hair salon that Izzy was now in charge of.

"He's good for business," Carmen snapped.

Stella's eyes went big. "I see."

"He's king of the assholes," Lola said.

"Who's good for business," Carmen said, her voice tight.

"Okay," Stella said, smoothing glue on another wine label. "This is fun."

"No, not okay," Carmen said. The tendons stood out on her neck as she glared at Lola. "Could you not, Lola?"

"Could I not what? She asked how things in the kitchen were."

Carmen pursed her lips. "Not everything is about you. It's about the business. I know that you're Lola and the big picture doesn't concern you, but if I wasn't running things, god knows where we'd be."

Lola's face burned. She'd gone way past annoyed with Carmen and would now love nothing more than to punch her in the face. "Seriously?"

"Yes, seriously."

"I'm sorry, Stella. I know this was your wedding thing for Carmen…" Lola said.

Stella waved her hands, leaning back. "Oh please, let's be real. Weddings are about fights."

Off went the gloves. "Carmen, where is it written that you run the winery?"

Carmen's eyes flashed. The closer they got to the wedding, the quicker she was to fly off the handle. "On every pay check. Who pays the bills? Who negotiates with the bank? Who runs personnel?"

"Oh right. Who hires people like Neil?"

"What exactly have you done, Lola, besides come up with half-baked ideas that would cost us a small fortune?"

"My ideas are great!"

"Like what?"

"Like the tiny cabins! If you would open your mind even the smallest amount and see the possibilities!"

Carmen jumped up from her chair, pacing, waving her hands theatrically. "Like the art gallery that just sat there outside the bar? How many people went there? Three people? And we wasted all that money on paint and lighting."

Lola crossed her arms, jutting out her chin defensively. "That was a good idea."

"Or wait, how about the sandwich stand? How did that go, Lola?"

Of course she'd have to bring up the sandwich stand. Everyone had a sandwich stand story in their past, right? Or one like it. Lola had talked Carmen into a Blue Hills Winery sandwich stand, but they'd ended up not making any money, even going into the red after Lola used some cheese that she thought was blue, which turned out to be spoiled and made people sick. They'd ended up handing out free dinner vouchers to the restaurant like popcorn. Since she'd used the winery kitchen, they'd almost lost their food license after someone had reported it. It had taken Carmen a great deal of time and negotiations to claw back on that one. Rodolfo called them the world's most expensive sandwiches.

Carmen, of course, had refused to even listen to Lola when she tried to defend herself, laying the blame on the local cheesemaker.

"That wasn't all my fault!" Lola simmered.

Carmen waved her arms. "Of course it wasn't your fault. That's my point, Lola. While I'm running everything, you're coming up with hare-brained ideas that make my job harder. And nothing is ever your fault. You get to flounce around being the artistic one, while I get blamed for stifling your creative nature."

Lola felt the sweat beading on her forehead. "That's not fair."

Carmen pointed a finger at Lola. "No, it's not fair. It leaves me being the one who has to say no to everything. Do you think I like that role?"

Lola pursed her lips, trying not to explode. "Are you kidding me? You love it. Being irritated is your default setting. Lists are your happy place. Carmen, you are a complete control freak. The only reason you're marrying Evan is because he's the first guy that you couldn't push around."

Carmen stopped dead in her tracks.

Stella reached for a potato chip, popping it in her mouth as if this had turned into quite the entertainment.

Carmen patted her chest. "My lists are the reason Blue Hills is still around. If it weren't for me, Papi would have lost the property to the bank. I threw everything I had into saving the winery. Everything."

Bam. There it was. Lola's head sank to her chest as the reality hit. Carmen saw herself as the single savior of the winery. Lola had merely been there to do Carmen's bidding. The whole time, Carmen had only been giving lip service to the concept of the two of them being a team—coming up with a way to get the harvest in when they were out of money, saving the land from the bank—even though they'd been side by side, coming up with ideas and working long hours and days. In the end, Carmen saw herself as the mastermind. She'd told Lola in the thick of it all that Lola had had a big part in saving things, in cheerleading the harvesters through bringing in the grapes. She'd said she'd make sure Lola had a role going forward. Instead, Lola had been sidelined until she'd interviewed to become a line chef. Carmen had locked herself in the office and forgotten everything she'd promised. Running her own show and leaving Lola to once again find her own passion.

Although Lola already knew it, the truth was hard to hear. The worst thing was that it would always be this way. In Carmen's head, they'd always be slotted into the roles they'd been born into, and there was nothing Lola could do to break free from the mold. It was called Youngest Child Syndrome. She remembered the first time she'd read a blog post on it. It was the lens through which your family would always perceive you. The family pet, indulged and tolerated. Lola was suffocating. She had to get out.

"I'm never going to be anything other than your spoiled rotten little sister, am I? The flighty one. I was stupid enough to think that when you said we'd have an equal share in running the winery, you actually meant it. I'm never going to be anything more in your eyes than what I was when I was sixteen, no matter how hard I work."

"That's not fair. I took a risk hiring you for the kitchen. Let's not forget that."

"I applied for the job, Carmen. Like everyone else."

Stella took a sip of her wine. "Well, this is fun."

Lola lifted a finger to quiet Stella before turning back to Carmen. "The winery is one third mine."

Carmen put her hands on her hips. "Oh my god. Then why don't you act like a responsible partner?"

"You mean your definition of a responsible partner, which is to do exactly what you say."

Stella sipped her wine again. "The tiny cabins sound interesting."

Carmen turned to Stella. "Whose side are you on, anyway?"

Stella lifted both hands. "I'm Switzerland." In a very slow voice she added, "But in Switzerland, we do enjoy our tiny cabins. Just sayin'."

Lola raised her eyebrows. Maybe a neutral party was what she needed. She lifted her chin, plunging in. "Tiny cabins are low-impact rental units that house two adults and maybe some small children. They don't require the same permits or foundations as cabins over five hundred square feet and therefore have less restrictive construction permits." She spread her fingers, warming to her theme. And the fact that Carmen was sitting back, arms crossed and listening. "Five of them would fit at the top of the vineyard. Close enough to drive breakfast up by golf cart. Staying in a vineyard has real appeal and it would further our brand awareness with wine tastings and word of mouth."

Stella blinked at Carmen. "Sounds nice. Carmen, do you want to say something?"

Carmen pinched her lips. "It does sounds nice. In theory. However. By having guests sleep on the property, we open ourselves up to all kinds of liability. Also, the amount of income they'd generate isn't going to be worth the added tax implications, staffing or headache."

Lola shook her head. "I'd do it all."

Carmen sighed. "Lola, you are so good at dreaming all this stuff up. You have the best ideas. But your ideas leave me holding the pieces when the inevitable problems come up. We run a winery and a restaurant. We host weddings. We're very good at all three. It's called staying focused. That's how businesses go under. They spread themselves too thin. They focus on things that aren't their core strength. We're really good at what we do. Why can't we stick to it?"

Lola swallowed the giant lump that had grown in her throat. "That's just it, Carmen. It's not we. It's you. Always has been. We're not good at anything. Especially at being sisters."

CHAPTER NINE

Water Hound

Chelan was in high summer mode. A fresh crowd of weekend tourists had infused the little town. Merchants pushed their wares onto the sidewalk, hoping to entice customers. The air was balmy and hot, fragrant with sunscreen and cooking tacos from the food truck parked in the gas station under the jacaranda tree. The overhead sun was slipping towards the khaki mountain bordering the west side of town. Boats buzzed on the nearby lake. Children dragged their parents towards the ice cream store adjacent to Señor Frog's. It was a Saturday meant for play.

A large party of raucous frat boys eager for an afternoon beer surged around Izzy and Gus as they met on the hot sidewalk outside Señor Frog's.

"They look like children," Izzy said as the frat boys were swallowed into the dark bar.

"Soon to be drunk children," Gus said, holding the door.

They went inside, entering the cool dim room, glowing with neon, redolent of fried food. It always took Gus a second to adjust his frame of mind, reminding himself that he was an adult. There was nothing to worry about. Although the bar sent a friendly vibe to most, this was where his father had spent their welfare money. Where he'd drunk away the infrequent pay checks. Gus had been sent here regularly by his mother to drag his father out of the bar. A fifteen-year-old Gus had had his face slapped when he'd told his father that his mom had sent him to find out what time he'd be home. When the bartender had said something, Gus's dad had told him to mind his own business. Gus had watched the muscles twitch in the bartender's jaw, hoping he'd use those ropey, muscular arms to deck his dad. But although the bartender had looked like nothing would make him happier than to jump across the bar and to break Gus's father in half, he'd just kept wiping the bar with his towel. Nothing had happened. Gus had left the bar with stinging skin, shrunken and defeated.

Soon they were seated with Diet Cokes and a bowl of hot wings between them.

"How's the job?" Izzy asked. She'd asked him to come out and celebrate his new job. It was important, she felt, to mark milestones and accomplishments. One thing she'd learned along the way was to make a fuss over life events. Even the small ones. Gus was learning a lot from Izzy, including to make each day count. Finding the joy in everyday life of work and errands and fresh coffee with real cream. She was a genius at excavating joy. When he asked how to thank her for all her help, all she'd say was to be there for someone else. Gus hoped he had the chance.

Gus opened his mouth then closed it again, before tilting his head, giving Izzy a look. She propped her chin on her hand as if he was the most interesting thing in the world. "Complicated."

Izzy took a wing and dipped it into the milky ranch dressing, holding the improbably red chicken over the bowl until it stopped dripping. "How so?"

Gus sighed. "It's on the Alvarez place."

Izzy raised one eyebrow, chewing slowly. "Hmmmmm." She wiped her lips. "Interesting." She stretched the word out, considering all the possibilities.

"That's one word for it. I had no idea I'd react like I did. I keep one eye out for Mr. Alvarez and his shotgun, and the other for Lola, who just about brained me last night when she thought I was a bear. The last time I saw her, we were seventeen and making plans to sneak out during Christmas break. Now I'm wondering how much to tell her besides I'm sorry."

Izzy frowned. "What else would you tell her?"

Gus winced. "Let's just say I didn't expect to feel the way I did when I saw her."

"Who else is out there with you?"

Gus chewed for a moment before putting the wing down and fastidiously wiping his fingers. "That's the thing. It's just me. The building site is way up at the top of the vineyard. Hidalgo didn't want to pull anyone off another job, so I'm up there, hidden away, hoping nobody actually knows that he hired me. There should be more people for a job of that size, but I wanted to be alone. I nearly got crushed putting the pre-fab log walls up, until I figured out how to do it safely. Also, a friend from high school who is a waiter told me she saw her out on a date with Hidalgo. It's a crazy situation."

"Or perfect, depending on how you look at it."

Gus scratched his beard. "On what planet is it perfect to be working on the property of a man who said he wanted to kill me the last time he saw me? The same night I'd been driving his youngest daughter around while I was high? A girl who, when I see her, I don't know whether to run from or to ask out on a date. Explain to me the 'perfect' in that."

Izzy took a sip of her Diet Coke. "Well, because you're right there. Literally at the scene of the crime. Any time you feel moved, you just march on down, find Juan and unburden yourself. Then move on."

"He's not exactly the first one I'd want to start with."

"Then Lola. You've already broken the ice."

Gus looked at the frat boys, who were hollering about something, pushing one another around, prompting their waiter to rush over and tell them to keep it down. He looked back at Izzy, sighing. "You make it sound so simple. I'm not sure I want to know how she feels."

"Gus, the longer you think about it, the worse it's going to be."

"The ice isn't exactly broken with Lola. I don't know how to describe it. It was night, in front of a fire. It felt completely unreal. I don't think it's going to be any easier when we see each other in the daylight. Also, I don't want to get fired."

"Ah." Izzy nodded. "Fair enough."

"Hidalgo is a good guy to work for. He trusts me. He knows about my background and took a risk. I don't know that most builders would do that around here. If their clients knew they had someone with a record working in their homes, they could lose jobs. Throw in my history with this family and it's downright messy. If old man Alvarez knows that I'm the one building those cabins, he's going to throw a fit."

"Unless he forgives you."

Gus leaned back in his creaking chair, eying the neon beer signs lining the wall over the pool tables. "That's a big ask."

Izzy wiped her mouth, nodding. As she reached for another wing, the silver bracelets on her arm jangled. "It is. But you need to leave that up to Juan Alvarez."

"And what if he says 'get off my property'?"

Izzy considered this for moment. "Then you hightail it as fast as you can, because I've heard that Juan is an excellent shot."

Lola didn't know why she thought Carmen would show some sympathy. But when she came back in from dragging Daisy away from snapping at the neighbor's sprinklers, Carmen was pacing in the living room with Rosie and Carlo perched on either hip, her face a twisted knot of frustration as both babies fussed. "You woke the babies up when you screamed at the dog!" she snapped.

Stella swooped in to take Carlo, looking anxiously at Lola. "Carmen—"

"He was in the neighbor's yard!" Her shirt was soaked from holding the wet dog.

"There's something wrong with that dog, you know."

"You know what, Carmen? There's something wrong with you. Daisy is a shelter dog. Who knows what she's been through? Just because she likes water, there's something wrong with her?"

Carmen rolled her eyes. "I didn't mean it that way."

"Oh. Wow. Your empathy is just overwhelming," Lola snarled.

"Don't make this about me, Lola."

"No. I'm sick of it." Lola felt kind of ridiculous cradling a wet dog while trying to have an argument, but Daisy loved rubbing up against furniture when she was soaking wet. Indigo Bay wasn't fancy, but nobody needed dog-scented couches.

"Sick of what?" Carmen looked stunned.

"Seriously? I'm invisible, Carmen. Every idea I have is shot down. I want to make my mark on the business, and nothing ever happens. It's all, 'Oh sure, some day when we're making money' or, 'No, that's not our focus.' But who decides on the focus? Who makes all the decisions? Is there ever any voting? Any meeting? Or does the buck stop and start with you?"

"Am I really going to have to spell it out?"

Daisy was getting really heavy. This argument could only last as long as Lola could hold her. "Sure, spell it out."

"Or not. Maybe we can like, have a glass of wine first," said Stella. "Bring this back to something, I don't know, less Real Housewifey?"

The sisters ignored poor Stella, who had somehow managed to get the twins back to sleep and returned to the living room.

Carmen raised an eyebrow at Lola. "You're not going to like it."

"I already know, Carmen. You don't have to tell me. You spell it out every single day. You don't even trust me to cook for your wedding."

"Okay fine. Ever since you were little, you've been spoiled. You got what you wanted as a little kid and it was cute. But then you put Papi through hell sneaking out when you were a teenager. I remember him calling me, nearly out of his mind. You know what he said? He said he could just stand losing his wife but losing you would be the end of him. You and that guy Gus? It nearly killed

Papi with worry. I get it, you were a teenager, but it was selfish. And it's the way you've operated ever since. You've never had to live with the consequences of your actions. If I let you run with half of these ideas—"

"That's the whole point. It's not up to you."

She shook her head. "Honestly? Do you really want to run Blue Hills Winery?"

"That's not what I said," Lola muttered.

"No, it's not. Because it's not about doing all these pet projects. It's not the fun stuff, Lola. It's ninety-nine percent stuff nobody wants to do. It's the spreadsheets and the budgeting and making sure our employees have health insurance. It's figuring out if we've bought enough bottles or hired enough pickers or if we're making the right kind of wine. It's market analysis and honestly, a lot of hedging my bets and praying I'm right. Because nobody tells you what kind of wine is going to be trendy next summer, and you'd better get it right because it's a really thin margin. It's working until midnight, one, two o'clock in the morning, making sure that everyone gets paid and that the food for the restaurant gets ordered and that yes, we manage to land the Instagram star chef from Seattle who, by the way, I know is problematic… But man, Lola, just handle it. That's what being a grown up is."

"A grown up?" Lola would have dropped her dog right there in the living room, but she was frozen. "Carmen, your lack of empathy is stunning. But you know what? I will handle it. And step one is moving out of the house. Because I cannot live for one more second under the same roof as you."

Before her sister could say another word, Lola marched out of the living room towards the front door before she dropped her own dog.

Righteous indignation was a tough look with a thirty-five-pound dog in her arms. Daisy was now asleep and she didn't want to put her down. Luckily, Stella came along behind her and let her out of the door.

"Okay, so that was super fun," Stella said with a wry grin.

"I'm really sorry."

"Don't be. I get it." Stella followed Lola out, opening the passenger side door. "What's a wedding without a good freak-out beforehand?"

Lola stood up from putting the dog in the car. "Sorry about the wet dog in your house."

Stella gave her a hug. "Of course."

"We smell terrible."

Stella grinned, lightly petting the dog's head. "Well, my house usually smells of dirty diapers."

Carmen was now standing on the narrow walkway at Stella's front door, her arms crossed, as if she couldn't quite believe this was happening. "Lola. Think this through. If you want to cook something for the wedding, fine."

"Seriously? You think this is about your wedding? This is about how you treat me. I'm not running away. I'm twenty-seven years old, Carmen."

"Then maybe you should act like it."

Maybe Lola was tired. Maybe she'd just had it. Maybe she just felt like flipping her off. So, she did.

Carmen's face contorted like she'd just bit into a lemon. "Well, that was mature."

"Apparently maturity is not my look. Isn't that what you've been telling me?"

"Where are you going?"

"Anywhere I'm guaranteed not to see you!" Lola stalked around to the driver's side. The car was suffocatingly hot, so she cranked the windows, trying to ignore the scowling Carmen, who was now right beside the car, watching her. Unfortunately, Lola's car was wedged between a hedge and Carmen's car. She had to execute a five-point turn to get herself facing the road. All the while, her sister and Stella watched her, saying nothing, like twin statues with matching folded arms. Of course, neither one of them backed up, so Lola was forced to pull up next to them with her window open, awkwardly saying nothing a total of five excruciating times. Stella was biting her lip, barely concealing her laughter.

It was the most undignified angry exit in the history of family fights. By the time she crossed the driveway, Lola's cheeks burned bright red.

All the while as she cranked on the steering wheel, she'd wondered where, exactly, she was going to live. At this point, it didn't matter, as long as it was away from Carmen.

CHAPTER TEN

Airstreaming

Pulling into Crystal Huttinger's farm was like going back in time. Crystal was a friend of Lola's parents who lived on a parcel of land overlooking the lake with her herd of goats. Lola had passed Blue Hills, thinking she'd drive up to Twenty-Five Mile Creek State Park and come up with a plan while she stared at the lake and talked to some ducks. Then she remembered Crystal and knew she'd find a sympathetic ear and more than likely, a glass of wine. Daisy was fast asleep in a bed of dry blankets on the front seat. Lola left her there with the windows cracked to catch a breeze in the shade of the small goat barn. The goats' peaceful bleating sounded like a distant lullaby.

Crystal came out of the Airstream that was her home. Time hadn't altered her in the slightest. Her hair was twisted into a low bun; her wide-open face was smiling. She opened her arms as she crossed the dry grass, her blue eyes twinkling. She smelled, pleasantly, of hay, rosemary and faintly of soil. Her overalls were sun-bleached to a soft blue the color of the lake shallows, rolled up over a pair of Birkenstocks. "Lola! What a nice surprise. I was just about to have a glass of wine. Now we have a party!"

Crystal brought out the wine and they settled under the oak tree at the edge of her field, overlooking the glittering blue of Lake Chelan, while Lola explained to Crystal what had brought her here. Across the lake were the straw-colored slopes that led into the foothills of the North Cascades, greenish-blue in the late afternoon. Dragonflies gleamed in the fields. Squirrels and birds scampered overhead in the ancient oak. They were deep in the cool shade with the heat shimmering around them. Lola took a sip of her wine, waiting for Crystal to comment on her tale of woe.

Crystal pursed her lips, nodding. "You girls have worked awfully hard on that place."

Lola was slightly deflated, thinking Crystal was about to discount her feelings. "We have."

"And Carmen…" Crystal looked off, across the lake, as if composing her thoughts. "She's a tough one. I remember your mother saying she'd have to marry a strong-willed man, because she was a fighter."

"Mom said that?"

Crystal handed her a bright blue pottery bowl of pistachios in their shells. "She sure did. Carmen used to tell her that she needed to speak English at home. That she'd be too hard to understand if her English didn't improve."

"That sounds like Carmen."

Crystal nodded, tossing the pistachio shells into the dirt. "From what I've heard, Carmen has met her match."

"What do you think I should do?" Lola asked. She couldn't spend one more night across the hall from Carmen. She was too mad and didn't want to back down. Not now.

A beatific grin spread across Crystal's weathered face. "My darling girl, you came to the right person. I have the perfect solution."

The next day, Gus was at the job site with Hidalgo, wrapping up their discussion over the bed of his truck, drinking bottled water and watching the sun sink behind the cliff overhead. This left plenty of daylight but mercifully, blocked the sun. Gus loved it when the cliff gave him respite from the heat. Both men turned their heads as they heard creaking and rattling headed their way. It was an old truck, straining to pull a large Airstream trailer.

Gus and Hidalgo stopped talking, watching with wonder as the two women came crawling up the hill in the old Ford, whipping up a cloud of red dust. Mrs. Huttinger, the old woman who raised goats out on a large piece of property north of Chelan State Park, was at the wheel. She waved a friendly salute as she passed. Lola was beside her, pointing ahead, not looking at the two men. Daisy jumped over the back seat, barking out the open window at the men with delight, her tail wagging ecstatically.

The men stared at one another, as if a circus had just passed.

"So that happened," Gus said.

Hidalgo took a long drink of his water, shaking his head. "Is it always like this?"

Gus thought of Lola thinking he was a bear, the whirling emotions after the fireside chat, the constant looking out for the old man with his shotgun. "Pretty much."

Hidalgo shook his head. "Well, let's go help them then, I guess."

Gus wondered if he should head out, which he had planned to do… But then he couldn't resist the temptation of seeing Lola and finding out what on earth she had planned. He grinned, thinking that some things never changed. Lola was still full of surprises.

Crystal Huttinger was forthright, offering her hand, introducing herself to Hidalgo, saying she'd seen his trucks around town. The women had rolled the old trailer over yellow plastic wheel blocks to level it. The spot Lola had chosen was out of the way, tucked behind a high row of staked vines. It was far enough to the south to keep it tucked out of sight of Orchard House. Gus stayed off to the side, noticing the way Hidalgo placed his hand on the small of Lola's back for a second, how he smiled at her. How he rushed to direct the backing up of the trailer, tugged endlessly at the rusty stairs when they wouldn't come out of the rig. Made sure to add WD40 to the shopping list on his phone. She'd need it, he said, happy to be useful.

"Nice to meet you, ma'am," Hidalgo said politely.

"Don't you 'ma'am' me. I'm Crystal. I'm a goat herder. Come see me sometime. I have the best place for cocktails on the entire lake. Ask Lola." She grinned mischievously as she offered her hand to Gus. "Gus Weaver, as I live and breathe. So nice to see you. And well, you know Lola…"

Gus felt himself flushing, looking down at the ground. "Yes, I do." Which hardly accounted for the riot of images running though his brain. All the ways in which he knew Lola. Lola remained impassive. Either Lola genuinely didn't care about him, or she was being political. Gus hoped the latter.

"Hi," Lola said, nodding.

Gus went to his truck and dug out more water from the cooler he kept in the backseat, handing one to Crystal before approaching Lola, who thanked him before making sure that Hidalgo was otherwise engaged making the sure the trailer tires were properly inflated.

"Maybe we should stay away—" Lola blurted.

He interrupted Lola before she completed the thought. "Agreed. Maybe we should." Although he wasn't exactly sure what she'd been going to propose, it sounded like it was to about keeping their distance. With Hidalgo here, it seemed like a good idea. It would be easier for both of them.

Lola's face flashed a multitude of emotions. Gus, who'd spent his youth following her signals, couldn't read one of them.

"Okay, fine." Her face flushed as she turned away from him.

Gus felt sadder than he'd ever felt in his whole life. This was how they were going to play it. She'd ignore him, and he'd pretend like he hadn't come back here for her. Although she seemed to be ignoring him in the way of someone who sensed, without looking, his exact location.

Or maybe he was projecting. It was almost animal, the way his senses became keener, how the hair on his arms stood up when she was near. The air caught her hair and for a second he could smell her mint shampoo. He felt weak with longing. Sick with the desire to touch her. Feel her skin. This would be hard.

Lola was prattling on to Hidalgo about how she'd sleep here, while Gus clutched his water, gazing out at the orchard. Crystal was studying him with concern. He glanced down at his water bottle, crumpled in his hand.

"Are you okay?"

Gus was shocked. He hadn't remembered crushing the bottle, but there it was. "Oh yeah. I'm tired. Just, um, could you please tell Hidalgo I took off?"

Crystal nodded, before placing a dry hand on his arm. "Gus?"

"Yeah?"

Crystal's eyes were warm. "Homecomings are never easy."

Gus nodded, not sure what to say. "Right. Thanks."

Gus drove down the hills through the Alvarez orchard, imaging Lola living in the trailer a few feet from him, pretending that he wasn't aware of her every move, the girl his boss obviously was falling for, thinking that a complicated situation had just gotten much more complicated.

The next morning, Gus sat in his truck drinking the last of his coffee. The old Airstream was still parked at the far end of the field, the silver aluminum reflecting the faint morning light. There was no movement from the trailer. The two chairs rested by the stone fire pit. Had Lola invited Hidalgo to stay? Did they stay by the fire until she led him by the hand up those creaky metal stairs into the trailer? Why was he torturing himself this way? Gus looked into the depths of his coffee, thinking that this was just about the weirdest job he'd ever taken. It was one damn thing after another. The dog appearing out of nowhere. Staring at him as if she were proxy for the old man. Lola mistaking him for a bear, then them having that one weirdly intimate night by the fire. The old man lurking out there with a shotgun in his imagination, but definitely with the potential to become reality if he knew that Gus was here. If Gus knew one thing about Juan Alvarez, it was that his fierce love of his daughters wouldn't dim with age.

Gus just about jumped out of his skin when his phone rang, shattering the silence. He had to dig around for a minute to find it, lodged in the back of the truck. Hardly anyone called him. He never understood people who talked about being addicted to their phones. There were too many other interesting things in the world. Like making something with his hands.

"Hey."

It was Hidalgo. "Hey. Are you at the job site?"

"Yeah." Gus kept his eye on the Airstream, wondering if he was supposed to keep quiet. It was six o'clock in the morning. Down below, the lake shimmered in the gray haze. A couple fishermen floated silently on the glassy surface in open skiffs. The cottonwood trees on Wapato Point were motionless, reflecting in the steel-colored water.

This was Gus's favorite time of day. Always had been. He used to wake up in the cold trailer and eat his cereal in the dark, hoping that nobody else would wake up. It was slightly annoying—okay maybe very annoying—that Lola had moved in, even if she was probably asleep right now. He'd looked forward to having the site to himself, interrupted only by Hidalgo, who seemed to stop by more than he needed. But now Lola was up here, too. How were they supposed to navigate their distance if she'd moved right the hell in next to him? What kind of mixed messages was she sending? Stay away, but I'm moving in?

"Is Lola alright?"

The way Hidalgo said her name worried Gus. Hidalgo sounded less like a boss and more like a middle schooler asking about a girl.

"I think so. Looks like she's still sleeping." Oh god, was he going to have to spy on Lola for Hidalgo? How many levels of awful was he descending into? Clearly, Hidalgo was worried about her sleeping way up here, but Gus had spent enough time here to know that the worst intruder would be coyotes or marauding raccoons.

"Okay, if you see her, let me know."

"Okay." Gus waited for Hidalgo to explain himself. To say, *I know it sounds like I'm asking you to spy on her, but I'm not.* There was an awkward silence, so he tacked on, "Will do," immediately thinking he sounded like a total ass. Why was it that everything to do with Lola made him sound like the sitcom version of himself? *No man is an island*, his therapist liked to say. *We all need help from other people. Our support system.* Gus felt like he could definitely be an island, if it weren't for the existence of Lola Alvarez. Even when he'd been behind layers of concrete, locked away like an animal, all he'd had to do was to become very still and he'd been able to feel her presence. It had been both comforting and alarming. All his life up until then, Gus had learned to do without other people.

What if he needed Lola more than she needed him?

If last night was the sum total of the evidence, then Lola clearly was doing just fine without Gus in her life. Lola had at least one man falling all over himself to help her. There were probably half a dozen more waiting in the wings.

The door of the Airstream creaked open. The hinges needed oil. He mentally ticked off the other maintenance items the trailer required: sealant around the windows, a good anti-tarnish scrub, better levelers on the wheels, a new propane tank and, if he had to guess, the roof needed scrubbing and coating. Airstreams would last forever, but you had to keep them up or they'd show their age. Hidalgo would get around to everything, but Gus would beat him to the punch.

Daisy trotted down the metal step of the trailer. She sniffed the air, sensing that something was different before spotting Gus's truck. She trotted over, her ears alert, her intelligent eyes on his. She was within six feet when she stopped, squatted and peed, keeping a close eye on Gus the entire time. It was a very clear message. Gus was on her territory. She was taking over for Juan Alvarez. Be warned.

After she'd finished, she scraped her back legs a few times, covering the muddied dirt, looking scrappy and tough in the process. Again, her eyes never left his face. Gus had the strange feeling that he was an intruder. With a pointed look that said, *I've got my eye on you*, the little dog ambled back to the trailer, climbed the metal step, scratched the door once, and after giving him a parting glare, was instantly admitted inside. So much for being BFFs with the dog.

Lola peeped out of the trailer window after she let Daisy back in. Gus was just sitting in the cab of his truck. She'd heard him pull up and had scooted over to the banquette to spy on him. He'd parked the truck and just sat there—although, what else was he supposed to do? Here she was, staring between the slats of the Airstream blinds like a peeping Tom… Although in this scenario, clearly Gus was the peeping Tom. Right?

Last night had been so awkward. She'd been so exhausted, moving her new home like a snail and then having both Hidalgo and Gus there. She hadn't even been sure what she and Gus had agreed to, except to ignore one another, which was all but impossible.

For one thing, he worked here. Of course, she'd known that when she'd told Crystal that she had the perfect spot for the old trailer, but what Lola hadn't anticipated was the intimacy of waking up in the morning and having Gus just a few yards away, looking shockingly sexy in his old truck, like some ad for manhood and beards. She hadn't felt like this in years. That buzz of anticipation. The hum in her body. Damn Gus. Why did he have to show up now and confuse things? She was focused, she was living her dream, and now Gus Weaver, of all people—all filled out and manly with that beard—showed up. Just when the first eligible man she'd dated in years was actually interested in her. How about showing up ten years ago, when she'd really needed him?

Lola snapped the blinds shut, thinking she'd better get a hold of herself. Gus was just some guy she'd known in high school. Then she laughed out loud at the idiocy of thinking of Gus as "just some guy." Gus was, and would always be, central to the person she'd become. Gus had anchored her at a time when she'd felt herself lifting off the known world. Papi and she had been rattling around in the big house, each grappling with losing Mami, then rearranging themselves when first Adella and then Carmen left. Every time she'd begun to feel settled, the family landscape had shifted and Papi had seemed to hold her tighter, becoming the disciplinarian he'd never been before. The more she'd longed to stretch her wings, the tighter his hold had become.

It had seemed like he'd trusted Adella and Carmen, but Lola was a different story. With Lola, he'd become the old-school Papi. Strict.

Anxious and controlling. Lola had lashed out, feeling unmoored. First Mami's death, then her sisters leaving, and then the distance from Papi. If she wasn't part of the Alvarez family, what was she? Gus had stepped into the void and seen her when she'd felt herself disappearing. Gus had turned it around for her. Reminded her that she was, despite Mami, lucky. And beautiful. And cherished. Gus had wrapped her up in a thick blanket of love and made her feel safe. And for that, she'd always have a place for him in her heart.

But would she trust him?

Probably not.

The people she loved disappeared. Lola knew that.

Lola busied herself now getting ready for work, focusing on how thrilled she was—despite the complication known as Gus Weaver—to be waking up in her own little home, away from all things Carmen. The particular freedom that came from having her own snug abode had been a long time coming. The last time she'd awoken to her own place had been the rare occasions in Seattle when all her roommates had been gone. She'd never been able to afford to rent her own place. As soon as Crystal had shown her the old Airstream tucked behind the goat barn, shining in a dusty beam of sunlight like something out of a hipster fairy tale, Lola had known in her gut that it was the perfect answer. Crystal had recently upgraded her Airstream, and was looking forward to getting this old one off her property. She'd refused to accept any payment, saying they'd talk about it after Lola had had a chance to try it out. Crystal had hooked up the old trailer to her truck, pulling it up her road from her lakefront property. Crystal, an inveterate flea market shopper, had also provided Lola with nearly everything she needed to kit the trailer out.

Waking up this morning had felt like she'd traveled to the other side of the rainbow. Birds calling in the vineyard. Buttery sunshine peeking through the blinds. Pushing back the covers and hearing… Nothing. Nature. No sharing a bathroom with Carmen, no stumbling downstairs to a kitchen full of people. Just the magnificent view of the vineyard and the lake and, mostly, the quiet. Give or take a handsome guy or two.

Daisy had taken to it as if she'd lived in a trailer her whole life. Last night, she'd jumped up on the foot of Lola's bed, circling around innumerable times, scratching at the covers, as was her habit, before finally finding the perfect position and tucking herself into a tight curl, her nose buried under her paws. A furry little cashew. And Lola could have stayed in bed all morning, admiring the perfect simplicity of the Airstream. The cupboards built into the curve where the walls met the ceiling, in a perfect union of form and function. The minimalist kitchen with the little window framed by hand-sewn curtains. Lola felt like Thumbelina, tucked into her perfect shell. Her sleep had been the deepest and most restorative she'd felt in months.

Now she sifted through her clothes, pulling on a T-shirt and jeans, waiting for her heart to stop beating so fast. She brushed her teeth, looking up at her face after she spit, examining her face for signs. How did she feel about Gus? Was being around him, even if they gave each other wide berth, a good idea? Would they stick to ignoring each other, even with nobody else around? How awkward would that be? Surely she'd have to talk to him, eventually? Last night had been beyond strange, but she just couldn't have it out with him. She couldn't tell him what she'd been through in the aftermath of his departure. Not in front of other people. Not now. Lola wanted to keep an eye on him. See if he'd gotten over his self-destructive impulses. See if it was worth telling him how she'd suffered.

What if Gus Weaver had changed?

What then?

Lola took a deep breath and opened the Airstream. Daisy trotted out ahead of her and Lola descended. All her worrying had been for nothing. Gus had made himself busy at the second cabin and was holding up one of the walls, already sweating. Lola watched him out of the corner of her eye, pushing the wall up, his head turned in her direction. His brown eyes seemed to be summing her up, making her heart do a quick flip. She quickly whipped her head away, inhaling sharply.

Shoot.

Ignoring Gus Weaver was going to be a lot harder than she thought.

Mid-morning, Carmen came into the kitchen to refill her coffee cup. Felicia nudged Lola. They both knew that Carmen could have gotten her coffee up at the winery office, where they had their own Keurig machine. Carmen filled her mug, walked to the refrigerator for half and half and looked at her sister as she said, in a loud voice, "Neil, can you come up to the winery office later? We need to talk about the wedding menu."

"Cold," Felicia whispered. Felicia knew everything. Sister drama was like reality TV. Strangely addictive and utterly entertaining.

"She so could have called him. She's dying to know where I'm staying." Lola spoke under her breath. She and Felicia had perfected the art. It kept them sane under Neil's rule.

"Make her ask." Felicia peeled hard-boiled eggs with her thumb, prying the shells off in halves.

Lola ran her favorite Santoku knife over some jicama, slicing it into fine straws. "She wouldn't give me the satisfaction. She'll ask someone else."

"Your mother must have been something else," Felicia said, placing the eggs into pickling vinegar with red onions.

"Why?" Lola asked, stilling her knife to look at her friend.

"More workee less talkee," snapped Neil as he sailed past on his way to the giant range at the end of the kitchen, his arms full of smoked ribs.

Lola stuck her tongue out at his back.

"Because her daughters have hella strong personalities."

After the lunch rush, just when Lola could stop to get a drink of water, she felt Felicia poking her in the side. She choked on the water, coughing until Felicia pounded her back.

"I'd ask you if you wanted a glass of water, but…"

Lola kept coughing. "Not funny."

"Actually, it is."

Lola shook her head, riding out the last few coughs.

Felicia pointed to the kitchen door where Hidalgo peeked in. "It's, um…"

Before Felicia could say his name, Hidalgo spoke up, looking a little unsure. "Hey, Lola. Can I see you for a sec?"

Lola instinctively looked at Neil, and then hated herself for it. She arrived at the restaurant before he did and stayed longer. She should be able to step out for a few minutes during a lull. Taking off her apron, she noticed Neil appraising Hidalgo.

As she passed him, he said in a leering tone, "New boyfriend?"

"I'll be right back."

"You'd better be," Neil said snidely.

Hidalgo gave Neil a sharp look, which made Lola supremely happy. Hidalgo was the kind of guy she needed to focus on. He was solid and could always be counted on to do the right thing. He seemed like the kind of guy whose past stretched back in one serene, unruffled path. No ghosts. No skeletons. Hidalgo, she sensed, would always have her back. Would always stop the Neils of this world.

"Hey," she said when she reached Hidalgo, surprised at the happy tone of her voice. Was it that she was getting out of the kitchen, or was it possibly the sight of Hidalgo? It could be Hidalgo, which was reassuring. Maybe she was finally making the right choice when it came to men.

"Can you come look at something?" Hidalgo asked.

She thought about it for a half a second before turning to Neil. "I'll be back in fifteen minutes."

"I don't think so," said Neil with arch skepticism, as if she'd been foolish to ask.

Lola could sense Hidalgo growing tense behind her. "I'll have her back as soon as I can," he said.

Lola knew she had to get Hidalgo out of there before he said something incriminating about the cabins or the building site. He wasn't the kind of guy who'd be okay with secrecy. "Neil, it will be fine. Felicia will cover for me."

Felicia turned to Neil and saluted. "Felicia will cover for her."

Neil's face twisted into an unhappy sneer. "If things get busy, I will not be happy."

Felicia looked away from him, hissing, "He's never happy."

Lola took out her phone and waved it. "I'm one phone call away."

Before Neil could ask any more questions, she pushed Hidalgo out the door.

"I'll go with you," Lola said, following him to the truck after he asked her if she wanted to walk and meet him at the hollow. It seemed to make him happy. She noticed him smiling down at his feet as he opened the door for her.

As she climbed into the truck cab, Lola thought she needed to hang out more with men who opened doors for her. Sure, she was perfectly capable of it herself, but it was more about the gesture. It demonstrated a certain kind of respect. An attitude. She was tired of guys who asked her out to sticky-floored bars and still talked about high school.

"That guy is a piece of work," Hidalgo said as he turned the truck around in the driveway. His arm, slung around the back of Lola's seat, was nearly around her back. She found it comforting. His arms were muscular. He clearly didn't spend all his time driving around from site to site.

"Oh yeah, Neil is a gem."

Hidalgo's jaw was tight as he glanced at her. "And your sister won't do anything about him?"

Lola rolled down the window, letting the wind press against her face, drying the inevitable sweat from her T-shirt. Even though the day was in the low nineties, it still felt cooler outside than in the kitchen.

"She thinks I'm exaggerating. To her, I'm the whiny little sister who can't take the heat. She automatically cuts everything I say in half. It's not that she thinks I'm lying about him, it's more of an old habit of hers. I mean, when I was a kid, I was spoiled and I gave my dad a hard time when I was in high school, running around. I was a little wild. But that was a long time ago."

"Families do that. They stick people in slots and keep them there."

"Yeah and people are fine with it, I get it. It's familiar and mostly, people don't mind it. And maybe that's okay for people who get together once a year for Thanksgiving. But we're running a business together."

Hidalgo took a left onto the main road and the next left up into the canyon road bordering the orchard. He drove with a calm assurance, one elbow slung out the window. Lola could feel herself calming down as the truck bounced up the hill. If she reached out, she could almost touch the red grit of the cliff wall. The dusty smell of sage and ripening grapes filled the truck cab. Behind them, a plume of dust filled the road. They passed a trio of deer lying in the deep green shade under a ponderosa pine, nearly invisible.

"No wonder you want to live up here," Hidalgo said.

Lola nodded, suddenly gratified that Hidalgo could see her point of view. She gave him a broad smile. He grinned, looking over at her. His eyelashes were absurdly and beautifully long. The kind women said weren't fair to waste on a man. They weren't wasted on Hidalgo. They made him look soulful. Lola felt her heart hitch a tiny bit, which was gratifying. Life would be so much easier, loving someone like Hidalgo.

Her heart did another flip though as they crested the hill, pulling into the parking spot beside Gus's truck. Her body reacted viscerally to the sight of the truck, as if dredging up memories from ten years ago. She tried to stuff it all down, to just enjoy being with Hidalgo.

"How's the trailer?" Hidalgo asked after he shut off the truck engine.

"Quiet. I didn't even know I'd end up here. Carmen and I got into an argument and I might have said I was moving out before I had an actual plan." As she climbed out the truck, she realized she sounded exactly like the person Carmen accused her of being. Impetuous. Irrational. Hot-headed. Why was she telling him all this now?

Hidalgo met her at the front of the truck. "I don't blame you," he said.

She felt immediately comforted and wondered why she couldn't give herself that small amount of grace. "Thank you."

Instead of heading directly for the building site, Hidalgo hiked in the opposite direction. Lola felt a tiny bead of worry rise as he went directly to the spot where Gus used to wait for Lola when they were young. How many times had she looked up from the vineyard to see him waiting there, peering down into the vineyard, his face cracking into a broad smile when he saw her? There was a slight rise at the end of the meadow before it sloped down to the vineyard, making it the best spot to enjoy the view. It was natural, Lola told herself, that this was where Hidalgo would go. Still, it made her uncomfortable to be in the exact same spot that she and Gus had once wrapped their arms around each other and pledged eternal love. She remembered thinking that she'd felt like Rose, from the movie *Titanic*. That had been her moment. It was etched in her brain forever.

Which is why she felt confused by standing here with Hidalgo.

Hidalgo, oblivious to her quandary, crossed his arms and breathed deeply, turning his head slightly towards her as she joined him.

"Gorgeous!" he pronounced.

Lola had to force herself with iron will not to look towards Gus. He was carrying two-by-fours on his shoulder from his truck to the spot where he had framed one of the cabins. Out of the corner of her eye, she couldn't help but notice the vivid blue of his Levi's, his suede work gloves and... Was that a wry grin on his face? Her neck felt weak from the task of holding it rigid. Everything in her being wanted to track him, but she was aware that he was just going about his business. She'd go about hers. That was the deal, right?

"This is my favorite place in the world." As if on cue, a red-tailed hawk floated overhead, shifting on the thermals in the cornflower blue sky. The lake was ruffled with wind, glimmering deep blue.

Then the peace was shattered by the whine of a table saw. Gus was sawing the two-by-fours with a nearly imperceptible wicked grin on his face. Lola was sure she could see it.

Hidalgo leaned towards her ear. "He has perfect timing."

Lola's lips twisted. "A little too perfect."

"I was being sarcastic but yes, he's not exactly setting the mood for us," Hidalgo said, shouting to be heard over the table saw, the noise of which was amplified by the cliff. "I hired him to do fine carpentry, but he's going to be working on the cabins until they're done."

Lola was staring at Gus, who was slicing a two-by-four into tiny chunks. "Great."

"Are you okay with him?"

Lola nodded, replying firmly. "Yes."

Hidalgo pointed to the stakes marking off the building sites for the tiny cabins. "I just wanted you to look at the layout before Gus got going. He had to move things around a little bit."

The table saw whine felt like a dentist drill in her head. "Can we sit in the truck and talk?"

Hidalgo nodded.

Once they were in the car, he turned to her. "Sorry about that. I could ask him to stop, but given our time considerations, I didn't think it was the best idea."

Everything about Gus drew her attention. If he was gone, she'd be less inclined to think about him. That was the hope. She twisted in her seat. "Do you really think he needed to do that?"

Hidalgo frowned. "I don't know."

"Using the table saw right while we were looking at the view seems, I don't know."

Hidalgo looked out the window at Gus, who was measuring the two-by-fours, making ticks with a pencil he kept behind his ear. "I really don't think he planned it this way."

Lola willed herself to be quiet, but the words came forth in a gushing torrent. "Okay but we were looking at the view and he's got a whole building site. I mean, surely he could have found something else to do until we'd, I don't know, moved on?"

Hidalgo shrugged. "I guess I'm just used to this kind of noise. I can ask him to stop, if that's what you want."

Lola waved her hand, wishing she weren't so irritated. Wishing that Gus Weaver wasn't ruining what should have been a nice moment and that he didn't look so strong and fit and downright irresistible. That he wasn't taking off his worn flannel right now to show off his arms, which were muscular and sported tattoos that made her way too curious. When had he got them? What did they mean? She shook her head, as if to free her mind of all things Gus Weaver. Why oh why had Hidalgo hired Gus of all of all people? What if Papi saw him? What if anyone saw him? That beard wouldn't fool anyone. Would it?

"No. It's fine." She tapped her fingers on the dash, willing herself to look away from Gus.

"Is everything okay?"

Lola looked at Hidalgo's face. He was so concerned. She knew he was moving heaven and earth to make this happen before Carmen's wedding. "Everything is great. I know that you didn't have to make all this work, and it's super sweet of you to do it. Really kind."

Hidalgo grinned. Lola looked out of the corner of her eye, making sure that Gus was watching before she leaned in to Hidalgo and kissed him on the cheek.

"I'd better get back."

Hidalgo turned the key and the truck's engine roared to life.

Lola could tell from the set of Gus's shoulders that he'd definitely seen what had transpired in the truck, and it gave her a happy little jolt. *Take that, Gus Weaver*, she thought. It might have been ten years, but she could still read him like a book.

Lola couldn't concentrate. She'd gotten ready for this date with all the concentration of someone anticipating a great night. She'd chosen her outfit carefully, applied makeup, then blended it until it was the merest hint, capitalizing on her bronzed skin. Getting ready for a date in the trailer was challenging. The lights in the bathroom gave her skin a bluish tint. She didn't have an iron or a full-length mirror. She'd nearly cracked the bathroom toilet when she'd stood on it to get a better look at herself. The end result was worth it, though, she thought. She was wearing her favorite sundress and the perfume Stella had brought her from Italy. After a long chat with Daisy, informing her that she was in charge and not to let any attractive carpenters inside, during which Daisy had fallen asleep, she'd locked the trailer, walked right past Gus—who'd ignored her in favor of a nail that suddenly needed extracting—and climbed into Hidalgo's truck.

On the drive over, she'd promised herself that she'd stop her mind from traveling the same obsessive track it had been running on since she'd realized Gus was back, reminding herself that she was here, with Hidalgo.

She couldn't do it.

Every time she tuned into what Hidalgo was talking about, they'd pass another landmark from her relationship with Gus. The big sign as they drove into town, "HOME OF THE CHELAN GOATS," the unfortunately named Chelan High School mascot. The bridge that they'd jumped off, holding hands, plunging into the night water, high on being alive and in love. The parking lot where Gus laid sleeping bags in the back of the truck and they'd watched meteors streak across the sky and he'd told her his mom was going to die. He'd cried and she'd felt responsible for him. It had felt like the most important moment in her life.

The wine bar at Wapato Point was one of Chelan's nicer bars, and Lola appreciated that Hidalgo had chosen it. It had a vastly different view of the lake than Blue Hills. Wapato Point was on Manson Bay, and the restaurant sat just above the busy dock with an expansive view of the small bay and the point, with its towering poplars and high-end resort homes to the left.

Everything should have been perfect, except that Lola's mind wasn't on the man in front of her. Not that Hidalgo could tell. Hopefully, he couldn't. Lola felt terrible. Here was the right guy in front of her. Successful, thoughtful, raised in the right kind of family. One that Lola could already tell that she'd slip into seamlessly. From what she'd gathered, Hidalgo came from a family remarkably similar to her own. Parents who had immigrated from Mexico to escape cities blighted by poverty and drugs. They had met while agricultural workers. Night school and some lucky breaks had led to success in a family-owned business. A warm, loving matriarch. A strict-on-the-outside, cuddly-on-the-inside father. Two chatty, gossipy sisters. One look at Hidalgo, and you could tell the man had won the family lottery. He had an easy way about him that spoke volumes. He had nothing to prove.

As much as Lola hated to admit it to herself, Papi was right. Dating a Mexican man would be easy. Familiar. And, also, fun.

But her mind was on Gus.

Always.

She shook herself. Told herself she was only thinking about Gus because it was weird living so close to one another, and also because she and Gus had a history, so seeing him again was always going to be charged. It meant nothing. The sooner she got this out of her system, the better. Then she could focus on Hidalgo, who deserved more. She wanted someone who saw her for the person she was today, not the version she was ten years ago. Hidalgo liked who she was in this moment. He wasn't chasing a girl who didn't exist anymore.

First, she had to resolve her past, which had arrived on her doorstep. How was she supposed to get Gus out of her system when they weren't even talking? Wasn't the best way to rid yourself of a fear facing it head on? What if she gave herself and Hidalgo a real shot by purging herself of Gus by attacking the problem instead of running from it? Not seeing one another for ten years hadn't worked. Maybe it was time for a new solution. Not talking wasn't working anyway. It was like the absence of talking led to obsession. Every time she stepped out of the trailer or hiked up from Orchard House, Gus suddenly found something entrancing in a piece of wood or walked inside one of the newly framed cabins. Or went to fetch something from his truck. And as soon as Lola had settled into her trailer, picked up a book or poured herself a glass of wine, or even thought about sitting outside by her hastily constructed fire pit, Gus would start hammering away.

Lola would slam her book to the table or stop her meal prep or whatever she was doing and try to ignore the noise. But the Airstream, for all its retro charm, was like living inside a piñata.

Lola had to fight the urge to stomp outside and yell at him. On the other hand, she couldn't stop spying on him. Or thinking about him. She found herself peeking through the blinds, thrilled whenever she caught him glance, ever so covertly, in her direction (unless, of course, it was all in her imagination), then chastising herself for caring. For noticing. For becoming the kind of woman who peered out of her windows. She was a catless cat lady.

She also spent a lot of time analyzing the pros and cons of talking to him. Of having it out, realizing that, no matter what, she'd cry. She'd turn back into that girl who had sat at home alone while her girlfriends met at Felicia's house to get ready for prom, giddy and excited. The girl whose eyes had welled with tears when the principal had called Gus's name at graduation, then had awkwardly tucked the diploma under his arm when nobody collected it. The girl who had heard he was out of jail and had hoped, in vain, that he'd come home.

Gus was stirring up a lot of emotion at a time when she couldn't afford it. But if she was going to have a future with Hidalgo could she afford ignoring it?

At work, Felicia had yelled at her just before she'd accidentally poured Béarnaise sauce on the grilled cheese and tomato sandwiches. She'd grabbed a tray of sweet potatoes out of the oven without an oven mitt, and had cut her knuckles while prepping food until they looked like they'd been attacked by piranhas.

The moment Gus had taken off his flannel shirt and exposed his arms in the black shirt with the sleeves cut off kept replaying in her mind, like a song you couldn't stop repeating in your head.

It was ridiculous.

At one point she'd come clean, telling Felicia when Neil had disappeared during the middle of the day for one of his smoke breaks. They both breathed easier, knowing they had twenty Neil-free minutes.

"Oh no, this is bad." Felicia had shaken her head. "He's back and he's working up there?"

Lola had put her finger over her mouth. "Yes. Shhhh. Right where I'm living."

Felicia's face had brightened as she tried to hide her smile. "Wait, Gus is the hot construction guy?"

"You've seen him?"

"Oh yeah. He came in to talk to Izzy while I was getting my hair done. Brought her a coffee and oh my oh my. You mean, you're living up there in the trailer, while he's working up there all day long? This is like a total country music video. There's no way you guys are not hooking up."

"Oh my god! Can you just shut it? This isn't a video, Felicia. It's my life. He's working there and if anyone in my family finds out, heads will fly. And probably more than that. I'm just lucky that Papi is going deaf and Carmen spends most of her time over at the Hollister Estate."

"Right. But I mean, have you looked at him? I mean, it's like all his hotness went to school and learned how to be super-hot. It's ridiculous. He's like Coke commercial hot. But better, because…" She dropped her voice to a whisper. "He's right here. In your backyard. Or front yard. Which is it?"

"Can you not?"

"I kind of have to. Obviously, you're not taking this on a superficial enough basis. Have you stopped freaking out long enough to look?"

"Of course I've looked at him. How can I not? He's there all the time."

Felicia's eyes went huge, implying the obvious. "I wouldn't tell anyone. I mean. You're practically living together."

Lola slapped her hand over her eyes. "Not even remotely."

"I mean, I feel like a hook-up is practically required."

"Leave it alone. Please. I'm dating Hidalgo."

"And I get that, but you and Gus? I mean, did you ever really finish it? Don't you feel like you need some closure or something? And by closure, I mean, just feeling those biceps…"

"Stop it. Just stop it," Lola had hissed. "We're done."

Felicia had pretended to zip her lips and throw away the key. But, nonetheless, had blurted, "Nobody would have to know."

"I would know! Me. I'm not making the same mistake twice."

When Lola came back to the present moment with Felicia's words ringing in her ears, Hidalgo was looking at her with questioning eyes. "Is everything okay?"

Lola took a deep breath. The waitress was there, and she hadn't thought about what she was going to eat. She hadn't thought about anything but Gus. She was a horrible person. She had to fix this.

They were both quiet after dinner, driving around the south end of the lake, enjoying the view as the sun set, painting the sky with vivid pastels. In Chelan, tourists crossed the street in clumps, laughing without paying attention to where they were going.

As they turned north, Lola felt compelled to say something. "That was a really nice dinner. Thank you."

Hidalgo turned to her, smiling. "My pleasure. I can't wait to see what Gus has gotten done today, you know? You should really see his portfolio. He's an artist. Makes me wonder what he's doing here."

Great. She'd just gotten Gus off her mind and now Hidalgo was singing his praises.

"He just came home," Lola said, eager to change the subject.

After turning the last curve along the lake before the towering cliffs, Hidalgo took a left. After the bumpy ride up the hill, he pulled the truck into the parking spot off to the side of the vineyard. Gus's truck was there but he was nowhere in sight. Pink clouds faded into the indigo sky as they sat under the dark shadows thrown by the cliff towering over their heads. Bats flitted across the orchard. A pair of deer moved slowly across the road behind them.

"This view never gets old, does it?" Hidalgo said. Although they couldn't see the lake just below the vineyard, they could see the hills stretching in the distance, the vast expanse of land slipping into darkness.

"No." Lola twisted in her seat to look at Hidalgo in the dim light. "You know, we almost lost Blue Hills a couple years ago. We didn't know my dad had Alzheimer's, and he was just letting things go. It's very tricky, running a winery. You have to be part chemist, part marketer and one hundred percent farmer. Anyway, we enlisted all these people to help us get the harvest in. City people. People who had no idea what they were getting into. It was Carmen's idea. Sort of a Hail Mary at that point, but you know what? Those people came through. And I thought if those people loved working in the fields, then people would love to stay in someplace more rustic, right in the vineyard. In the heart of Chelan."

"It's a great idea."

"Yeah, try telling my sister." It slipped out.

"What do you mean?" Hidalgo tilted his head, curious.

Lola grit her teeth. That was a serious slip. Might as well start with the truth. "Carmen sees me as her little sister. Nothing I do makes her see me as a valuable part of the business."

"Well, this will." Hidalgo put his hand over hers. "It's the perfect place for your cabins."

She grinned, pinching her fingers together. "Tiny cabins."

His teeth were white in the dark cab. "Tiny cabins."

"Do you want to stay a bit? I could make a little fire," Lola suggested, feeling more than a little guilty for being not fully present during dinner. Hopefully Gus would stay scarce. She'd heard him moving around in the distance but nothing more.

Hidalgo nodded. "For a little bit. Yeah. That would be nice."

They walked past Gus's ancient truck, which Lola thought was the perfect comparison for the two men: Gus's was admittedly a classic, but had hundreds of thousands of miles on it and was more than a little banged up. Hidalgo's was gleaming, solid, and new. It would never break down. It was one hundred percent safe.

"There's some paper and wood over there," Lola said, as she went into the trailer to get some wine. She poked her head back out. "I'll be right out to get it started."

"I don't mind," Hidalgo said easily, lifting the tarp where Lola had stashed her firewood.

Daisy bounded out of the trailer, disappearing into the vineyard to chase hidden rabbits. She returned quickly, running off again to run the perimeter of the building site, as if making a nightly inspection. As Lola collected a bottle of wine, the opener and a couple of jam jars for glasses, she thought about Hidalgo's easy nature. He'd build a fire, take her out to dinner and not mind when she was slightly absentminded. As Venus appeared in the night sky, Lola made a vow to herself to be more present. To push Gus back to the corners of her mind, where he belonged.

Lola opened the bottle of wine, placing the glasses on a rickety table she'd found in her father's old barn in the orchard, where he kept cast-offs from Orchard House he couldn't bear to part with. Things his wife had bought.

Ten minutes later, they were having an easy conversation about Hidalgo's childhood in Wenatchee, when Gus strode into the meadow, planting himself thirty feet away. He flicked on a work light, which lit up a ten-foot diameter around him. He was sawing some molding by hand. Hidalgo stopped talking, smiling at Lola awkwardly.

"Uh, do you want me to say something?"

What the hell? Why did Gus have to plop himself down so close to them? The sawing noise cut through the peaceful silence like ripping silk.

But still, she shook her head. "No. That's okay."

Hidalgo turned towards Gus, trying to catch his eye, but Gus was sawing away, seemingly oblivious of the moths fluttering around his face.

"Are you sure?"

Lola frowned. "Yeah."

"What were we talking about?"

The sawing grated on her ears like fingernails on a chalkboard. "How you used to pick apples with your parents after school?"

Hidalgo shook his head. "Yeah, this is… Well…" He stood up. "Hey, Gus? Gus!?"

Gus put down his saw, giving Hidalgo his full attention.

"Isn't there something else you could do right now?"

Gus's mouth hung open in surprise, as if he'd just realized that he was inserting himself into their date. "Oh. Right. Yeah. Sure."

Hidalgo had just settled back down into his chair when an industrial vacuum started up in the cabin. Or maybe a sander. Whatever it was, it was ten times louder than the sawing had been. Hidalgo stood up as if he was going towards the cabin, but then he turned around.

"You know, we're the ones that gave him an impossible deadline. You can't blame the guy."

Lola was thinking that she could blame him for wrecking this conversation—and a lot more—but she wasn't about to say anything. Instead, she fantasized about marching over to Gus and asking him if he really thought this was going to work. Did he really think that making a bunch of noise was going to endear him to her? She'd tell him that unlike him, she didn't live in the past. She'd moved on. She'd end it with dumping the remains of her wine on his stupid head. The vision was enormously satisfying.

Hidalgo shrugged. "I've got an early morning."

The vacuum shut off. Gus came out of the cabin. "Too loud?"

Hidalgo shook his head. "I'm just leaving."

Gus nodded—and quite possibly smirked. He damn well knew it was too loud, thought Lola, gritting her teeth. She downed the last swig of wine before taking Hidalgo's hand. "I'll walk you to your car."

She made sure they passed right by Gus, and although he didn't look up, Lola was sure she could see him looking at their joined hands from the corners of his eyes.

Good, she thought. *Let him look.* Gus Weaver needed to know the lay of the land. Things had changed. Lola wasn't going to make the same mistake twice.

Daisy, however, had other ideas.

CHAPTER ELEVEN

Kitchen Rats

"Daisy! Come on, girl. Daisy!"

Lola had said goodnight to Hidalgo, making sure to position herself in clear view of Gus in case he looked up. She wanted him to see her kissing Hidalgo. Although she had mixed feelings about why, exactly, it was important that Gus witness it. She made sure that if he even turned slightly towards them, he couldn't help but notice.

Also, she couldn't help but feel that he was tracking their every move.

Now that she'd poured water on the fire, brought in the wine and was ready to call it a night, Daisy, who was usually the first one in the trailer, was nowhere in sight. Typically, a long evening of chasing rabbits left her exhausted and eager to bed down for the night.

"Daisy!"

Lola went down the trailer steps, double-checking the fire to make sure she'd gotten every last ember. She called the dog a few more times, ducking her head as bats fluttered close. Walking in a circle, she saw the dog's shape near a pile of lumber and called her again.

"Come on, girl. Let's go."

But Daisy stayed there, unbudging. Lola took a step closer and
noticed that Daisy was leaning against Gus, who was crouched
down, rubbing her ears.

Lola crossed her arms. "Daisy, come on."

Gus stood up, waiting for the little dog to obey her mistress,
but Daisy stayed there, leaning against Gus. "Go on, girl. Go on."

"You little traitor!" Lola whispered under her breath. Daisy hardly
allowed anyone else to pet her, let alone this. It was completely
awkward, calling her own dog, and also not knowing if she should
talk to Gus. But he remained silent. She wasn't going to be the first
one to talk. No way.

"Daisy!" Lola hissed. This was embarrassing. She climbed the
steps of the trailer, leaving the door open. She didn't know what
else to do, so she brushed her teeth, slipped on a nightshirt, and
sat in the kitchen banquette, staring at the door. A few moments
later, Daisy pushed the door open with her snout, trotting in and
proceeding to the back of the trailer, where she hopped up onto
the bed and curled up as if nothing was the matter.

Lola sat a while on the cold vinyl before making her way to the
bed, giving her dog an accusatory look. "How could you?"

Daisy sighed with deep contentment.

"Look, you don't know my history, but he is the enemy."

Daisy burrowed her snout deeper into the blankets, blissfully
happy.

Lola lay in bed as the crickets chirped their symphony and the
vineyard settled into a deep quiet. She waited for the sound of Gus's
truck. It took a long while. First, she heard his footsteps tracing a

path around the work site. He did this every night. Making sure everything was in order. Despite her feelings about Gus Weaver, Lola found it deeply reassuring.

When his old truck fired to life, Lola finally drifted off to sleep.

Daisy trotted out of the vineyard and sat on the dirt, tracking Gus's every move from a safe distance. Gus found it amusing how the dog didn't lie down, just kept an eye on things, as if Lola had sent her up here to make sure Gus didn't goof off. A canine supervisor. She'd move a little closer gradually, until Gus was passing within a foot of her. Gus had unwrapped the leftovers of a breakfast sandwich and a piece had dropped on the ground.

"Whoops," Gus said. "I know how dogs hate bacon."

Daisy stared at the food, drooling, until Gus had insisted. She'd edged a bit closer, sniffing the air, then taken a few more steps. When she'd finally snuck close to him, she'd daintily sniffed the bacon, keeping an eye on him, before wolfing it down with evident pleasure. From then on, they'd been buddies.

Gus looked forward to the little dog's arrival. He'd be working away in a cabin, nailing down molding, or sanding the floor, when the familiar white and brown speckled head would poke through the open door, her bright, oddly colored eyes meeting his with obvious intelligence. She was good company. Alert and companionable until it grew too warm, at which point she would find a shady spot to curl up, one eye kept trained upon him. He'd pour a bowl of water in the shade, which she sniffed before drinking, burying her snout deep into the water to cool down.

Gus had always liked dogs but had never owned one, at least not for very long. His father had brought home a dog once wrapped in an old sweater, but the dog had run off within a few weeks. Gus had been heartbroken, but didn't blame the little animal. His mother hadn't exactly made the little guy feel welcome. He'd slept in an old box under the trailer, shivering under thin blankets until he lit out for greener pastures. Gus remembered comforting his little brother, telling him stories about how the dog had found a lonely little girl who needed a friend. They didn't need friends, Gus had said, since they had each other. The dog had left to help the little girl.

Since then, Gus had befriended all kinds of dogs on work sites. Fancy pedigrees in waterfront mansions, who'd follow him around, lonely in their palatial surroundings, their nails clicking on the stone floors. Scruffy neighborhood dogs near the apartments where he'd lived in Seattle, some of whom he'd taken care of, bring them along to job sites, talking to them as they rode in the cab of his truck, wishing he had the kind of life that could include a dog. In one way or another, they'd all offered him the friendship and comfort he'd craved during those lonely but rewarding years as he built his craft. Found his place in the world.

Now, Gus habitually saved part of his breakfast, unwrapping it and offering it to Daisy when he arrived on site. She took it daintily, as if doing him a favor. She ate with evident enjoyment, but also with a fastidiousness that Gus found charming. She moved around the site with him as he completed his jobs, checking on him if she went off for a nap. He enjoyed the company. She knew, with some canine intuition, exactly when Lola was getting off work, and disappeared into the deep green of the vineyard at the same time every day. It was like a bell went off. She'd cock her head, perhaps listening to something Gus couldn't hear. The slam of a door. The scrape of pans. Gus wondered if Lola knew what her dog was doing while she worked. Somehow, he doubted it.

"What am I supposed to do now, huh, Daisy?" Gus asked, watching the dog enjoy the scraps of bacon, licking the paper to get every last bit. "I mean, she's dating my boss."

Daisy sat on the newly installed hardwoods, her ears pricked up, listening politely. The hollow smelled of freshly cut cedar, mixing with the ripening grapes and the salty earth, creating what Gus thought was one of the most intoxicating smells on earth. Each day, he stopped to look at the grapes, tracking their progress from dusty purple to deep merlot. It was like watching an artist at work. The magic of nature: both complex and mind-bendingly simple.

Unlike his personal life.

"It doesn't get more cut and dried than that, right? I mean, Hidalgo is a nice guy. But for Lola? I mean, come on." Gus removed the worn sandpaper from the sander, clamping in a fresh piece, enjoying the stiffness of the paper against his rough fingertips. "She's… Lola. She's never wanted the whole traditional thing. People change, but not that much. When we were up here, she wasn't a daughter or a little sister. She was free." He took off his flannel, draping it over a chair in the corner. "Well, honestly, I was a terrible influence back then. But a lot's happened in the last ten years. Therapy, for one thing, courtesy of the state of Washington. That's a game changer, right? What if…" Gus let the sentence trail off, scratching the dog behind the ears before checking the fit on the sander, plugging it into the extension cord. "Hidalgo really likes her. Who wouldn't, right? And the guy gave me a chance, right? Not everyone would hire an ex-con to work on people's homes. He's a good guy." He turned on the sander, working down the length of the floor before stopping to brush off the sawdust and examine the grain. "But am I going to let her go just because of a job?" He shook his head. "Life's not fair, is it?" He sighed. "You think you're on the straight and narrow and bam, it swerves."

He rubbed his hand down the length of the pine floor, enjoying the way the oil from his hand exposed the grain, hinting at the beauty to come. Once these floors were stained, they'd complement the Scandinavian look he was going for. He'd studied the pictures that Lola had posted on her blog and thought he could improve upon what she'd found. He'd already ordered some lighting fixtures inspired by a ski cabin he'd worked on at Stevens Pass. Gus enjoyed building furniture, but had never thought much before about the final phases of building a home. His current apartment was just a place to sleep in. On his way back to it, he'd sometimes pull over at the beach just to run down the hours until he felt sleepy—and to keep himself away from the noise of people drinking. If Izzy hadn't given him some blankets (that he suspected she'd bought and washed and pretended they were used), he'd be sleeping under an old sleeping bag.

"Here's the thing, Daisy. Am I going after his girl, or is he going after mine?" He shook his head. "You're right. I can't exactly call her my girl when I left ten years ago in the back of a Washington State Corrections van. My brain is definitely not focusing on what my therapist and I agreed on right now. I was supposed to be apologizing and moving on."

He gave the dog another quick pat and got back to work. The sun was heating up the meadow quickly. Even though the cabins didn't have windows, they were like saunas in the afternoon.

Maybe if he got far enough ahead, he could drive down to the lake for a quick dip during lunch. Not that he took lunch. It struck him that both he and Hidalgo were trying to impress the same girl. Hidalgo was going about it the traditional way, with dates and fireside conversations. Gus was throwing everything into her impossible deadline, trying to make these cabins something worthy of the Blue Hills name, which, now that he thought about it, meant something to Gus, too. Even if he'd infuriated Lola's father, he'd always felt a special fondness for Orchard House. If she was going to turn the place where they'd both fallen in love into a vacation spot, then Gus was going to make sure that everything was perfect. He owed her, and her father, that much.

And somewhere in building her dream, he was going to have to apologize to her father, too. Gus rubbed his beard, wondering if there was ever a perfect time to make amends.

The whole point was to get away from Blue Hills. From Gus and Neil and all the complications of Lola's business and life. Felicia and Lola had managed a rare day off together. Neil, of course, didn't know, but they'd made some promises to other staff and it was all arranged. It was a sunny morning and they were at the Manson Farmers' Market in the leafy parking lot at the Manson Grange. People spread their wares—jewelry, baked goods, candles, and jams—on makeshift tables, or in the case of the pie lady, off the back of her truck. One man had three tables of concrete yard ornaments. Another woman made bracelets from shotgun casings. Felicia had been bugging Lola to come with her to buy one of the cherry pies before they sold out, but Lola was looking at two Hudson Bay blankets that would look really nice in one of her cabins. Most of the linens were fancy and not her style, but the blankets were thick and cream-colored with the classic yellow, red, green and black stripes on either end. Very luxe, but rustic. Perfect for the tiny cabins.

"Two hundred apiece or three-fifty for both," the older woman with a plastic sun visor said.

Lola frowned. "That's a lot."

The woman shrugged. "They're real. I could sell them online for a lot more, but it's too much work. I don't like things online anyway. I like people."

Lola thought she didn't act much like it, barking out prices as if she were annoyed.

Someone who'd come up beside Lola pointed at the Hudson Bay blankets. "I'll take them both."

The woman's face lit up as if her slot machine was spewing quarters. "You came back!" She turned to Lola. "Sorry, dear," she said, without sounding the least bit sorry. "This man was here first."

A familiar voice leaned down to whisper, "Sorry, dear." He smelled of sawdust and soap.

Lola squinted into the green sunlight filtering through a massive oak tree. It was Gus. Of course. She couldn't hide from the man. Daisy did a little dance, licking his hand, jumping up on his leg. The woman made a big show of refolding the blankets, flushing, grinning at Gus like a sixteen-year-old meeting her movie idol. "I knew you'd be back. I just knew it." She pointed her gnarly finger at Gus. "You know quality when you see it."

Gus winked at her. "I sure do. The blankets are nice, too."

Lola thought she'd vomit. "Hey, wait a minute. I was going to get those blankets."

The woman shook her visored head. "No siree, Bob. This cute young fella was here first."

"But he left and I showed up. My money is just as green as his."

Gus glanced between the two of them, highly amused.

"Well, I said I'd save them for him," the woman said. Lola knew she'd promised no such thing from the way the woman ducked her head, blushing a deeper scarlet.

Felicia had joined them under the tree, where the woman had spread her wares over an old table and some magazine racks. She crossed her arms in obvious delight.

Gus smiled at her. "Hey, Felicia, nice to see you."

"Nice to be seen, Gus. I see you're stirring up trouble."

"Trying to stay out of it, but it's hard when this one's around." Gus smirked.

"I'm buying them for my cabins," said Lola, but the woman's eyes never left Gus.

"Well, aren't you fancy?" the woman said, handing Gus a large plastic bag containing both blankets. He passed over a wad of cash she didn't even bother counting. "There you go, sir. Enjoy."

Lola fumed at the old bat.

"Gus, you want to help us eat a pie from the pie lady?" asked Felicia.

Gus lifted his eyebrows at Lola before shaking his head. "I'm sorry, I have a job, you know. Best get back to it." He nodded at them, saying, "Ladies," before weaving his way through the idle groups of shoppers enjoying the sun.

Felicia watched him leave with obvious appreciation. "Oh, the irony of you two fighting over blankets."

Lola sighed. "Don't make something out of this."

Felicia laughed as they strolled over to the truck covered in home-baked pies. "Oh, trust me, I do not have to make something out of this." She pointed upwards. "There are astronauts on the space station who could read the tension between you two."

"Stop it." Lola studied the pies on the tailgate of the old Ford, each one more delectable than the last.

"Oh, please. I was not the one who was practically sending out sparks. Listen, you forget. I was there. I listened to you cry about that man." Felicia pointed at the sidewalk where Gus had disappeared. "I picked up the pieces, and if you think there isn't something unresolved between the two of you, then we need to get you a Seeing Eye dog. Look, I like Hidalgo, but I don't think you two stand a chance in hell until you and Gus have some closure."

"How about we start by changing the subject? That would be good," Lola said, pointing at a cherry pie decorated with sugar-coated cherries and golden pastry leaves. Too pretty for stress-eating, but what the hell.

Felicia grinned lasciviously. "Closure with a guy like that should involve very few articles of clothing…" Felicia lowered her voice. "And a lot of aerobic activity."

Lola paid the baker with a credit card. "Very mature."

Felicia smirked. "Again. Have your eyes checked, Lola. You might need glasses."

What was the precise definition of a stalker? Lola needed to know. Because on her way into town to buy supplies for the restaurant, she spotted Gus's truck. It was parked on a side street. At first, she rationalized turning right on the pretext of random curiosity. It wasn't so much about Gus, she said to herself. It was checking up on an old friend. Or his truck. Or something.

When Gus then crossed the street near Mystic Pizza, coffee in hand, Lola slouched into her seat, driving with her eyes just above the steering wheel, making a left turn at the Riverwalk Inn before stopping in the middle of the street. No one was behind her, so she sat there for a moment, trying to talk herself into running her errands. Pretending she was a normal person who didn't want to follow her ex-boyfriend's truck just to find out what he was doing. She sat there in the middle of the road, having a pointed conversation with herself. Sure, following Gus would be fun, but it was also following her baser desires. Hadn't she gotten over him a long time ago? After a billion tears?

On the other hand, what was the harm? It wasn't like she was vaulting over a fence and pulling out binoculars. Gus was probably going to the laundromat or the grocery store. Something utterly banal.

With a smile, she executed a U-turn, thinking the wide old streets had been made for this very task: spying on ex-boyfriends.

Gus's truck was pulling out of the parking spot as she turned onto the street, which was also very handy. It was as though the universe wanted her to do this. This wasn't stalking. She was merely interested in Gus's life, she thought, taking a right at the sheriff's station, continuing down the wide street flanked with broad maples and dotted with cottages. Lola's entire life was on display for him when he arrived every day at work. This was fair game.

Lola was following him. He'd seen her as he crossed the street from the café, had done a double-take but no, it was Lola, looking like something out of a sitcom. He'd laughed to himself as she'd slouched low in her car seat, barely able to see over the steering wheel. He hadn't thought she'd take it any further than that, but now there she was in his rear-view mirror, following him down the street in her little Toyota. She'd make a terrible spy. She'd slowed down so much when he'd been crossing the street, it had been impossible to ignore her. If he'd kept up his pace, he'd have bumped right into her car. Chelan was a hard place to hide, but she couldn't be doing a worse job if she tried.

Gus was sorely tempted to drive all over the valley just to mess with her, but he was meeting Izzy. He took a left and then another right until he was on Izzy's street, slowing down to see if Lola would pass him. She didn't, which was laughable.

He pulled into Izzy's driveway. Three dogs jumped off a wicker bench on the sagging front porch of her bungalow. They scampered into the patchy yard, yapping away. Gus got out of the car with his hands up, letting them sniff him. Izzy came out onto the porch, amused by the sight of Gus surrendering to her three mutts.

"Hey, there," Izzy said, coming down her front steps.

"Hey. Check it out." Gus pointed as discreetly as possible to Lola's car, which was cruising past. She was so far down in her seat that the top of her head was level with the middle of the steering wheel, which of course did nothing to disguise her. They could both see her through the passenger window. She looked like an octogenarian out for a Sunday drive, holding herself erect with the steering wheel.

"That is a very short person," Izzy said, handing Gus a cup of coffee.

Gus grinned. "That is Lola, trying to hide."

"Why would she be trying to hide?" asked Izzy, as the car disappeared from view.

Gus bent to pet each dog, submitting to their involved vetting. "She's following me."

Izzy took a long drink of her coffee as the dogs completed their inspection. "Why?"

Gus shook his head, bemused, and rather pleased. "That is a very good question."

"Come on in," Izzy said. "Seems like we've got lot to talk about."

Gus followed Izzy up her wobbling front steps, making a mental note to bring his tool kit next time. "We do. Like how I'm going to talk to Juan Alvarez without getting my head blown off."

CHAPTER TWELVE

Tattooed

Felicia came running into the kitchen like her hair was on fire. She zoomed up to Lola, who looked up from wiping down her station, spray bottle and white rag in hand.

"Oh. My. God," Felicia panted, waving her hand in front of her face.

"Now you've got my attention," said Lola.

Felicia pointed to the restaurant door through which she'd just run. "He's out there."

"Who?" Lola went back to wiping, crouching down to make sure there were no streaks on the stainless steel. Neil had gotten in the habit of writing little messages in the streaks left from bleach water on the counter. Needless to say, they weren't love notes. "Slob," "You Disgust Me" and "Loser" were three recent mementos.

"What do you mean who? Him!" Felicia said, breathlessly.

Lola blew a stray strand of hair off her face. It had been a long day. All she wanted to do was get off her feet. "Unless George Clooney stopped by for a glass of wine with Chris Pine, I'm going home."

"It's Gus Weaver!" Felicia hissed excitedly. "In the bar."

"Where?" Lola asked, suddenly all ears.

"First it's your eyes, now it's your hearing. The. Bar."

"Yes, but where in the bar? I can't run in there and like, spy on him."

Felicia nodded vigorously. "Yes, you can. That is how situations like this work. And for god's sake, you've been spying on him since he first set foot in town."

"I'm not interested in him."

Felicia glared at her. "You keep telling yourself that, while meanwhile, back in reality, your eyes practically fell out of your head when I said he was here, and you dragged a four-thousand-pound hunk of aluminum up a very steep hill and started living in it just so you could spy on him."

"That is not how that worked. I needed a place to live."

"Denial much? In the meantime, he's sitting in the bar."

Lola threw the rag into the laundry, following it with her apron. "Where in the bar?"

"By the window near the walkway. Middle table. I don't think anyone recognizes him."

Lola raised her eyebrows. "What makes you think that?"

Felicia frowned slightly. "I don't know. He just seems… super subdued. And that beard. And the fact that he's filled out, to say the least. Anyway, nobody is talking to him."

"Did it ever occur to you that you could, in fact, act like a normal human being and go talk to him yourself? We did go to high school together."

Felicia nodded. "Honestly, no. Because I am too busy totally freaking out at the fact that he's sitting out there, having a drink like he wasn't run off with a gun ten years ago."

"There's that."

"So you're not going to spy on him?"

"Oh, I'm totally going to spy on him. I just wanted to make sure you were in on it with me."

"Are you sneaking drinks?" Luke the bartender gazed down at Lola and Felicia with thinly disguised contempt. They were crouched behind the counter like fugitives.

They both shook their heads. Lola put her finger over her lips. "Shhhh."

"Hiding from Neil?" Luke asked.

Felicia shook her head. "No. From someone else."

"Look, this is all very junior high, and I don't want to break my nose falling over one of you, so can you please move?" His hand did a sweeping movement.

Felicia put her hands together. "We're spying on someone."

"And that is supposed to sell me on whatever this is? Um, no. Now get out from behind my bar before I kick you out." Luke went about making drinks while shooting malevolent glares in their direction. The girls scuttled over to the end of the bar.

Felicia peered around the side before whispering to Lola, "Okay, he's not looking. Now!"

They dashed across the entry out the side door, doubling over with laughter.

"Oh my god, this is fun!" Felicia said. "You should have old boyfriends come to the bar more often."

"Old boyfriends? Who?"

Lola stood up, glancing into the shadows under a trio of apple trees that bordered the driveway. Carmen was standing there with a clipboard clutched to her chest, staring at Felicia, while carefully avoiding looking at her sister.

Lola and Felicia exchanged panicked glances. Lola shook her head nearly imperceptibly.

Felicia patted her chest. "Me. My old boyfriend."

"But you said *you* should—"

"I said *we* should. We should have old boyfriends come to the bar more often. Because that is a thing we should do," Felicia insisted.

Carmen's brow furrowed. "Okay… Who are we talking about?"

Felicia tilted her head, squinting slightly. "You don't know him."

Carmen pursed her lips. "I probably do."

"Saaa—ah—manual." Felicia stretched out each chunk of the name as it came to her.

Carmen frowned. "Samanual?"

Felicia nodded like a bobble head. "Yes, good old Samanual."

"Good old Samanual who?" Carmen asked.

"Samanual Gussss—tav—erson—itich—son," Felicia said. Carmen and Lola studied her while she went through his last name one long syllable at time. It seemed to take hours. This was getting weirder and weirder, Lola thought. Not only had she and Carmen not been talking since they'd gotten into the argument at Stella's house, now Felicia was apparently losing her mind.

"Sounds like every Scandinavian in the valley got in on that one," Carmen said.

Lola scowled at Felicia as she doubled down on the ridiculous name, tossing off a thick parody of Scandinavian accent. "Ya, sure, you betcha."

Gus Weaver pushed open the door, then stopped short and nodded at the trio. "Good evening, ladies," he said pleasantly, gazing at them with an amused look in his eyes. Nothing about his appearance was lost on the women: his well-muscled arms, his tan, his thick hair above inquisitive, intelligent brown eyes that lingered a second longer than they needed to on Lola.

Carmen nodded at him pleasantly and said hello while Felicia and Lola held their breath. Lola prayed he wouldn't turn toward the light near the door and give Carmen a good view of his face.

"Nice night," Gus said. Lola thought she'd explode from tension. Despite her anxiety, she did notice the fragrance of her mother's roses hanging in the night air. They mingled with the freshly cut grass from the upper orchard. She remembered the way Gus used to notice everything at Blue Hills. The smells, the ever-changing shadows and light on the lake, the sounds of the orchard and, most noticeably, the peacefulness. Gus had always said he felt calmer at Blue Hills. None of Lola's friends had appreciated it the way he had.

"Beautiful night," Carmen said. "Thanks for coming in."

"You bet," Gus said, nodding politely before ambling down the driveway, whistling, hands shoved deep into his jean pockets. As he passed, Lola got a whiff of clean cotton. His hair was damp at the neckline, curling up on his shirt. He must have gone swimming.

"Samanual Gustaversonitichson?" Carmen asked, watching Gus's tall form slide into the shadows from the apple trees.

Lola was thanking her lucky stars that Gus hadn't taken a right after leaving the restaurant and hiked right up the vineyard to the work site. There would have been no explaining that.

"Yep," Felicia said, shooting Lola a look as they both waited for Carmen to recognize Gus. In the distance, Lola heard the unmistakable rumble of Gus's truck, low and guttural.

"Never heard of him. You'd think I would have. Kind of weird, don't you think? It's such a small town," Carmen said. "I thought I knew everyone."

Felicia almost started laughing. "Oh, not everyone."

Lola stomped on Felicia's foot, which made Felicia's eyes water, but she didn't look down.

Carmen tilted her head in the way she did when she had a delicate matter to settle. "Um, Felicia, do you mind if I talk to Lola for a second?"

Felicia shrugged. "No. Go ahead."

"Alone," Carmen added.

"Oh, right. See you tomorrow," Felicia said, giving Lola a tight grin.

Carmen sighed into the night air, holding the clipboard to her chest. "Do you want to talk about anything?"

Lola frowned. Had Carmen recognized Gus? Was this supposed to be her chance to come clean? "What do you mean?"

Carmen rolled her eyes. "Lola, I know we're different. And that I've been saying no a lot to you. I get that. And maybe someday when things are more settled on the winery, we can experiment more. Maybe even on menus."

Lola clenched her jaw. Could her sister sound any more condescending? Her whole body flushed with anger and excitement, happy that she'd taken a risk. Because Carmen would always see her ideas as experiments, no matter how much money they had in the bank. They could be rolling in dough, and anything that came out of Lola's mouth would be risky to Carmen. "Right. Someday." When hell froze over.

"Don't be like that."

"What? Don't have feelings? Don't want something more than being stuck in the kitchen with an absolute nut job all day? Don't want to be an equal?"

Carmen took a long, exaggerated breath, as if in the middle of a yoga class. "Lola, I understand what you're going through."

Lola rolled her eyes. "Right."

Carmen shook her head. "Okay, fair point. Maybe I don't. But I do understand what it's like to feel like the underdog. When I worked in Seattle, I had a boss who was such a bitch. She didn't want people leaving work for their parents' funerals, let alone to take care of them when they had Alzheimer's. It was awful."

"Okay, you're not that bad."

Carmen spoke through gritted teeth. "I was talking about Neil." "Right."

"Lola, I'm getting married. Really soon."

Yes. You run the winery. You are engaged to the handsome millionaire next door who thinks you invented sunshine and I am fending off a creep by day and sleeping in a trailer by night. "I'm aware."

Carmen was quiet for a long time, watching the bats flit around the three apple trees across the gravel driveway. "Do you even want to be in my wedding?"

Lola waited just long enough to think it through. Would she love to stick it to Carmen in an extremely dramatic way? Absolutely. But was it worth letting her entire family down? She could hear her mother prodding her, telling her to calm down, think rationally. Think of the future. The family. "Of course I do," Lola said gently, thinking they were about to have a moment. That, perhaps, Carmen was having second thoughts about the generic wedding menu, had realized that Lola had a point. That it should reflect her personality. Their family heritage. Blue Hills.

"Then act like it," Carmen said, walking past her into the bar, letting the screen door slam behind her.

"Okaaaaay," Lola said to the night sky, wishing that every interaction with her sister didn't leave her feeling three inches tall.

Lola stepped out onto the patio, gulping in the dusky air as if it could cleanse the kitchen and all its smells from her system. And it did. Stepping out into the vineyard was like being enveloped in a hug. The leafy vines rustled in the evening breeze off the lake. A lone hawk drifted on the still warm air as the sky faded from bright blue to shades of purple. The vineyard was at its most verdant green, spreading up the hill, highlighting the glowing orange pink of her mother's Tropicana roses in the planting beds. They seemed to glow in the dark, their fragrance mingling with the ripening grapes. There was movement in the nearby vines, which turned out to be a family of raccoons waddling down to the orchard. Their eyes glinted in the dark as they stood on their feet to appraise Lola before continuing on their way.

On the patio, Rodolfo was shoveling ash out of the pizza oven, his face dripping with sweat. His white T-shirt sleeves were rolled up, his apron colorfully spattered. "Hey, there. Long day?"

Lola locked her arms behind her back, stretching them backward, her chin pointing to the sky. "I'm pretty sure someone snuck extra hours in this day and they were all filled with way too much Neil."

"Oh man. That guy," Rodolfo said, dumping another shovel full of gray ash headed for the compost pile into a wheelbarrow. "He came out here to tell me that there was too much sauce on the pizza. On an olive oil and herb pizza. Not one drop of red on the entire thing."

"He's jealous."

Rodolfo shook his head. "I'm a pizza cook. He's a famous chef. I'm not even on anyone's radar."

"You're assuming that he's a nice person."

Rodolfo sighed. "I don't know how you put up with him."

"I don't have any choice."

Rodolfo looked like he was about to say something, but then changed his mind. Lola let it go. He'd heard her complaining to Carmen. "Well, you're doing an excellent job. Working in any commercial kitchen is really rough and this one is… Well, I don't have to tell you it's hard. You're a tough cookie, Lola. Keep it up."

"Thanks, Rodolfo." She tried to take it in. To feel the compliment and allow herself to feel good. She couldn't let Carmen get to her.

He nodded, lifting the handles of the wheelbarrow. "I mean every word."

Lola scanned the vineyard, looking for Daisy. Where was she? "I'm going to put my feet up and try not to think about anything kitchen-related for at least eight hours."

Rodolfo nodded. "You do that." He navigated the wheelbarrow across the patio towards the compost bins. "Hasta mañana."

"Hasta mañana."

To reassure herself that this was all worth it, Lola went into the first cabin Gus had built. The curtains she'd hung glowed in the work light, crisp white with an eyelet trim. The cabin smelled of varnish and the floor glowed with its final honey-colored coat. The cabinets were white with blue handles. Neatly draped over a bed with a white painted driftwood headboard was one of the Hudson Bay blankets. Lola's eyes welled with tears. It had been so long since someone had made such a big effort for her, let alone surprised her. Gus had bought the blankets for the cabins. For her. He'd seen them, and had thought the same thing she had: that these blankets would add something to her vision. Lola sat down on the bed, feeling the rough wool against her fingers. This felt like a validation. Gus could see what she'd imagined. It wasn't just another one of her fantastical schemes.

And it worked. The whole room came alive with the combination of creamy white, the texture of the wool, the thick lines of color. She rushed into the second cabin. Draped over a chair that Gus had just finished was the second blanket. Lola lifted the blanket, noticing the driftwood spindles on the chair, wondering how much she'd have to pay for it. He probably didn't charge enough. Gus never had believed in himself the way she had. His furniture was gorgeous. She sat on the edge of the bed, listening to Daisy bark at random things in the night outside. She shut off the light, and watched the stars blanketing the inky dark through the window. Why couldn't Gus just be selfish or immature or stupid? Lola smoothed her hand over the soft wool, thinking it was impossible, because Gus Weaver had never been any of those things. She shut the cabin door, realizing that Gus had laid out the blankets and then left early. As if he didn't want to be thanked.

Lola was waiting for him after work the next day. Gus had been avoiding her, or at least trying to. Hidalgo wasn't coming over because he'd been to a site over in Wenatchee all day and wouldn't be back until late. Knowing that Lola wouldn't be going out with Hidalgo, that she might be hanging around by her fire all evening, Gus packed up his truck. He just about jumped out of his skin when Lola said his name. He whipped around and there she was, holding a cherry pie.

"Holy cow, you snuck up on me."

"It's cherry." She grinned, looking like she'd swallowed the sun.

He pointed to the crust. "Yeah, there's little cherries right there."

"That was the nicest thing. The blankets."

"Okay, well—"

"No really, Gus. They look so perfect and you spent way too much money. I mean, seriously. But it's like you understand what I want. And those driftwood headboards. Wow!

Why was it so hard, taking compliments? He just wanted to make her smile. "I wasn't sure painting them was the right way to go."

"It worked so well." She forced him to take the pie.

He looked down at it. "This looks good. Thank you."

"You have amazing taste."

His smile was soft and a little sad. He looked directly at her with, "Yeah." Making her happy was the best thing in the world.

"I've built a fire. We could, you know. Have a slice. Unless you're busy."

Oh, shit. He was in for it. She knew he didn't have any place else to go.

Oh man, what an idiot he was. After everything he'd promised himself, he had ignored what he'd learned about temptation. He'd just turned around and been swallowed whole. *Sure, just one piece*, said the drowning man. He walked towards that cozy ring of firelight. To her. Had he known what he was doing when he'd bought her the blankets? Probably. Just thinking about surprising her had had him walking on air. He was still utterly infatuated with Lola. Always would be. The image of her from years ago, sitting in the passenger side of his truck, her long hair streaming against the cracked leather, damp curls pressed against her cheeks, the radio playing some dumb song she loved while her hand surfed the air. That one moment when she'd turned to him and smiled. Even in the middle of his hormonal fog, he'd known enough to tuck that moment away. Sear it into his brain. That image was what had kept him alive for all those months, when the only color in his life had been the orange jumpsuit he was forced to wear.

Nobody had ever looked at him like that besides Lola.

Nobody.

They ate pie, and she drank some sparkling wine. Gus had water. She kept thanking him until he said, "All right, I'm glad you liked them." For a moment, they just grinned at each other like two fools.

Then they started talking about the past, and Gus wondered if this was the part where he'd get up the nerve to apologize for being stupid enough to go along with his cousin. For letting her down.

"It was scary," he said, in response to her question about jail. Lola never bothered with small talk. She found it boring and trite, which was probably why she'd ended up riding around with him all over the countryside, instead of hanging out with her friends after school. If she wanted the answer to something, she'd flat out ask. There was no fishing, no sideways navigating—not like some of the women he'd worked for, who'd slipped in personal questions that left Gus stammering, unsure of how to respond.

He loved the way Lola leaned over to pet Daisy and stayed there, elbows on knees, looking at him as if there was nobody else in the world. Eyes settling on his like magnets. Of course, he knew that was just the way she was. When she listened, Lola threw her whole being into it, as if paying attention was a sport. Her body stilled, as though she'd gone into hibernation, except for those bright, warm brown eyes. She'd always been that way. If she was bored, there was nothing you could do to get her to settle down, but capture her attention and she was a statue.

For a moment, he considered telling her that she was the only thing that had stopped him from giving up in jail. Not the idea that they'd get back together; just the notion that she was out there, living her life. Graduating. Smiling. Breathing. But then again, why risk scaring her? He'd been frightened of his own reaction the moment he saw her.

"I was the youngest guy in the whole rehabilitation center," he said. "Once they'd built a place specifically for juvenile offenders, they shipped everyone else my age off there, but because my cousin left his gun and I'd touched it, I wasn't eligible. Lucky me." It had also meant that he'd stayed further away from his younger brother, who could have perhaps visited at the other facility, which was closer to Chelan. It would have meant something: seeing him, encouraging him to do well in school. To take himself seriously.

"I'm so sorry, Gus."

That was the thing with Lola. She was one of those people who could infuse "I'm sorry" with real meaning. You could cut into the very heart of Lola, and you'd see the exact same person through and through. She was, Gus thought, rare. He wasn't about to mess her up again. Even if he had to nail himself to the cheap lawn chair to prevent it. Even if her beauty made him a little bit breathless.

Gus remembered he'd not been able to believe it when he'd seen the Alvarez sisters together for the first time. They'd all come to some event at the high school. When Gus had seen Lola approach with her family, it was like watching a play where each actress was more beautiful than the last. The oldest one, Adella, had angular features and slightly paler skin. Carmen's features were rounder, and her dark hair was curly. Lola had wavy, lighter brown hair and the same wide dark eyes as her sisters. She had high cheekbones and long legs that she hadn't quite gotten used to. Gus had felt as though he could stay in the shadows of the auditorium and spy on them all night. Lola was so animated and clearly comfortable around them in a way he could only imagine. Old man Alvarez had escorted his family out the door, saying he had reservations at Campbell's. They'd walked past Gus in a haze of perfume and chatter, their bracelets jangling, their shoulders touching. It had seemed like Lola came from royalty.

"It was probably a good thing, you know?" Good for him, that was. Not good for Jason, his younger brother.

"How's that?" Lola took a sip of wine.

"Well, I spent all my free time in the wood shop and learned to make furniture. The guy who ran the place looked at some designs I'd sketched and said I could have some wood and a space, and that was all it took. For the first time, I was good at something."

Lola grinned. "No, it was the first time anyone told you that you were good at something. You were always good at lots of things."

He gave her a devilish grin. "Like what?"

She bit her lip, trying to stop smirking. "Things. Anyway, I'd love to see some of the stuff you built."

He pointed into the dark across the lake. "I have a little studio in Manson. It's just a corner in a warehouse, but Hidalgo lets me use his machinery. I've brought some of the stuff I built and didn't want to sell. It's pretty cool."

Her eyebrows shot up. "Can I see it?"

Daisy jumped up as if ready to go.

"Wait, you mean now?"

Lola laughed because it wasn't what she'd meant at all—but apparently, the dog was now in charge. "Sure, why not?"

Gus took a deep breath, willing himself to refuse her, to listen to the voice in his head that said this was a bad idea. Lola was dating Hidalgo. She deserved a stable life and didn't know how Gus felt. There was a torrent of ideas churning through his brain that all pointed him towards home and his lonely little apartment, but what came out was, "Why not?"

*

Once Lola climbed into the familiar cab of the old truck, she was right back in high school. Although the old truck had definitely been fixed up, the smell and worn leather seats evoked a specific, happy time in her life. The summer between junior and senior years, they'd driven up lake to secluded beaches, diving off logs and collapsing in the late day sun. Gus had been working for his uncle painting houses, but they knocked off at four. Lola would buy hot dogs and chips, then wait for Gus at the bottom of the driveway, telling her father that she was going to a friend's house. Not because Papi didn't like Gus. He hadn't even known Gus at that point, but Lola hadn't wanted anyone to know how much time she was spending with one boy. Particularly not one with the last name Weaver.

The truck might have brought back memories but it couldn't turn back time. Gus was pretty quiet, talking about the years he'd spent traveling and his time in Seattle when Lola asked questions, but otherwise falling silent. She didn't ask the one question that burned inside of her because she wasn't sure if she wanted to hear the answer. Why was he back? If she was perfectly honest with herself, she didn't know if she'd be relieved or devastated if the answer had nothing to do with her. Chelan was his home, after all. But the question wouldn't go away.

Gus pulled his truck into the empty parking spaces in front of Ruiz Construction. Manson was a two-dog town with a handful of touristy shops, a bakery and a convenience store with narrow aisles and wooden floors. Unlike Chelan, which was primarily retail space, Manson was one of the few places where small businesses could find affordable warehouses. Hidalgo rented the storefront and the attached small warehouse behind, which had a separate entrance.

Daisy trailed along behind Gus, trotting around the side of the building as if she'd done this a thousand times. Lola followed, finding the way the little dog attached herself to Gus more than slightly annoying. Daisy had always been fiercely loyal and protective, offering even Lola's best friends like Felicia no more than a few snuggles before returning to her side. With Gus, though, she was behaving like some wanton hussy, cozying up to him in the front seat of the truck, trotting along at his side. What was it? Daisy hardly knew the man.

Was Lola jealous?

It took Gus a moment, in the wide, dark street with the nearest streetlight halfway down the country block, to find the key. Daisy sat beside his dusty work boots, shooting Lola a look as if to say, "Isn't this great? Such an adventure!"

"Okay, here we go," Gus said. "Finally." He opened the garage-style door from the bottom, pulling the handle until the door was above his head. "Hang on. Let me get the light."

He disappeared into the dark. A second later, an overhead caged lightbulb illuminated the shadowy room. "Come on in. Watch your step."

It took Lola's eyes a moment to adjust to the inky dark because the light from the bulb only reached the inner part of the cavernous room. Large pieces of construction equipment crowded the front of the warehouse, near the door.

Gus walked back towards her, offering his hand. "Come on, I don't want you to trip. There's a lot of sharp edges in here."

Lola studied his outstretched hand for a beat too long.

"Lola, I don't want you to get hurt."

She felt foolish for her hesitance, taking his warm hand, feeling instantly more secure, wishing she didn't notice how his skin felt rough at the fingertips and smooth on his palm. Worse still, she had a flash of those same hands running all over her body until she wanted to scream. She stopped, shutting her eyes.

"You know what would help?" Gus said. "Opening your eyes. Fun fact: a hundred percent of people who open their eyes see better."

"Smart-ass," Lola said, happy he'd said something that distracted her train of thought.

"Says the girl who shuts her eyes in a dark room full of sharp-edged machinery." He pulled her deeper into the room.

"Is this where you hide the bodies of clients who won't pay?"

"I'm assuming yes." He nodded, completely deadpan. "I haven't been here long, but it is industry standard."

"Good to know." What about clients who were lying?

They'd reached an open space hardly bigger than a walk-in closet. Gus dropped Lola's hand and she immediately missed the feeling of connection. He whisked the white covers off several large shapes. The pieces looked lit from within, soaking every bit of golden light in the room, seemingly glowing.

Lola took a fast, involuntary breath. "Wow."

"Okay, that was neutral," Gus said.

Whenever he felt judged, Gus turned into a different person. Lola remembered that he'd always thrown away pieces he'd made in high school shop. His teacher had fished them out and saved them, never commenting, but placing them around the room. An Edwardian-style bird cage. A jewelry box with inlaid quartz. Gus had told Lola he found it annoying, but he'd never asked his teacher to put them away. Lola had seen them one night during an open house with neatly typed labels with Gus's name. For all Lola knew, they were still there. Although he never specifically talked about it, Lola knew that his life at home had been full of harsh words, criticism, and spite. No wonder he'd turned inward.

The two chairs were crafted from teak; Gus had carefully burnished the wood until it shone. They were simple and yet breath-taking. The backs were curved, the top frame bent gracefully in a wide half circle. The slats tapered on each side in an elegant shape. There was a rocking chair of polished gray driftwood, sanded to a smooth luster where it would touch the body, and left gnarled on the legs and back. A side table had a driftwood inlay that had been stained to match the teak, highlighting the texture of the wood. Lola had never seen such classic and yet imaginative furniture.

"I didn't even know you could make furniture like this," she said.

"You thought I spent ten years getting high?"

She was alarmed until she saw the grin on his face. "I didn't think anyone could make furniture like this. To be honest, I never thought about furniture other than something to keep me off the ground."

Gus nodded. "Most people don't. Which is why it is so gratify-ing to do more with it. We all need furniture, so why not make it beautiful?"

"You're right." She walked around each piece, noting all the small details hidden within the design. A piece of wood sanded down to its core, exposing a pattern that had a matching counterpart on the other side. It was clever artistry that still looked solid and comfortable.

"How long did it take you to learn how to do this?" Lola was overawed that Gus could turn wood into something so fluid and beautiful. It was as if he'd shared a completely new side of his personality—

which, she supposed, was exactly what he'd done. Maybe that's called growing up, she thought, but holy cow. Gus was an artist.

"I don't think I ever learned how to do this," Gus said, rubbing his hand down the back of the rocking chair, pushing it lightly, making it move effortlessly, with the lightest touch. "I just start building and go with it. This is all stuff I do for myself. When I start a piece, I just have the barest idea, except"—he pointed to the matching chairs—"if I get really ambitious, I'll do a dining room set."

She glanced at him. "You mean for your own house?"

Gus looked away, suddenly self-conscious. He lifted the white muslin covers, dropping them lightly on each piece. "Something like that. You wanna help me with this? I should get you back."

Lola wondered if he was thinking the same thing as her. The old vision of the house they'd dreamed of sharing. On a hillside. The garden. The fireplace. They'd been kids, but she could still picture it clearly.

Lola spread the covers carefully, tucking them in at the bottom.

Gus watched her. "They're not children, Lola. It's fine."

She smoothed the fabric before giving it a light pat. "You're really talented, you know that, right?"

Gus fished the keys out of his pocket before reaching for the string hanging from the overhead light. "I've got an early morning, so..."

"You never could take a compliment, could you?" Lola asked.

They stepped out onto the dusty sidewalk in the dim light. The garage door groaned as Gus pulled it down to the floor. He locked it and stood up. "I haven't had much practice."

Lola took one of his arms at the elbow, turning him toward her, then gripped his other arm. "Try this. Gus, that furniture belongs in a museum."

He rolled his eyes. "Maybe turn it down a notch."

"Gus, you are creating art in there."

He lifted one of her hands, holding it in both his for a slight beat, before lifting the other off him. "How much wine did you have?"

He started walking down the street. She followed. "You're terrible at this."

"Thank you," he said, smirking. "Is that better?"

He opened the passenger side of his truck. Daisy hopped in.

"And you're a dog stealer."

"Get in the truck, Lola."

She climbed in.

He smiled. "Let it be noted that Lola Alvarez, for once in her life, actually did as she was told."

When he got into the truck, she squeezed his knee. "Let it be noted that Gus Weaver is really talented."

Gus turned around to make sure there weren't any cars coming before he backed out, but Lola was pretty sure she saw a satisfied grin on his handsome face.

They drove through town in silence, watching the clusters of tourists wandering the sidewalks, holding hands and laughing. Just past Campbell's Resort, a couple teenagers were poised on the railing of the cement bridge, right by the sign that said "No Jumping."

"Remind you of anyone?" Lola asked, raising her eyebrows as the kids leaped off, splashing into the lake below.

Gus nodded, glancing at her with a tentative frown. "Yeah. Remember how we used to go to Skeet Carlson's house after we swam?"

The Carlsons had a modest house near the bridge and his mother made them all sandwiches, no matter how many kids showed up. "Yes. His mom was the best."

They were quiet for a minute, lost in their memories. They'd reached the floating trampolines on the lake when Gus spoke up. "I'd look in the Carlsons' fridge and think, look at all that food. They must be rich." He was quiet for a moment. "I've been thinking a lot about growing up the way I did. You absorb all this stuff and think it's normal. I was in therapy for a really long time. It helped me figure things out from my childhood. And forgive myself, which I know sounds corny."

She studied his hands, sure and steady on the wheel. It made sense. Gus seemed different. There was a calmness about him. He seemed to have lost the anxiety that had plagued him when they'd been younger. The only time Gus had seemed at peace as a teenager had been when they were alone, high up in the vineyard, with the wind whistling through the grape leaves.

"Not corny at all," Lola said. "It sounds real."

He nodded. "I thought Izzy might have told you."

It was her turn to frown. "No. Why would Izzy tell me?"

"She's been helping me."

"That sounds like Izzy."

Gus stayed quiet. "I went to my first group therapy meeting in jail. It's been really good for me. I stopped drinking so much. Reality kind of sucks sometimes, you know?"

Lola found it heart-breaking, imagining young Gus talking about his past to strangers.

"But it made me accountable to someone."

"I don't know much about therapy," Lola said.

Gus nodded. "This guy named Jeremy was assigned to me, along with a parole officer who was actually really nice. Better than family, in my case. Jeremy said that I'd been raised to think that intimacy was a weakness. The last step was coming here and facing the people I'd wronged, because I'd turned it into much more in my head, according to Jeremy. He called it self-blame and said once I'd apologized, I'd be free. Well, as free as anyone, I guess."

"Facing your demons."

He nodded. "Yeah. I told Jeremy for years that he was wrong, until one day I just knew I was ready. Or, as he says, I faced my own bullshit."

"*That* sounds like Izzy."

Gus laughed, slowing as he approached the turn past the vineyard. The truck swayed as he drove up the rutted road. "Are you sure you're okay up here all by yourself?"

"Are you offering to keep me company?" The minute it was out of her mouth, Lola regretted it. "I'm sorry. I shouldn't have said that."

Gus glanced over at her. His face was hard to read.

*

Gus pulled into the parking spot near the ponderosa tree. Through the open window they could hear crickets, and somewhere far off, an owl. The old engine gurgled as it cooled. Pine-scented air mingled with the ripening grapes. The lake spread out below them like a glimmering mirror. Gus turned to rub Daisy behind the ears. The little dog melted into his lap.

"Look, I'm sorry—" Lola began, but he cut her off.

"No, it's okay. It's just that a lot has happened. To both of us. I came back to Chelan because I have unfinished business here. And when I arrived, that's all I had. A plan to deal with my past, and that was it. And I know it might seem easy getting a job in construction, but with my background, it isn't. At least, not when you're applying for jobs where you'll be in a client's home or on their property. I've lost out on a lot of jobs because of my history. Even if the company owner wanted to give me a break, they knew that if something happened and their client found out about my past, it wouldn't go down well. But Hidalgo didn't even flinch when I told him. He's a good guy, and I'm not going to let him down. This job means a lot to me. For multiple reasons. I didn't want to leave here, Lola. You know that. But I can't pretend that my past is like everyone else's. I have to play the hand I've been dealt."

Lola clenched her fists so tightly that her fingernails dug into her skin. Had he ever thought about calling her? Writing? Anything? Had he thought for one second what it felt like on her end? That she'd been there that night, at the sheriff's office?

Gus cleared his throat, as if the words were stuck. "Hidalgo likes you."

Lola nodded, wondering what he was going to say next, but instead of speaking he just opened his creaking door, climbed out, walked around the front of the car, and opened her door. As she stepped out, she caught a glimpse of something on his arm, where his shirt sleeve had been rolled up. It made her breath stop. She looked at him, but he quickly put his arm down, rolling down his cuff and buttoning it as if he was cold.

It was the infinity sign. Something Gus had pointed out looked like two teardrops end to end, which reminded him of her name. Her full name, which was Dolores. She'd always hated her full name, which came from "Our Lady of Sorrows." On her first day of kindergarten, when the teacher had her full name printed on a name tag, Lola had come home and told Mami that her name was sad and she didn't like it.

Mami gently held both cheeks and kissed her forehead. "No, mi querida. What you don't understand yet, mi amor, is that in sorrow, we know great joy. And you, Dolores, are the greatest joy."

Lola had told Gus this, and he'd come up with the infinity sign, tracing it in the sand, explaining that it meant he would love her forever. "No matter where we are or what happens to us." He had traced it in the dirt on this very meadow; he had traced it in the snow, wherever they were, as a reminder, a promise. Once, she'd noticed it at school, on her locker, scratched into the paint: small, but visible.

Lola could still see his young, wolfishly thin face, glancing at her from under long bangs—

needing a haircut and a good meal, but shining with love when he looked at her. Wherever they went—a party, the beach, even in the privacy of this spot—his eyes had followed her, as if he hadn't been able to believe his good luck. As if he stopped looking, she'd vanish.

Which, of course, was exactly what he'd done.

Lola could barely remember the month after he'd been arrested. Unable to face the pain and worry, she'd curled up on herself like an anemone. Slept. Lived in a fog. Eaten no more than a few bites of all the favorite dishes Papi had cooked for her: Mami's enchiladas, sopa de tortilla, homemade tortillas with butter and cinnamon sugar. Had gone through the motions, until, bit by bit, despite herself, she'd resumed living. Years later, the pain had diminished, but she'd never stopped wondering about him, thinking about him. And yes, she'd worried too. She'd known that he was living in Seattle, but nothing more.

And now, this tattoo.

Gus walked slightly ahead of her in the dark. He glanced back for a second, looking troubled, but staying quiet. The dry grass crunched underfoot. Lola had left a light on outside the trailer, faint and fragile against the inky dark. A speedboat raced down the middle of the lake. Gus watched the boat's green and red running lights tracing their course, waiting for Lola to climb the steps to the Airstream and open the door. She tried not to notice how her body responded as she passed him. How his smell reminded her of burying her head in his shoulder, wrapping her arms around him, and pulling him down into grass. Whispering that she would always feel this way.

"Thanks, Gus. For showing me what you're working on. It's beautiful."

He nodded, as though to get the compliment over with, tapping the hollow metal door. It sounded like tin. "Don't you ever lock this thing?"

She gave him a half grin. "I'm pretty sure if anyone wanted in, it's cheaper just to leave the door open."

He dug his hands further into his pockets. "Maybe you should let me work on that."

She gave him a warm smile and patted his shoulder, leaving her hand there. "Maybe I should."

He looked at her hand and gingerly lifted it off his shoulder.

"Okay," she said. "Goodnight."

"Goodnight, Lola," he said, looking up at her with intensity until he turned around abruptly, crossing the clearing in long-legged steps. He was in the truck and turning around before Daisy had climbed the trailer steps.

Lola knew exactly what had made him take off. Three words that had always followed, "Goodnight, Lola." Words that hung, unsaid, in the night air.

CHAPTER THIRTEEN

Buzzing

Monday was Lola's day off, and here she was, in the Blue Hills restaurant, having dinner with her family after a late lunch with Hidalgo. They'd used to have Sunday dinner at home, before the restaurant had opened. Then Sunday had become Monday: the one day the restaurant was closed. But Lola never felt like cooking a big meal on her day off, and Carmen never had time. Instead, they shared several pizzas whenever Carmen could make it, and everyone was much happier. Including Evan Hollister, Carmen's fiancé, who wasn't used to watching family members scream at each other when things got tense. Evan's parents, Carmen had learned, were bottled-up tight WASPs who expressed their feelings by phoning their lawyers and changing family trusts.

The Alvarez family were biologically incapable of hiding their feelings from each other.

Lola chewed on a crust of the pizza, reminding herself to tell Rodolfo that he'd outdone himself with the lemony ricotta and basil topping. He'd left her a few pizzas to cook in the restaurant oven. Not as effective as the wood-burning oven, but delicious nonetheless. She stared at the printed menu Carmen had handed her when they'd all sat down. Evan, who sat to Lola's left, kept changing the subject whenever Carmen brought up the wedding menu. Unlike the rest of the table, he had been able to hear Lola's groans when she'd read the menu, and had noticed how she'd winced as her finger ran down the printed page. There was a storm brewing, and Evan didn't want to be anywhere near his fiancée when she went at it with his future sister-in-law.

"What do you think?" Carmen asked, leaning across the table to pluck one of the last pieces of pizza from a platter.

Lola grimaced, snatching the only piece left. "What do you think?"

Evan put his hand over his eyes. "Oh no," he muttered.

"Calm down, Evan," Carmen spat. "She just asked my opinion."

Evan looked between the two women, as if wondering how thick his fiancée could be. "It's a rhetorical question. You planned the menu."

"Neil planned the menu," Carmen replied.

"Aka Satan," Lola said.

Evan lifted his hands. "And we're off."

Carmen's eyes flashed daggers at Evan, scanning the table for anyone else looking at her sideways, before finally landing on her sister. "Believe it or not, this isn't about you. It's about me. And Evan—I guess."

She winked at Evan, who quipped, "Nice to be included."

"And this isn't the time to bring up your grudge with Neil," Carmen added.

Lola flushed bright red. "First of all, it isn't a grudge. It's a heck of a lot more than that. And second, this menu is all about Neil."

"What's wrong with the menu?" Carmen asked.

Lola frowned. "Nothing, if your parents were Martha Stewart and Prince Charles."

"What is that even supposed to mean?" Carmen snapped.

"You were raised on what is basically a farm, by two Hispanic parents, and this"—Lola shook the paper—"is a menu for the martini drinking, plaid pant wearing, white bread country club set."

"So basically me," Evan said cheerily, helping himself to more salad, making Lola love him even more.

"Yes. Which is totally fine, but this wedding is on a vineyard owned by a Hispanic family, and I don't see why the menu can't reflect that." Lola flicked her finger at the paper. "This isn't about you, Carmen; it's about Neil showing off."

"What is wrong with"—Carmen squinted down at the menu—"poached quail tartine and zucchini foam?"

"Foam? Who even eats foam? It's not even food. Foam, Carmen. It's what polluted rivers produce. Not cooks. If you step outside our kitchen and look in the garden, in the actual dirt, I grow all the peppers and herbs Mami used to make her enchilada sauce. Guajillo for the sweetness, ancho for the smokiness, pasilla for the fruitiness and arbol to kick it up a notch. On my days off I used to char the skins, slow roast them and make the sauces Mami used to make. Look in the family pantry. There are rows of them. I kept thinking that one day Neil would give me a shot. One dish. An appetizer, even. I even grow my own garlic. But he's one hundred percent against anything the slightest bit original—or maybe it's even anything Mexican. But what about you? Why not have a celebration that says something about you? Our family? Our heritage?"

Carmen tossed her pizza crust on the plate, taking a slug of wine. "You know what says something about our family? The fact that when they play the wedding march, I'll be walking down the aisle. The fact that my sisters and my father will be right there with me. We don't have to turn this into some kind of fiesta, Lola."

"But why wouldn't we?"

Lola saw Papi studying Carmen with neutral curiosity. She didn't blame him one bit. Why poke the bear? But Lola just couldn't help it. Yes, this was Carmen's wedding, but it was also a family celebration. A celebration that should reflect their family—and they weren't a foam or tartine-eating bunch. Neil had designed a menu that people would eat. Lola wanted to cook a meal that people would remember, that would elevate the party. It could be her gift. An unforgettable one. Lola wanted to bring the Alvarez family full circle. Back to what Mami had stood for: Mexican home cooking. Something Mami would have planned. Lola wanted this to be a family celebration, that ended up with her finally sharing the cabins. First, she'd get Carmen on her side by giving her a wedding feast, then she'd share the news of the cabins. She could already see Carmen looking at them, nodding her head in grudging admiration and saying something about being in the hotel business now.

As the table settled into an uneasy silence, Carmen glared at Evan. "I suppose you're going to just sit there?!"

Evan grimaced. "In my defense, it was working out pretty well for me."

"You approved this menu too," Carmen snapped.

"Darling, if you like it, I like it." He looked at Lola. "That line really works wonders."

"Traitor," Carmen hissed.

"Well, it works most of the time," Evan whispered to Lola. "That and a huge diamond ring."

Juan Alvarez lifted his hand. "Lola, Carmen, please." He turned to Carmen. "Un minuto por favor. Soy curioso." He glanced at Evan. "I'm curious."

Evan smiled, pouring both himself and the old man very full glasses of wine. "Thank you from the idiot who took German in high school."

Juan turned to Lola. "What would you cook? If the choice was yours. I'd like to know."

Carmen had been about ready to leave, but she crossed her arms: irritated, but listening. Waiting. "Fine. Let's hear it."

"Well, I'd make three kinds of tamales," Lola began. "Little ones. Roasted tomatillo and goat cheese. Eggplant with charred peppers and shredded beef tips. I'd do one classic enchilada with a red sauce and one with a green. An entire roasted pig. In the ground, like a real fiesta. I'd string up colored lights. I'd have serapes on the tables. And a tres leches cake."

The table was quiet. All eyes turned to Carmen.

"What?" she said.

"Let me do it, Carmen," Lola whispered, but everyone heard.

"Lola, when you asked me before, I told you what I didn't want to say in front of everyone: you simply don't have the experience." Carmen's eyes softened as she turned to Papi. "It's a nice idea. Lola always has good ideas. The problem is making them reality." Nobody spoke. Carmen glanced around, looking for backup, before turning back to her sister. But Lola was already gone.

Lola was still steaming the next day. She'd spent the morning chopping vegetables as if they were her personal enemies. Later in the day, she cleaned her station as if it were a boxing match.

"If throwing pans made them cleaner, we'd have the cleanest kitchen in the valley," Felicia observed as Lola slammed another pot into the sink, splashing water everywhere.

Ruelle held both hands up in surrender, stepping back. "Let her get it out," he said to Felicia.

"I'm fine," said Lola, wiping the dishwater off her face.

"Yeah, totally," said Felicia, making the universal sign for crazy.

"As if it's not bad enough that my own sister won't trust me to cook her wedding dinner—which, if she'd wanted to, she totally could have. I mean, what did she know about running a winery before she quit her job and took over? Huh? What?"

Felicia nodded. "Have you been hitting the cooking wine?"

Lola nodded, taking a mug out from under her cooking station. "Yes." She took a sip. "As I was saying, as if that's not bad enough, do you know what's worse?"

Felicia cringed. "The fact that you're drinking on the job?"

"I'm off the clock."

"And surrounded by fire and knives. But anyway. What's worse?"

Lola pointed out the window in the direction of the vineyard. "*He's* worse. He's up there every single day, and do you know what's not fair?"

"That he's even hotter than he was ten years ago?" Felicia asked.

Lola frowned. "How did you know what I was going to say?"

Felicia pointed at herself. "I have eyes. Two of them."

"Yes. But Hidalgo is so nice."

Felicia nodded. "Very nice."

"And I have a tendency to do the wrong thing," Lola said, drinking deeply from the mug.

Felicia grabbed the mug from her, spilling red wine on the stainless work counter. "Case in point."

"I'm going to ignore all this…" Lola ran her hand up and down her body. "What all this is saying to me in very clear terms. Do you know what it's saying? What I should be one hundred percent ignoring?"

Felicia grinned. "I'm pretty sure I don't need it explained."

Hidalgo, who had just stepped into the kitchen from the restaurant, cleared his throat.

Felicia spun around, relieved to be distracted from this particular conversational twist. "Hidalgo! Perfect."

Lola tossed another pan into the sink, fighting the urge to ask him who he was with in the restaurant. What if he'd been talking to her family and mentioned the cabins?

"Everything okay?" he asked.

Lola's face brightened as she set about washing the pan. A blob of soapy foam rested on her eyebrow, to which she seemed oblivious.

"Hidalgo. We were just talking about you. You're nice, you know that? Really, really nice."

Hidalgo glanced at Felicia with his eyebrows raised. "Okaaaay."

Felicia untied Lola's apron, took it off over her head and pushed her friend towards Hidalgo. "Hidalgo, Lola might have tested a little too much cooking wine."

Lola shook her head, tilting towards Hidalgo until she had to press his chest to avoid falling into him. "Nope. Was just drinking it." She got so close to him their noses touched. "FYI, my sister is a bitch."

Hidalgo tried not to smile. "Okay. Maybe some food."

Felicia held the door open. "Excellent idea."

At Mystic Pizza, Lola ordered a beer and drank it while they waited for the food. They sat at the little strip of counter at the window, watching clumps of tourists stroll down the street on their way from window shopping or the beach. They all had the relaxed demeanor of people without schedules or obligations.

Early evening sun slanted in the windows of the pizzeria. Hidalgo took a sip of his beer while Lola picked at the beer label, methodically peeling it off. "I'm glad I got you out of the kitchen."

She grinned at him. "Me too. Thanks for getting me out of there."

"You're welcome."

"I'm so over everything. Yesterday, I pretty much put it out there and asked Carmen, again, in front of the whole family, if I could cook her wedding dinner. The answer wasn't just no, it was a slap-in-the-face no. As in: 'you have ideas, you just can't execute them.' Which is pretty much saying I'm worthless."

Hidalgo winced. "Um, but haven't you had a lot of ideas that didn't work? You told me about the sandwich stand. Maybe it's about biting off more than you can chew rather than not being able to do it."

Lola snorted. "Wow, you're not going to sugar coat it, are you?"

Hidalgo lifted his hands. "I'm not saying she shouldn't let you cook the wedding dinner, but honestly, Lola, do you really want to? It sounds like a horrible amount of pressure to me. A huge, complicated meal like that? People expect so much on their wedding day. Wouldn't you rather enjoy your sister's big day?"

Irritated, Lola didn't want to look at him. Instead, she ripped off the last of the beer label and curled it around her finger. "If you had the chance to build this amazingly complicated showcase of a house and it's like, nearly all glass, so there is nowhere to hide your mistakes… And say it's right downtown, or someplace where everyone will see it, do you say: 'No, I've never done that before,' or do you throw everything you've got into it because you know it will take you to the next level?"

Hidalgo nodded. "No question. Option B."

Lola nodded. "Exactly. Because, sink or swim, it's your chance. And this is a chance to not only show my family what I can do, but to give something to my sister. I want to use my cooking to make her wedding dinner something special. Food is so much more than something to eat. It's a way to nurture people and tell a story. And it's about including our mother in the wedding. Mami was always about the big fiesta. If she were alive, that is what Carmen would want." Hidalgo's eyes stayed right with Lola, nodding. "I want to tell the story of my parents, coming to America and making so many things possible, including a beautiful wedding on a vineyard that we've all helped create." She wiped a tear from her eye. "Wow, someone must be cooking peppers."

A waiter pointed to a pizza box at the counter. Hidalgo stood up, patting her shoulder. "Yeah, that must be it." He looked like he had something else to say.

She looked up at him. "What?"

"The thing about option B, Lola, is that if it ends up being a rush job, it might not be the story you want to tell."

After Hidalgo had collected their pizza, they walked outside the tiny restaurant, taking a left, heading down the street to the grassy slope near the river. Hidalgo found a picnic table in the shade, opened the pizza box, and placed a warm slice on Lola's paper plate. By this time, Lola's annoyance at Hidalgo's warning had calmed down. All she wanted was food.

Lola bent her head to smell the fragrance of the perfectly charred crust, sweet tomatoes and curling green basil. "This is exactly what I needed."

"I thought so," said Hidalgo. "We both spend too much time working."

"I love cooking. I really do. It's dealing with Neil that's sapping my energy."

Hidalgo had a comforting effect on her, Lola noticed. Maybe this was what she needed. Not complicated and wild…

"That would do it. Hopefully seeing the cabins come together is cheering you up. How's it working out with Gus?"

"Gus? What about him?" Lola's cheeks flushed. She was still a little buzzed, her emotions swirling on the surface. She swallowed a mouthful of pizza, trying to recover her composure. "What do you mean?" Her words came out too quickly.

"I mean, you're living there. He's there full-time. Probably more, given all he's doing. How's it working out?"

"My dog loves him," Lola blurted.

Hidalgo frowned, putting down his slice. "You're having issues with him?"

She shook her head. "Oh, no. I'm not. No issues. He's fine."

Gus looked at her closely, wondering what was going on. "So, why exactly don't you like him? I'm going to need an explanation, Lola."

Lola took a long sip of water. "It's a little weird, going to sleep and not knowing if he's still around. Waking up and having someone there. He's very respectful. You know, keeps his distance. Do you know Daisy has stopped coming to get me from work?"

"You're jealous because your dog likes him?"

She shook her head, lifting a finger. "No. Because I know that she loves me, but he thinks it's funny, and that's annoying."

"He thinks it's funny that your dog likes hanging out with him?"

"He thinks it's funny that I'm jealous."

"You just said you weren't jealous."

"I'm not. Totally not."

Hidalgo shook his head, watching the paddle boarders on the river. "I'm not really following this, Lola."

"No. Someone with a normal brain wouldn't. But, bottom line, everything is fine. Gus is just doing his job. Perfectly normal. Hunky dory."

"Hunky dory?" Hidalgo raised his eyebrows.

"Yep." Lola opened her bottle of water, taking a deep gulp to settle her nerves. "You know, the cabins are cheering me up. They're going to be beautiful."

"Gus is a talented guy. You should see what he's got going on in our warehouse."

"Can we not talk about Gus?" It came out way too aggressive. Lola forced herself to slow down. "I mean, yes. He is. Talented. And all that. But let's not talk about Gus. Because you're the one that's making this happen, and I'm really grateful. I'm being blocked at every other point in the Blue Hills business, but the cabins are finally happening. You are making them a reality, and I just want to say… Thank you."

As she spoke, she'd leaned towards him in a friendly manner. He took the opportunity to kiss her.

Lola held back for a second, then kissed him back. It was nice. Soft, warm and an invitation to more. A pizza-tasting kiss turned out to be surprisingly pleasant.

As Hidalgo's truck pulled into the dirt parking area at the top of the vineyard, they both saw Gus's truck backed into the clearing, much closer to the Airstream that he normally parked.

"Okaaaaay," Hidalgo said, clearly annoyed.

Now, as they got out of Hidalgo's truck, they had no choice but to pass right by Gus, who'd set up a table saw off the back of his pickup, using the truck bed to support a large piece of lumber while he worked. He lifted a hand while they passed, but otherwise kept his eyes trained on the saw.

The noise was astounding, bouncing off the cliff behind them, which seemed to act as an amplifier. Hidalgo walked Lola to the trailer, waving up at the red cliff, saying something about the noise.

"What?" Lola yelled back.

"Never mind." He glared at Gus, but his back was facing them. "Do you want me to tell him to stop?"

Lola nodded. "Sure, it might be messy but come on in."

Hidalgo laughed, following her into the Airstream, glancing around. "This is nice."

Lola nodded. The noise wasn't nearly as bad inside, but it was still irritating. Her teeth were on edge, as if someone were dragging a nail across cement. "It's actually perfect."

Daisy scratched at the door and Lola let her in, rubbing her ears when she hopped up on the banquette. "Daisy loves it. Thinks I bought it for her."

Hidalgo smiled, patting the seat beside him. "Here, Daisy." The little dog studied him across the table. "Here, girl." Daisy didn't move.

"Don't worry. She takes a bit to warm up," Lola said. She reached over to the tiny refrigerator and handed Hidalgo a dog treat. "Here. Give her this."

Hidalgo held out the dog treat. "Here, Daisy. Look what I've got."

Daisy hopped off the banquette, jumped up beside Hidalgo and took the treat, allowing her head to be scratched before jumping back down and scratching at the door. Lola let her out, turning back to Hidalgo, feeling like she had to apologize for her treat-snatching dog. "I'm sure she just had to go to the bathroom."

"Right." The table saw stopped, and they smiled happily at each other. "Much better."

"Want some wine?" Lola asked.

She had just opened the fridge when there was a loud knock at her door. Glancing at Hidalgo, she opened the door. Gus stood on the ground, shifting uneasily. "Hey, sorry to bother you."

"I bet," Lola said under her breath.

"What?" Gus asked, before plowing ahead. "Anyway, there's something I wanted your opinion on before I take off."

Hidalgo moved into view.

Gus looked at Hidalgo, as if considering his response. "Oh, hi, Hidalgo. I thought you'd left."

Hidalgo frowned. "My truck is right there."

Gus nodded. "Right. Sorry. I can't see it because of my truck."

Hidalgo rested an arm over the door frame. "Now that Lola's living here, maybe we need some work hours."

Lola, feeling the rising friction between the men, didn't want to be responsible for it escalating. "No, it's fine. I wanna get these cabins done."

She climbed down the steps. Gus didn't step back until Hidalgo followed, which left Lola standing very close to him, looking into his eyes until Hidalgo joined her. She took Hidalgo's hand, as if reminding herself of what she wanted.

"What did you want to show me?" Lola asked Gus.

"Hang on," Gus said, in a manner that struck Lola as aggressive.

Was he annoyed because she was holding Hidalgo's hand? She had a right to hold any hand she wanted. She squeezed Hidalgo's hand with such force that he shouted "Ow!", letting go of her.

Lola gave Hidalgo a piercing glance.

He rubbed his hand. "You just cut off the circulation or broke some bones, is all."

Gus covered a smirk, but not before Lola saw it. "Everyone okay?"

Lola shot daggers at him. "Are you going to show me the issue, or are we going to stand here all night?"

"It can wait until morning," Gus said cheerfully.

"Go!" Lola snapped, following him.

"What exactly are we looking at?" Lola asked, as she and Hidalgo peered into the snug cabin. It was the first cabin and nearly finished. Every time Lola went inside, she felt like levitating when she saw the interior, complete with the gorgeous Hudson Bay blanket that she couldn't resist touching, smoothing down an imaginary wrinkle. Sometimes she went in and just stared, hardly believing they'd come this far. She'd added some pottery on the open shelves over the sink. White cups with matching saucers. Everything in the room was harmonious, inducing a sense of serenity. As if you could lie down on the bed and drift off in utter bliss. Gus had absolutely nailed it. These were cabins with everything you needed, yet nothing superfluous. They'd appeal to minimalists, and to couples looking for something different. They were just what she'd dreamed of yet better.

Lola wanted to lavish praise on Gus, but felt it would be better to wait until Hidalgo and his swollen hand had left. She and Hidalgo peered in the door from the deck, admiring the cabin by the light of an industrial lamp. Broad windows flanked the door, which would allow guests to enjoy the view. To the right was a miniature kitchen with open shelving and a curved snug eating nook. To the left, there was a queen-sized bed, with a bedside table. The front of the bedroom area had a small couch facing the window. Gus had insisted on the furniture being delivered ahead of completion, so he could make sure that everything fit properly.

Gus sat on the edge of the mattress on the Hudson Bay blanket, with Daisy curled up beside him. Occasionally, she opened one eye, seemingly keeping watch on Hidalgo.

"Shelving," Gus said, pointing to the half wall dividing the kitchen and the bedroom. There were three long open shelves on the wall.

"This really couldn't have waited?" Hidalgo said, glancing at his phone.

Gus shook his head. "I'm sorry but I have to order tonight if you want more shelving. If you keep this design, you're guaranteed that the person sleeping here won't hit them, but if I move some down here, we can put in two more. But, that eliminates the possibility of bar stools."

"Bar stools?" Lola asked, intrigued despite her determination to be annoyed.

"Yes. I know you were thinking of summer visitors, but in the winter, when people aren't sitting on the deck, you might want the option of two bar stools here so people could sit here while someone else cooks. Or whatever."

"Oooh. I like it," Lola said. "Hidalgo?"

"I like the bar stools. Good thinking, Gus. Lola, I'll talk to you tomorrow."

Her big plan for kissing him goodnight fell apart as she followed him outside. A thousand stars shone overhead as she said goodbye to Hidalgo, kissing him lightly, wishing she could slow this down and not have Gus so close. "Thanks for a great night."

Hidalgo looked down at her, tucking a strand of hair behind her ear. "It was fun." He smiled—somewhat wistfully, she thought. "Are you sure you don't want me to set some work hours so he's not bothering you?"

Lola sighed. "He's just doing his job. He can't help it."

Gus would always unsettle her, on some level, she thought. She returned her attention to the man before her.

"I had a really nice time," Hidalgo said.

"Me too."

Daisy trotted out onto the porch, watching them. Hidalgo bent down to call her over. She came and let him pet her head. Lola silently thanked her dog for being gracious. She wasn't normally this accepting with strangers… Unless the stranger was Gus.

Daisy joined Lola, watching the truck drive away, wagging her tail. The truck disappeared from sight, leaving a ghostly trail of dust in the night air.

Lola turned around to see Gus locking the huge bin he kept at the site for his equipment. He looked up at her and he rose, dusting off his hands with a wry grin on his face. "Have a nice time?"

"As a matter of fact, yes, it was lovely. No thanks to all your noise."

Gus smiled. "My noise? You mean the noise I create when I'm doing my job? Because it's not like I'm out here yodeling, Lola. Construction is noisy."

She stomped up to him until they were inches apart. "Not always. Things seem to get very loud when Hidalgo is here. You just happen to turn on table saws and hammer like a madman."

Gus pointed to his truck. "Not a table saw. A buzz saw. A table saw is much louder."

"Well, thank god for small mercies."

"I'm always making construction noises, because, Lola, that is what I'm hired to do. If you want me working nine to five, I'd be happy to oblige. And your shrinky dink cabins will be done around Christmas time."

"They're tiny cabins," she growled.

"Adorable, the way you say it."

She crossed her arms, glaring at him. "Just build the cabins."

"I will." He leaned down to pet Daisy, who flopped over for a belly rub.

"And stay away from my dog!"

Gus lifted his arms and stood up, face to face with Lola. As he lowered his arms, he looked down at the lake. "Lola, we can't pretend we don't have a history."

"Oh yes we can."

Gus shook his head. "Lola, you're a lot of things, but a liar isn't one of them."

"Who said anything about lying?"

Gus licked his lips and Lola hated herself for noticing that one gesture. "That's what you do when you ignore your feelings."

Lola looked him evenly in the eye. "I do not have feelings for you."

Gus smiled. "Now that's a lie." She tried to object, but he lifted his hands. "No, wait. Let me explain before you run up one side and down the other. You're still mad at me."

"That was a hundred lifetimes ago, Gus."

Gus crossed his arms and looked up at the sky for a long moment. A shooting star traced a fading light across the inky sky before he looked back at her. "The first time Jeremy, my therapist, said I needed to apologize to forgive myself, I thought of you. I could see you driving away with your dad in the parking lot right before Christmas, the day school got out. You were wearing that red hat with the…" He flicked his fingers around the top of his head.

"The pom-pom?"

"Yeah, the fluffy thing. And your dad had hot chocolate for you. You had this nice, safe life and I…" He bit his lip. "And I came between you and your father." He wiped his eyes, his voice cracking. "I wasn't good for you, Lola."

Lola put her hand on his arm, touched that he remembered her drinking hot chocolate back then, instead of coffee. "We were kids."

He lifted a hand. "Just listen. I can't do this halfway, Lola. I have to face facts. I endangered your life. I made your father worry. He was nice to me. Most people in town thought I was trash, and your father—until I didn't deserve it anymore—was really decent, you know? He said hi. He looked me in the eye. He shook my hand. And it meant a lot to me, you know?"

Lola felt her chest tightening up. "You couldn't help it."

Gus shook his head. "I could have. You saw me drinking but I smoked some weed too. I might have been a kid, but I was very deliberate about hiding the weed from you." Lola frowned. "Yeah." He took a deep breath. "I didn't know my cousin was going to rob that convenience store, but I knew what he was like. We weren't going to a Boy Scout meeting." Lola thought about the weed. She'd known. Instead of feeling angry, she just felt sad. She squeezed his arm, giving him space to talk. The open sky and warm summer air made it seem like they had all night. "Where I ended up was inevitable. But I'm sorry I hurt you. I should have called you when I was settled in Seattle. I just thought I should let you go. But it was wrong."

Tears streamed down Lola's face. "It's okay."

Gus wiped his eyes, then put a hand on her shoulder. "No, it's not. That's not what I need, Lola."

"Gus? What do you need?" Her voice was nearly a whisper.

Gus smiled wistfully. "Oh, everything." He shook his head. "I'm sorry. I guess I just need to finish apologizing. This is a start."

"And after that?" Her voice was hoarse with emotion.

Gus was still for a long moment, letting the noise of the crickets soothe him before reaching out. He touched her cheek with his fingertips very gently. "Goodnight, Lola." He opened his mouth to say something more, but stopped, swallowing whatever it was that he was going to say, and walked away as fast as his long legs would move.

Lola watched his truck disappear down the hill, the rumbling engine echoing off the cliffs. She leaned her head back, gazing into the peerless sky before gathering Daisy into her arms, burying her head in the dog's thick fur, comforting herself. Putting the dog down, she slowly made her way to the Airstream, locking the door behind her. Kicking off her shoes, she fell onto her bed, slid open the curtains and gazed out at the star-blanketed sky. Gus Weaver was back in her life. Hidalgo Ruiz was a good kisser. Carmen was going to figure out what her little sister was doing. Things were about to get very, very complicated.

CHAPTER FOURTEEN

One Drink

Lola wiped her station until it gleamed, thrilled that she wasn't going to be subjected to tonight's drama. It was her night off. She'd take Daisy for a long walk, tidy up the Airstream, maybe see if the Town Tub laundromat was open, walk down to Tin Lilly during the wash cycle and have a glass of wine. The evening stretched in front of her like an empty beach.

Neil passed by her, placing his hand on her shoulder, and whispering, "Not so fast, hot stuff: you're working a catering shift." A perfect moment for the camera. That wasn't there, because Neil had found it, thinking they were spying for another jealous chef. Only Neil could make up something like that.

Lola whirled to face him, stepping back so they weren't toe to toe. "Nope. It's my night off."

Neil rubbed his knuckles under his eyes. "Boohoo. My catering line cook has food poisoning. You're it."

"Find someone else," snapped Lola, taking off her apron.

Neil handed her a clean apron. "We're plating in one hour."

"You have other people you could call."

He grinned at her. "I do, actually. But you're right here and, as much as it pains me to say this, you're not half bad. And if you can't stand the heat? Get out of my kitchen."

"It's my kitchen."

Neil smirked. "That's not what your sister says."

Lola didn't have time to stew in her hatred towards Neil. There wasn't time for anything but moving with the precision of an assembly line robot as plates flew out the door. Outside, a quartet played as relaxed wedding guests in low-key elegant summer attire chatted, sipped wine, and enjoyed the fragrances wafting from the kitchen, blissfully unaware of the frenzied workers laboring to produce their meal. Lola leaned over snowy white entrée plates as big as Frisbees, drizzling a glossy herb-tinged wine reduction onto the delicate lamb chops. If one drop of sauce migrated on the plates, the entire tray was carefully lowered and a designated touch-up server wiped the plate clean before the tray was lifted and whisked out to the racks positioned around the patio. All this happened with such speed that Lola's mind whirred.

A server came in with empty trays, snapping her fingers, saying one half of her table had meals. "They're sitting there in front of their food. I have to go now!"

Lola plated so fast that a chop skittered off the plate, across the stainless steel and onto the floor—just as Neil was passing by. He held up the offending chop in one hand.

"You're costing us time and money, Lola. Two things caterers do not have to spare." He studied her with beady eyes until she felt her heart was going to explode. "Do better!" he said, through gritted teeth.

Carole noticed Lola's hand shaking and patted her back. "It's okay. He's always like this."

Lola had worked brunch catering services before, but her schedule had until now miraculously spared her this fresh hell. Wedding dinners were a different beast altogether. Neil was bad enough in everyday life. This version of him was horrid.

He stalked the kitchen like an angry bear, holding up a wine glass and touching it to Ruelle's nose. "Would you drink out of this?" Ruelle blinked, moving his head back, looking slightly amused. Neil hissed. "Would you?"

Ruelle, nonplussed, knowing he could walk out the door and have another job within an hour, shook his head and replied in his thickest Mexican accent: "I'm a beer drinker."

"That's not the point!" bellowed Neil.

After a hundred years, the cake, which had arrived midway through the dinner, was served. With what little energy Lola had left in her body, she cleaned her station to the point where it would pass muster, although not as thoroughly as she'd like. Tomorrow, she'd start fresh. Tonight, she just had to get off her feet. After she'd given the stainless counter a last polish, she looked up, aware Neil had come to stand in front of her. Felicia, who had her purse hiked up over her shoulder, ready to go, lingered, although she'd already said goodnight.

Neil gave Felicia a nod. "It's okay. Believe it or not, I'm here to deliver a compliment."

Felicia gave him a dubious look, but Lola nodded that it was alright.

"See you tomorrow," Felicia said, squeezing Lola's arm protectively before slipping out the back door.

Ruelle, Lola knew, was making himself busy just to ensure that Lola wouldn't be left alone with Neil. They were a tight little crew and she loved them. Especially tonight.

"Right," Neil said. "I know it was your night off and you'd worked a long week. You did well." Lola waited for the other shoe to drop. "That's it." He walked off, returning a second later. "Look, I know I'm hard on you, but you have a future as a cook. You do. I'm just trying to prepare you." He made to go again, but doubled back a second time. "I know you think you know everything there is to know about me, but you don't." He jerked his thumb towards the bar. "Buy you a drink? To thank you?"

"No thanks, Neil. I'm wiped out. I'm calling it a night."

"Fair enough." He patted the stainless. "You did well."

Gus must have left early because Daisy was waiting in her usual spot, curled up near Rodolfo's station, where she'd be conveniently available for any spare pizza scraps. The pizza oven was out of commission due to the wedding, but Daisy kept to her habit, jumping up and spinning happy circles at the sight of Lola climbing down the kitchen steps.

Lola's legs ached as she bent to rub the dog's head. "You little traitor. Your first love is off for the night, is he?"

Lola tried to ignore the tug of disappointment at knowing that she wouldn't find Gus working in the fourth cabin, eager to show off his latest flourish. Each cabin had its own distinct features. One had an old log running down the side of the kitchen that added a deep, rich color and a touch of nature. Another had a front door framed with boards carved with flowers that Gus had found in the back of the Ruiz warehouse, salvaged from a tear-down. The last cabin would have a door that Gus had found sitting in a back alley, seemingly belonging to no one. The door had been a bear to move, comprised of thick board with an arched top, and a handle that, when polished, had turned out to be brass. Gus thought it might have been sitting in the alley for decades, hidden behind some boards. He was building a special frame to fit the door which Lola thought would lend the cabin the air of a hobbit dwelling from the outside.

Every day Lola found herself looking forward to the progress on the cabins and, if she was honest, Gus himself. They discussed each development with growing excitement and pleasure in seeing the project coming to fruition. It was a pity that he wouldn't be there tonight because discussing the cabins was often the highlight of her day. It was all about the cabins.

When she arrived at the meadow, it was still. Crickets chirped and the occasional bird cried, but there was no wind. The vineyard spread like a dark green sea around her, as it always had and always would. A lone boat travelled the lake, its motor humming far away. Lola went into the Airstream, thinking she'd plop into bed, but her body felt sticky from working with food. The smells, smoke and sweat. She opened a drawer and pulled out her bathing suit. "Daisy, how about a swim?"

*

The swim was more of a dip. The moment her head was submerged, Lola felt her body relax. The water was a pale turquoise, turning a deeper shade of blue as the sun slipped further behind the mountain. The cliffs above the road were reflected in the lake, wavering in the glassy blue. The sky was a purple-hued bowl filled with puffy pink clouds. Lola waited until Daisy found the courage to hop off her rock and swim out to join her. Then together, they swam back to the shore, scrambling up onto the rocks, refreshed and ready for home.

Towards the end of their walk Daisy became more alert, slowing her pace, creeping carefully onto the rise at the top of the orchard road. At first, Lola thought maybe there was a deer near the Airstream, but as they neared, she saw that someone was sitting in one of the old lawn chairs. Lola tugged her towel closer.

Neil stood up from the chair, stooping to gather a bottle that had been sitting by his feet. "I brought wine. I was going to leave it, but thought I'd wait, since your car was still here."

Lola hesitated for a moment, remaining at the edge of the clearing.

"I won't stay long. I know you're tired. One glass. I promise. Do you have an opener?"

Later, Lola would see how Neil had distracted her with the task of getting the opener. He saw her hesitation, and moved her brain to something tangible: finding a wine opener. He knew exactly what he was doing.

"I do," she said, going into the Airstream, making sure she returned wearing baggy sweatpants and an old T-shirt, her hair wrapped up in a towel.

She handed him the opener and thought to herself that this was the moment to say she'd just realized she was too tired to sit up. Or had a headache. Or any excuse that would get him out of here. But she didn't. She could handle Neil. He'd bitch and moan and wobble home. She sat down in the tatty chair across from him and took the glass of wine.

"Cheers," Neil said, offering the glass.

"Cheers," Lola said back, wondering if she was making a mistake.

CHAPTER FIFTEEN

More Than One Drink

It was getting late and Lola had grown slightly cold from staying so still. She'd left her sweater in the Airstream, not thinking that she'd actually stay outside this late, but Neil would not stop talking. Already, he'd told her about how he'd built his restaurant from the ground up, funding it with the last chunk of his college student loan after he'd dropped out of school. How he'd slept in the office more nights than not. How he'd married a waitress who'd put family money into the place. "Then, poof," he said, flicking his hands into the night air. "She divorced me, and took the controlling share of the restaurant with her." He took a long sip of his wine. "All those nights at the restaurant had been"—he used his fingers as quotation marks—"abandonment." He rolled his eyes theatrically.

Lola stared at him over her nearly full glass of wine, sure that there was much, much more to his ex-wife's side of the story.

Neil lifted the bottle, but it was empty. "Time for me to go." He shook the bottle over the glass. "Unless you have another one hidden in there…?" He pointed at the Airstream. "If it's getting cold, we can go inside."

As if it was his trailer and not hers.

Right.

Lola stood. "I'm going to call it a night."

Neil pushed himself up as if to leave before drunkenly falling back. The straps of the chair strained to hold him. "You know, I have tried to support women in the kitchen."

Lola nearly spit out her sip of wine. "Uh-huh."

He stood up, taking a step towards her, pointing in a preachy manner. Daisy got up from where she had been sleeping and stood at the ready, by Lola's side, her ears flat to her head. "I have. You think, because I push you, I'm being too hard on you. But…" He stabbed his finger in her direction. "But. You see? I'm toughening you up. Getting you ready." He thought. "For battle."

"That is not it at all," said Lola.

Neil tilted his head, looking genuinely interested. "Okay. Tell me, then. What does little Lola Alvarez think of the way I run my kitchen? Do tell."

Lola swallowed, trying to hold back her burning anger. "Your flirtatious manner, your whispering, the way you call women 'sexy' or 'hot' or violate our personal space. It's demeaning. It's harassment."

Neil threw up his hands, letting out a series of short, barking laughs. "Listen to yourself, Lola. It's a kitchen! There are seven people coming in and out of a space as big as a walk-in closet. There is no personal space. And as for joking around, it's part of the culture. Look, I know this is the first professional kitchen you've worked in—and I'll let this one go because of it—but honestly, stop being such a snowflake. Welcome to the real world. You millennials. I swear to god."

"It's not just me, Neil. It's everyone."

Neil took another step towards her, tossing the wine bottle in the fire pit. "Oh, for god's sake. Now you're speaking for everyone? Of course you are. It's your kitchen, right?"

"You asked me what I think." This had been a huge mistake. Why had she opened her dumb mouth?

Neil rolled his eyes, shaking his head. He looked very drunk. Lola wondered how long he'd been sitting at the bar before he'd made his way up here. "I'm going. And if you're lucky, I'll forget about everything you said tonight. You're tired. I get it. You're not used to this level of work."

He had to step by her on his way to the path that led down through the vineyard. Thinking she was safe, Lola spat out: "I won't forget."

Neil stopped, standing in the dark, a hulking figure with sloping shoulders, a ferocious scowl and, Lola noticed, a fighter's stance. He slowly turned and stalked back to her. He grabbed her arm, yanking her towards him. "Don't you ever threaten me," he growled, with real menace. "Ever."

Daisy launched herself into Neil, snapping her jaws at him. Neil shook Lola once before dropping her arm. Stepping back from Daisy, he tried to kick her, but she danced out of his reach, barking hysterically.

Sometimes, Lola thought to herself, giving yourself a break meant drawing a line in the sand.

"You're fired," Lola said, massaging her arm.

Neil laughed. Not the barking, sarcastic laughter of earlier, but a real guffaw. "Good one, Lola. Do you really think your sister is going to fire me right before her wedding? And do what, have Happy Meals for her guests?"

Lola patted her chest. "I'm firing you."

He shook his head. "You don't have the authority."

Lola wanted him gone more than anything in the world. She decided to lie. She held up her phone. "You thought we were stealing your ideas? We were recording you. We have videos of you harassing us. Right here."

He took a step in her direction. "Show me."

"I don't have to. Bottom line, Neil, you know we have more than enough to put a serious roadblock on your career. My sister might not have thought what I was telling her was enough to fire you, but when she sees it for herself, she'll know exactly what to do. This was always going to happen sooner or later. You just hurried it along. You're fired. If you don't pack your knives and leave right now, I'll post the video on social media. Do not underestimate me, Neil."

"You're lying. You would have told Carmen."

Lola shook her head. "She's getting married. I thought it could wait. Guess I was wrong."

Neil lunged towards her, making a grab for the phone. There was a noise in the bushes. Neil and Lola both turned as a dark shape hurtled towards them. Lola was about to grab Daisy and dive under the Airstream, then she realized what was happening.

It was Gus.

CHAPTER SIXTEEN

Taking Out the Trash

Gus didn't arrive so much as land in front of Neil like a boulder. He might not have been an actual bear, but he had all the menace and physical presence of one. Neil wasn't stupid. He threw up his hands and stepped cautiously away from Lola with a sneer on his face. "Well, Lola, if it isn't your old flame."

Lola frowned, confused. "What?" How could Neil know anything about her past? Unless he'd eavesdropped on her and Felicia…

"Go home, Neil," Gus said in a low, even tone, standing close to Lola. Daisy wedged herself between them, looking inordinately pleased, as if waiting for Neil to get his ass handed to him. She appeared to be wagging her tail in gleeful anticipation.

"Out delivering some of the family merchandise? Perhaps for your brother?" Neil said to Gus, with one raised eyebrow.

Lola looked between the two men, trying to figure out the connection between them. How on earth could Neil know about the Weavers?

"I'm going to lose my patience very soon," Gus said quietly.

Neil grinned at Lola. "Don't be so surprised. I've lived here long enough to know about the illustrious Weaver family and their various illicit endeavors." Gus took a small step towards Neil. "From what I've heard, having anything to do with the Weaver family leads to no good. He glanced at Lola. "Isn't that right?"

"That's it," Gus said, stepping closer with a threatening stance. "You're off. One way or another."

Neil tilted his head. "I don't think ex-cons are supposed to beat up people now, are they? I think, given your background, you'd better think this through. You wouldn't want to land back in jail, now would you?"

Gus darted behind Neil, pinning his arms and lifting him up, turning him toward the path. "Some people are just worth it, you turd."

"Put him down, Gus. We've already got him."

Gus gave Lola an unreadable look before dropping Neil.

Neil somehow found his feet and dusted himself off. "Lola, I'm sure your family will be thrilled with"—he waved his hands between Lola and Gus with a disgusted look—"whatever this is."

Gus stepped so close to Neil he was nearly stepping on his toes. He lifted a single finger, punctuating each word with a tap to Neil's chest. "Pack your shit and get out of here. Tonight." Gus shook his head. "You don't want to know what will happen if you stay even one more day. It's a very deep lake, Neil, and you said it yourself: I know all the best people in town."

Even in the shadowy light, Lola could see the color drain from Neil's flushed cheeks.

Daisy followed six feet behind Neil, making sure his loose-limbed form was well on its way down the path before she turned to trot happily back to the campfire.

Lola and Gus stared at one another across the expanse of the fire ring, each lost in their own thoughts, not wanting to break the moment which hung suspended between them. The gravity of the previous moment had brought them closer—although in what sense, neither could be sure. There weren't words for what they were feeling, so they both remained quiet as a billion stars illuminated the sky and bats flitted over the vines. An owl hooted in the orchard, filling the night with sound.

Daisy's return broke the spell.

Lola rubbed her arms, taking a deep breath. "Do you, uh, want to come inside?" She nodded at the fire pit area. "I'm going to have to burn those chairs now."

Gus nodded with a slight grin. "Good idea. Sure, I'll come in, for a bit. I don't think you should be alone, do you?"

Lola understood that he was being tactful. Neil could come back. Gus had ordered a new lock set for the Airstream, but it hadn't yet arrived.

"How about some tea?" she said, holding the trailer door open behind her.

Gus had to duck his head at the entry, but could stand up once inside. He seemed to fill the space, making the trailer shrink in size. Lola plugged in the kettle while Gus settled into the curved bench around the table, studying the tiny kitchen, the snug bed, the compact overhead cupboards and the yellow Swiss dot curtains. "This is nice."

Lola, gathering cups and tea in the kitchen nook, turned to him. "Why were you here?"

Gus nodded, as if he'd been waiting for the question. "I was in the bar, trying to work up the courage to talk to your father. But I didn't want him to notice me first. I thought if he did, he might ask me to leave. Neil was sitting at the bar too. At the other end. I heard him talking to the bartender. Going on and on about how he wasn't just an award-winning chef, he was a mentor. And how nobody, especially you, treated him with the respect he was due. You had an attitude. You were entitled. It was such garbage. I realized that the guy was completely mental when he started describing himself as 'Anthony Bourdain meets Picasso.' What does that even mean? Yeah, so when I finally left, I just had this feeling in the pit of my stomach. Guys like that get themselves all revved up and they need somewhere to spend it, you know? So I thought I'd check on you. Just to make sure."

"Thank you." Lola placed Gus's tea on the table in front of him. "So much."

He looked up at her, and their eyes locked for half a second too long. He nodded, breaking the spell. She collected her tea and sat across from him, making sure that her fragile emotions wouldn't get the best of her. Daisy, of course, hopped right across Lola, scooted around the bench, and curled up next to Gus, who scratched her behind the ears.

"I'm going to miss her when I'm done," Gus said, looking down at the dog, stroking her soft fur.

"Yeah," Lola said absently. She hadn't thought about Gus packing up and leaving. The idea left her suddenly bereft. She had to remind herself, again, that her emotions were all over the map tonight. "She'll miss you."

Gus raised his eyebrow suggestively, glancing at her across the table. "Is that a fact?"

"We're talking about the dog, Gus."

"Listen, do you want me to spend the night here?" He didn't look at her as he said it, paying attention to Daisy. "Just in case." He patted the table. "Doesn't this fold down into a bed?"

The word "bed" shifted things. Lola studied him, to see if there was any hidden meaning in his offer. "It does."

Gus dragged his hand through his hair, as he always had when he was agitated. "I'm not…" He frowned, searching for the right words. "Trying to take advantage. If that's what you're thinking. It's just in case."

Lola sighed. She knew that as soon as she closed her eyes, she'd hear Neil's footsteps. He could have easily gone back to the bar and continued drinking. "You know, that would help me get some sleep." She got up from the table and found a sheet and blanket. "Which I'm going to need if I'm taking over the kitchen tomorrow."

Gus drained his tea, passing very close to her on his way to the sink. They each turned sideways, as if looking at one another at this distance would be too intimate. Gus broke the silence with awkward jocularity. "Heck yeah, you will."

Lola watched Gus crouch on the floor, lowering the table to the correct height, and reminded herself that it didn't matter that his broad shoulders fit him better now, or that his shirt slid up, revealing a well-muscled back. So what if his tattoo meant he thought of her every day? Those things meant nothing to her.

Gus Weaver was spending the night in her trailer. Within breathing distance. It meant absolutely nothing.

Nothing at all.

CHAPTER SEVENTEEN

Kitchen Meeting

"I know you're awake." Gus was facing the opposite direction, pulling on his shirt in the early morning dark. Even in the dim light, Lola had been enjoying the sight of him walking around the trailer half dressed. She'd never thought of him as scrawny when they were together, but he'd become a powerful-looking man. Lean, yet strong. Something she'd been admiring through squinted eyes.

Lola pulled the sheets over her head. "Uggggggghhhhh. It's too early." She tried not to think about his body, but it was damn near impossible. She was only human. There was, she rationalized, no harm in looking. She peeked back out of the sheets.

Gus took a drink of water. "Don't you have a kitchen to take over?"

"Oh god!" Lola sat up straight.

"Uh—" Gus traced a low neckline on his own chest, his face flushed.

Her tank top was very low cut, with oversized arm holes. She pulled the sheet up to her neck.

Gus looked out the window over the tiny sink. "Don't worry, I'm leaving."

"I'm not worried," Lola said, annoyed at the huskiness in her voice.

Gus turned back at the door and winked at her. "You should be."

And with that, he was gone.

Gus Weaver had kept her safe, and opened her up to a new kind of danger.

"Stop it. Stop it. Stop it," Lola muttered as she hurried to the vineyard from the Airstream with Daisy trotting happily beside her. Lola had a thousand things she needed to think about, and not one of them could make it through her swirling thoughts from this morning about Gus. He'd winked. He'd all but said he was interested in her. Or strongly suggested it. Right? "Stop it!"

She hated that she was flustered. That her emotions, always hard to rein in, were dragging her along unwillingly. During Carmen's courtship, she'd seen her sister infuriated, stomping around the vineyard like a charging rhino, cursing Evan while she spied on him. They'd very publicly waged a war that had led to infatuation. It had been fun to watch, but it wasn't the kind of thing anyone wished upon themselves. Lola found herself thinking of Hidalgo. His tender kiss. Their dinners and conversation and the way he calmed her, knowing just what to say when her emotions spiraled. A man like Hidalgo could give a girl a very happy life.

Daisy reached the spot where she normally turned around to head back and join Gus. She sat down, her tail beating, whipping up dust. The vineyard shone with early morning dew. The lake was glinting steel in the early morning mist, dotted by the same three fishing boats that appeared every morning. Crows fought over apples in the orchard. Normally Lola would stop and take in the serenity. Today she barely noticed her surroundings.

She stopped to secure her tennis shoe to the back of her heel, giving the happy dog a look. "Don't look so smug. Hidalgo is a nice guy, too."

At the word "Hidalgo," Daisy cocked her head, as if questioning Lola's judgment.

"Knock it off, Daisy. He is. He's kind and sweet and…" She put her hands over her face. "Oh god. I like both of them." She peered at her dog between her fingers. "Did you see Gus? I mean, come on." She glanced at her phone. "Gotta go. I've got an insurrection to lead." She scratched the dog behind the ears. "Wish me luck." She gave Daisy an extra pat. "And don't worry. It'll always be you and me. Dogs before dudes, right?" She crossed her fingers, kissed them, and patted the dog's head.

Lola had hoped to beat all the staff into the kitchen, but when she walked in, Ruelle and Mike were already there, placing stacks of clean glasses and silverware on trays for the wait staff. It was everyone's favorite time of the day. Quiet, clean, and calm. Mistakes had yet to be made. There wasn't a room full of hungry waiting customers next door.

Lola made coffee while Mike unpacked a linen delivery. A half hour later, Felicia rolled in, hung up her purse, donned a clean apron and helped herself to coffee. She stood by Lola at the stainless cooking station, pouring in the cream, stirring, and peering into the mixture with appreciation. It was general knowledge that Felicia wasn't to be spoken to until she'd finished her first cup of coffee. Anything before that was just asking for abuse.

Nonetheless, Lola whispered, "I fired Neil."

Felicia pursed her lips, nodding. "Mmmmm-hmmmm. And I spent the night with Zac Efron. We just had bagels."

"He came to the trailer last night."

Felicia's eyes went wide as she turned to face her friend. "What?"

"Yeah. It was bad, but Gus was there."

Felicia took a sip of her coffee. "This gets better and better."

"It wasn't anything like that."

"What was it like?"

Lola sighed. "He heard Neil talking about me in the bar and got worried."

Felicia shook her head. "Wow, so he's…" She looked at the clock on the kitchen wall. "Not here. Holy… God. What are you going to do?"

"Replace him." Lola stared at Felicia, until she blinked several times in recognition.

"Oh. Geez. Wow."

"What? You don't think I can do it?"

Felicia hurriedly drank three gulps of coffee to buy herself time. "Well, I mean, the restaurant, maybe. But Carmen's wedding! And Neil's menu is intense. As much as I hate to say this, he knew how to get it done."

"I'm scrapping Neil's menu."

Felicia's jaw hung open. "Oh. That's… a lot, to put it mildly."

Lola took a deep breath and let it out slowly, gripping her friend's shoulder, still whispering while the rest of the staff trickled in. "I cannot do this without you. I know that I'm the one that got myself into this, but I need your help."

Felicia shook her head. "No. You did not get yourself into this. This is all a result of Neil's behavior. And that's what you're going to tell Carmen."

"Uggghhh. Here's the thing…"

"Please don't say what I think you're going to say."

"I'm not telling Carmen."

Felicia looked up at the ceiling fan. "And there it is."

The assembled kitchen and dining room staff, including Luke, sat in the restaurant at a few round tabletops by the window. Pale, buttery sunlight streamed in from the French windows facing the stone flag patio. Butterflies flitted gracefully on their namesake tree, covered in clusters of purple blooms, planted because the flowers had reminded Mami of grape clusters. Lola could see a few deer grazing in the shady orchard before the midday sun beat down. It was nerve-wracking, facing the staff, but they seemed patient and eager to see what this meeting was about. There was a sense of anticipation.

Normally, Carmen talked to the staff once a month, updating them on any new employee benefit information and business changes. The Alvarez family treated them not just as restaurant employees, but as part of the whole vineyard enterprise. They had wine tastings, seasonal parties and, whenever she could, Carmen brought in experts to educate all of them in the business and art of food and wine. Lola wondered if they thought she was just pinch-hitting for her sister, but there was a low buzz of rumor that suggested otherwise.

Lola clasped her hands, looking at Felicia, who nodded encouragingly. "Okay. I fired Neil."

There was murmur around the room, which turned to speculation. Connie started clapping and Zoey joined her.

"About time," Connie said.

Rodolfo raised his hand before speaking. "He's not coming back? At all?"

Lola shook her head, exhaling, before allowing herself a small grin. "No. And if he does, let me know right away."

Zoey nodded. "Uh, who is cooking? I mean, I know you and Felicia are, but who is going to take Neil's job?" She raised her eyebrows expectantly.

Lola took a very deep breath. In a few hours, hungry people would come in expecting lunch. A great lunch. "I am." The room went deathly still.

"For the restaurant?" asked Connie, who was a long-time employee—and, Lola realized at that moment, friends with Carmen. Oh, golly.

"And my sister's wedding. But for now, I don't want to tell Carmen." Lola waited for reactions. Some people raised their eyebrows, or smiled, incredulous.

Zoey laughed. "Dang, girl. You're putting your big girl pants on today."

Lola studied the group to see if she was losing people. This was critical. She needed to start out confident. Prove that she could lead. "Obviously, I'll tell her later, but this isn't the kind of thing anyone wants to hear right before their wedding. And I'm asking you to go along with it. Trust me, I didn't plan this, but Neil left because he had to leave."

Connie seemed to be thinking it over. "You mean, we pretend like Neil's here?"

"I don't know. I haven't gotten that far. I fired him last night," Lola said.

"After he left the bar?" Luke asked.

Lola nodded.

Luke frowned, putting it all together. "Okay, I saw him last night. When he left here, he was in quite a state." He shook his head. "We have to get behind Lola." He lifted his coffee cup. "Lola, whatever you need. Count me in. I'm sorry, I should have escorted him off the property last night."

Lola nodded her head in acknowledgment. "Thanks, Luke. It worked out. He's gone."

After exchanging some quick words, the rest of the staff nodded in agreement.

"Sí, está bien."

"We can do this."

"Okay, Lola. You got it."

Felicia stood beside her friend, wrapping a protective arm around her as Lola's eyes misted. She quickly gained control.

"Can we fake it for a week?" Lola asked.

Connie patted her arm. "Sweetheart, I've been faking it most of my life."

Lola snorted. "Thank you."

"Well, darling, thank you for taking out the trash," Connie said.

Lunch flew by with some surprising hiccups. Turned out, Neil did actual work. Lola assumed his position at the large range and monitored the kitchen, troubleshooting when the ice maker broke or the sour cream needed for the sauces tasted off. Lola realized that much of Neil's job, besides cooking, was checking on staff, making sure everyone was able to do their job, keeping the entire enterprise running. It was like an orchestra. While meat seared on the range, Lola darted to her own station to help Felicia, who was also struggling with the new load of work. The same amount of food had to go out the door, with fewer people to cook it. Neil had taken care of the minutiae that allowed everyone else to do their jobs. It was shocking, really, that a man who spent so much energy harassing other people could get so much work done.

Lola didn't like admitting it, but by the end of lunch, she turned to Felicia. "I didn't realize how much he did."

"Right? It's kind of horrible to admit it."

"Yeah, and I fired him. How are we going to keep this going?" Lola looked at the devastation of the stainless cooking station and the range. Normally everyone kept their station spotless by cleaning as they went. There was an endless supply of cloths to wipe up spills, sweep debris into buckets and lift hot pans. Today, they hadn't had time to do anything but cook food as fast as they possibly could.

"I can't believe we have to do dinner," Felicia moaned, sitting on a stool they used to reach the back shelves in the reefer.

"Do you think I made a mistake?" Lola whispered.

Felicia waved her hands and pulled herself up with the edge of the counter. "The only mistake both of us made was not doing something about him sooner."

Lola nodded, thinking that the best way to solve problems wasn't to reinvent the wheel. Burgers. Lamb burgers were one of the most popular menu items, and the easiest. That was it. She ripped off the piece of paper, waving it in the air. "I've got it. We're going to simplify the menu."

Somehow, they made it through dinner, collapsing onto each other when the last entrée had been sent out the door. Felicia said she'd clean up their workstations so Lola could run up and feed Daisy before bringing her down to join her for a long night of menu revision. Just as Lola was opening the door, Carmen stepped into the kitchen from the patio. The sisters nearly collided.

"Hey!" Lola said.

"Hey yourself," said Carmen, peering around the kitchen. "Where's Neil?"

Mike dropped a large pot, splashing water over himself. "Neil is gone," he fairly yelled in a flat, agitated manner.

Carmen frowned. "Gone where?"

Lola glared at Mike, whose eyes went big. Who knew he was such a terrible liar? "He's at his house."

Carmen nodded. "Okay. I wanted to talk to him about some of the appetizers for the wedding."

"He's agreed to do some of mine," Lola said.

Carmen looked up from some salad garnishes—pickled vegetables—that she was picking her way through. "He did? Really? Hmm. Like what?"

"Goat's cheese in endive. Empanadas. Mini shrimp tacos."

Carmen raised one eyebrow, a gesture that Lola had always envied. "That's generous of him."

Lola, who'd been expecting a fight, cocked her head. "Wait… You mean, you don't object? You trust me with the menu?"

"Don't get ahead of yourself, Lola. Appetizers."

Shockingly, it worked. Lola streamlined the entire restaurant menu to something less pretentious, more beach-inspired. Fish tacos with homemade tortillas and lime crema. Ceviche on a mini fried tortilla. A hot dog basket—a real risk. A wine bar with a hot dog basket was a reach. Even the waitresses said so, but Lola asked them to try it, and from the second it appeared on the menu, it was surprisingly popular. It was a Niman Ranch hot dog. Or, as Zoey said, "A hot dog that went to college." It had real flavor. They complemented it with homemade ketchup—something that sounded impressive but was easy—and found fancier baskets at Walmart than the red plastic ones used all along the lake at burger places. Theirs were more reminiscent of bread baskets, and came with a mini crudité-filled ramekin and ranch dressing, something Felicia thought would make the parents happy. The lowliest menu item received the most thought. The staff were consulted. There were taste testings and arguments. Lola knew that if she was going to keep this fragile enterprise afloat, it would take everyone buying in. Mike had contributed the recipe to his grandmother's sweet and spicy relish. It was a hit.

The menu change wasn't without bumps. Regular customers asked for their favorite dishes and were disappointed. Happy hour regulars moaned about their missing scallops and risotto patties, both time-consuming dishes. When customers complained, Lola was brought out front. She listened and offered them samples of new appetizers on the house. They started by tweeting about hot dog happy hour. Families, returning from the beach with young children in tow, were drawn by the chance to have a glass of wine sitting in front of a serene lake view, while their children stuffed themselves with pricey hot dogs (it was vacation, right?) and then wandered in the orchard afterward. When Carmen asked if Neil approved the changes, Lola glanced at Felicia. "He didn't say anything but for every hot dog we sell, the adults order at least two glasses of wine per table," Lola said, knowing what would placate her sister. Carmen, distracted by a call from Evan, nodded and left. A friend of Neil's turned up to see him after a hiking trip. When he was told that his friend had suddenly left, he nodded, seemingly not at all surprised. Lola got the sense that this wasn't the first time this had happened. She bought Neil's friend a beer, telling him that she wished his friend well, but he wouldn't be working for her again.

Saying the words made her feel better.

*

"Please don't say you're leaving me. I can't deal with it if you start your own catering business."

Carmen was reacting to Lola reading her a supposedly fictional menu—one that, in theory, if Lola was going to cater a wedding herself, she'd serve. Tamales in three varieties, tiny crispy fish and pork tacos, a salad with avocado, and jicama with lime, cilantro and honey.

"It sounds like something Mami would make," Carmen added. The sisters sighed, looking around the kitchen that still, even in its industrial iteration, seemed to be missing something without Mami. This had been her home kitchen long before Blue Hills had opened a restaurant.

"I'm not leaving you," Lola promised.

Carmen clasped her hand over her heart. "Thank god."

"I can cater a wedding, though."

Carmen ignored the last comment. "Where's Neil? I should have talked to the rental people by now about seating arrangements, and the florist. Wait, should I have called the florist?" She looked down at her clipboard. "Okay, no. Neil's handling it. He's told me nothing and vanished."

Rodolfo came in from the patio, patting her back. "He was right here."

Carmen's face brightened. "Where?"

"Oh, but then he left. Poof," Rodolfo said.

"This isn't normal," Carmen fretted. "He's not answering his phone."

Rodolfo clucked his tongue. "Not to worry." He took a sheet of paper from his back pocket. "You see this? It's a list of all the things. We all have one. He gave us the instructions, and now we follow them. You see? Nothing to worry about. Now come outside and try the fig and blue cheese pizza. It sings." He ushered her outside, leaving his list on the counter. "Really, it sings. The cheese pops and it sounds a little bit like a song. A little."

They went outside. Lola looked at the piece of paper.

It was a checklist from Rodolfo's service station of repairs done to his car.

Lola clutched the edge of the counter. She had to call a florist? And a rental company? What were they renting? Lola swallowed the lump of fear rising in her throat. She could cook. She knew she could cook enough food. And maybe even get it out to the tables on time. But planning an entire wedding? A wave of fear was poised to crash down on her head. She needed help. It was time to call in the cavalry.

The question was, who were they?

CHAPTER EIGHTEEN

More Than a Prayer Group

"The dog can come too," Hidalgo said at the hopeful little dog who was wagging her tail at Hidalgo's truck. He had pulled up just as Lola had been crossing the pebbled driveway to head up the hill to change and come back to the restaurant. They hadn't seen each other in a while, and she'd felt happy when she'd seen his truck.

"Hidalgo, I'd love a little surprise, but I can't do anything until after the wedding. It's nuts."

Daisy glanced between the two of them as if this were a tennis match.

Hidalgo marched to the passenger door and held it open. "I know. Get in." Without waiting for Lola, Daisy hopped in. Hidalgo laughed. "You see? She trusts me. Trust me."

"Papi always says to watch out for men who say 'trust me.'"

Hidalgo's smile was warm. "Papi is a smart man, but he also introduced us."

Lola wavered. Hidalgo wasn't the kind of guy to whisk her away on some kind of romantic adventure in the middle of a work crisis. He understood work stress. They came from the same kind of background. Nobody understood the importance of work like someone from an immigrant family. It was what kept their families together. She decided to trust him.

Lola had to push Daisy into the center of the truck to find space for herself.

"She certainly makes herself at home."

"She loves trucks," Lola said. "When Papi goes to the Apple Cup Café, he sometimes takes her just because she loves going in the truck."

It was nice to get away, Lola thought, even though her mind was spinning through the list of catering duties, wondering what she'd missed. She assumed they'd have a quick drink somewhere, sure that Hidalgo was trying to help her have a moment away from the restaurant. So she was surprised when he took a right after the Safeway. He pulled into St. Francis de Sales Catholic church, found a parking spot and turned off the engine. They sat in front of the low beige concrete block building. The heat rose in shimmering waves from the blacktop parking lot.

"I don't think I've reached the praying phase yet," Lola said, quietly.

Hidalgo lifted his finger. "Wait."

She followed him out of the car and into the dim community kitchen where her mother's prayer group was cooking, as they did every week. The group of women, friends since they'd moved to the valley, had helped each other through discrimination, bad marriages, raising children and death. They were the first ones at the door with food when there was bad news and the first ones to raise a glass to good news. They'd raised dozens of children together and buried a few of their members, including Mami. Now they served the valley by cooking for the elderly and sick, providing a week's worth of frozen entrées delivered by a van owned by the church.

Hidalgo took Lola by the hand and introduced her in Spanish to a pretty woman with short gray hair and bright pink lipstick—his mother. Hidalgo's mother gripped Lola's hands with warm, firm assertiveness, beaming at her son, clearly happy that he'd found someone like Lola.

"I am so lucky, getting to come here and join my sister's church group." She beamed at Lola. "My group"—she clutched her chest emotionally—"we all got so old, there wasn't enough people. Now this is my group! I come once a week and spend the night with my sister." Hidalgo's mother spoke in Spanish, clearly enamored of her son and this group.

Lola was introduced to Aunt Flores next, who spoke little English and was as shy as her sister was outgoing, nodding and saying "Sí, sí, sí," while gazing at Hidalgo.

Although the two women were charming, Lola felt a growing uneasiness at meeting a parent this early in a relationship. Too early, although clearly, she'd been right about Hidalgo's family. They were warm, friendly, and tight knit.

With the introductions out of the way, Lola said a quick hello to her mother's friends and, as soon as possible, joined Hidalgo. "Okay, this was really nice, but I do have to go."

"They want to help," Hidalgo said.

"Help what?" Lola asked impatiently. She was itching to get back to work. She had to go through Neil's lists, figure out who he'd tapped for rentals, flowers, and supplies—and hope he hadn't sabotaged them by canceling.

"The other day you said you were short-handed. That the whole banquet was overwhelming you. So, when you said you wanted to do a Mexican-inspired wedding menu, I thought of these ladies." Hidalgo waved his hand around the room. "They love your family and they're amazing cooks. And they can churn out the food."

Lola felt a wave of emotion as she glanced around the room. Love and compassion beamed from the warm brown eyes of these small, seemingly inconspicuous women. They weren't people typically recognized for their quiet heroism, but they were, Lola thought with growing emotion, a river of strength that lifted their community, carried them along. These were the women who had fed the Alvarez sisters after Mami died. Who'd quietly cleaned the house and done the laundry, who'd dropped off casserole and soups and groceries until Papi had been well enough to return to the world. They'd slipped Lola money for her birthday so she could host a pizza party in town and left a cake at the restaurant that was brought out with candles and tears because everyone knew her mother and this was the first birthday after her death. They'd quietly made sure that the Alvarez family had more invitations than they could handle that first Christmas. They'd helped life go on.

Tears streamed down Lola's face. She wiped them away with her hand before Hidalgo offered her a handkerchief. "Really?"

All the women nodded in unison.

"Por supuesto!"

"Of course!"

"Será divertido!"

"It will be fun!"

Lola took Hidalgo's hand and let the warmth wash over her. Standing on her toes, she whispered into his ear. "Thank you. Thank you so much."

He put his arm around her while his mother and aunt beamed. For that moment, Lola allowed herself to feel happy.

Late in the afternoon, on an impulse, Lola grabbed her bathing suit off the chair outside where it had been left to dry. She should have gone back down to the restaurant, but a quick swim would clean more than the day's cooking grit; it would clear her brain. That was the plan.

But was the plan something to do with the fact that Gus had taken off his shirt and was working on the porch of the last cabin, installing the railing? Did her desire to be floating free and untethered, temporarily, from her worries, come from that moment when she'd crested the trail leading up through the vineyard and her breath had caught at the sight of him? She'd had to mutter "Stop it," to herself, which had become a habit. Stop what? Sometimes, she woke up in the middle of the night and imagined Gus opening the door to the trailer.

No. No. No.

She headed down to the lake, crossing the meadow in her flip-flops and an old guayabera shirt of her father's, sun-bleached to a snowy white, sleeves rolled. It smelled faintly of her father's aftershave. Bay leaves and lemon. Comforting.

Gus straightened, wiping the sweat off his brow. Lola wanted to stop and tell him that the railings, inlaid with salt-colored driftwood, were a nice touch. More than a nice touch. Artistry. But she didn't trust her voice or her face not to belie her. What kind of person was she? Meeting Hidalgo's family one day—in a church, no less—and lusting after her old boyfriend the next. Did Hidalgo know by now about her relationship with Gus? He might be removed enough by his work from small-town gossip, but his mother and his aunt weren't. Gus was living above Twig, for god's sake. Izzy was Gus's friend. Gus literally lived above gossip central for the entire valley. He might as well have hired a plane to drag a banner across the beach: "Single. Back in town."

"I'll be right there. Chill," Lola called to the shivering dog. Daisy had paddled happily around her once, chin jutting bravely from the water, before returning to shore, shaking, to sit nervously on her rock until Lola was safely ashore. It was all show, Lola knew. The shivering always stopped as soon as Lola approached the shore.

But the water was that perfect shade of cerulean blue, reflecting the cloudless sky. It was a reminder of all the happy times spent down here with a bag of sandwiches and a friend, the day open like a fresh piece of paper, waiting to be filled. The quiet was a drug she hadn't even known she craved until she'd noticed that the only sounds were birds and the gentle lapping of waves against the rocks. By some miracle, all the jet skis had gone to buzz frenetically on other parts of the lake. Lola was left blissfully alone in the peace of the yawning blue, floating on her stomach with her eyes open, gazing into the blue-green at the boulders dotting the white sandy bottom which she'd long since committed to memory.

It used to drive her mother crazy, the way Lola could hold her breath, floating face down, legs and arms splayed like a starfish. Mami used to think that she did it to scare her, but she did it to immerse herself completely into the liquid world. Lola took a breath now and resumed her peaceful float. There was a splash, and she waited for Daisy to swim up beside her, grown impatient, coming to hurry her along.

A few seconds later, missing the sound of paddling paws, she lifted her head to see Gus's face. His beard, dripping with water below blinking blue eyes. She lifted her hand. "Hey. Nice, isn't it?"

Gus wasn't smiling. He didn't even look particularly happy to be in the cool water, despite having labored most of the day in the hot sun. Shirtless.

He trod water, taking a deep breath before he spoke. "I thought I could come back here, and things would have changed, but they haven't." He seemed to be choosing his words carefully. "I think maybe that's why I came back. To prove something to myself. Because even though I've changed in so many ways, my feelings for you are the same. I knew it the moment I saw you. I'm just going to be honest. I love you. And I know I should stop, but I can't. I don't want to. Loving you is the best thing that's ever happened to me, and it will always be part of who I am." Gus stared up the hill to where the dirt roads led to the cabins. "And maybe this is me trying to get you out of my system, but I had to tell you, Lola. I had to."

Lola stared at him, willing herself to say something, but he turned and swam to the shore before she could pluck something from the thoughts racing through her brain. She floated there, watching Gus pull himself from the water, wrap himself with a towel, pat Daisy's wet head and cross the street to the orchard without looking back. Lola was stunned. Here was the speech she'd wanted so badly ten years before that her body had ached for it. Everything she'd wanted. Gus had come back. Wanted her. Loved her. Right when she'd met another man. A good one.

The lake didn't feel comforting at all.

Even knowing that Mami's prayer group would be cooking for the wedding, running a restaurant and a catering business was no joke. Lola found herself waking up at night remembering something, leaping from her bed, and writing down a menu item she'd forgotten to source, or a final head count, or to replace a waiter who was trying to weasel out of the gig. She'd told the wait staff to wear white pants and black shirts, then realized that was a mistake and reversed it. She needed more aprons. More water jugs. Daisy would groan and shift on the bed, giving her the stink eye as the light went off. Sometimes Lola would have trouble going back to sleep, which is why, that lunchtime, she found herself staring at a pan of lamb burgers when Felicia pushed her aside to get to the deep fryer. The alarm had gone off, and they'd nearly lost four servings of sweet potato crispy puffs thanks to Lola's spaciness.

Felicia was dumping the crisp orange barrels into a nest of paper towels, giving them a generous shake of garlic rosemary salt, when yelling erupted in the dining room. The two women exchanged glances.

"Is that…?" Felicia asked, before Zoey pushed into the kitchen, waving her free hand at Lola.

"You'd better get out there. It's your dad."

Lola frowned. "My dad?"

Sure enough, she could hear Papi bellowing in the combination of Spanish and English that he only employed when furious. The last time Lola could remember her father yelling like this was when a warehouse worker had hit a stack of wine barrels with a forklift and destroyed thousands of dollars-worth of wine. Which was why she now left the expensive burgers on the burner with nothing more than a vague nod at Felicia before running into the dining room, passing a worried-looking Zoey.

It took Lola's eyes a minute to adjust to the darker dining room, which used mostly natural light streaming in from the open patio doors and windows. It was a pretty room with bright walls, a lovely old turn-of-the-century bar and round tablecloth-topped tables with flowers. But the scene in front of Lola didn't match the casual elegance of the restaurant. Papi was facing Gus, who'd shaved his beard and was nodding at the old man, clearly trying to explain himself, his hands lifted in supplication. Lola's heart ached for him in the split second she used to catch her breath.

"Get out!" Papi was yelling.

The restaurant staff were racing from table to table, soothing the customers, while shooting pointed "do something" glances at Lola. Lola couldn't move for a moment, shaken at seeing Gus's clean-shaven face, the same face that she'd caressed a thousand times. She hesitated just long enough to need a push from Luke the bartender, who muttered something about her taking action before he did. It was all she needed to rush to her father and pull him away, still angry and muttering in Spanish.

"Outside, Papi. Please," Lola insisted. "The customers."

The concept of paying customers seem to wake up the old man, who allowed his daughter to pull him outside. Gus followed. Lola wasn't sure what Gus was up to, but she was flustered by the dramatic change in his appearance. Once outside, Gus stepped to the far side of the hard-packed dirt driveway, near the trio of apple trees that Lola had always thought of as her friends when she was a child. The fragrance of the ripening apples filled the night air, calming Lola.

Gus took a deep breath, turning to Lola. "I'm sorry—"

Papi burst forth. "You don't talk to her."

Lola grabbed her father, muttering to him under her breath. "Papi, you can't cause another scene. There are people on the patio of the restaurant."

Lola wasn't sure they could hear, but if there was one thing she could count on, it was her father's desire to be a good host.

"I told him to get off my property," Papi said, more quietly.

"I was trying to apologize," Gus interjected.

"We don't need your apology," the old man spat.

"Papi," Lola pleaded. "Maybe you don't. But I do."

Her father was taken aback. He frowned. "What do you mean?" he asked in Spanish.

Lola glanced at Gus, who seemed to be holding his breath. The confession in the water, combined with his newly revealed face, gave her a feeling in her gut that she had to ignore. There were too many things that needed dealing with before she could process what, exactly, Gus Weaver meant to her. But she could do this.

She closed her eyes for a moment and took a breath. "Papi, I know that it was a lot, having a teenage daughter with a boyfriend who went to jail. You had to pick up the pieces and it wasn't easy. But we can't keep judging him for the way he was when he was seventeen. Would you want the world judging you for the way you were at that age?"

Papi snorted. "At seventeen, I was working to build a life for myself."

Fair enough, Lola thought. "Papi, Gus has served his time. He came back here to apologize. You have always told me that people deserve a second chance."

"Not for everything," the old man grumbled.

Lola took his hand. "I'm a grown woman, Papi. I can take care of myself."

To her surprise, her father wiped his eye. "I know."

Carmen came out of the restaurant. "Hey, the florist called and said…" She reached them and did a double take, looking closely at Gus. "Hey, what are you doing here?"

Lola saw it before her eyes, like a car crash happening in slow motion. She opened her mouth to try to stop it, but it was too late.

Gus was clearly happy to change the subject. He brightened. "I'm working on the cabins."

Carmen shot a look at Lola. "What cabins?"

Gus waved towards the corner of the house where the vineyard covered the hill, dark and glossy in the dusk. "At the top of the vineyard. You should have a look. They're almost done."

Carmen gritted her teeth, glaring at Lola. "Oh, I'll have a look. I'll have a look right now."

And she was off, running up the hill, her legs pumping with fury, Lola chasing after her, leaving a confused Gus staring after them both with a sick feeling in his gut.

Carmen stalked around the cabins, throwing her arms up into the air. "I don't even know where to begin. How did you get the money?"

Lola, breathless from running after her sister, put her hands on her knees to catch her breath. Daisy was barking from inside the trailer. "I had investors."

"You took money for cabins that weren't even built?" Carmen crossed her arms, watching Lola climb the stairs to her Airstream and let the dog out. Daisy ran straight to a bush near Carmen, squatted, and let out a long stream while gazing at her. The symbolism did not seem to be lost on Carmen.

"People asked me about it. On the blog," Lola said.

"Oh, the blog," Carmen sneered.

"There it is. The patently superior attitude whenever something that's my idea comes up. It's like you have to hate it because it's my idea."

"We're not a hospitality business," Carmen said in an overly loud voice.

"We're a restaurant. That is hospitality. And that was your idea. If it doesn't come from you, then it's not Blue Hills. Well, the reason I did this was that you gave me no choice."

"Ha! That's priceless. I gave you no choice but to go behind my back and lie to people…"

Lola waved at the cabins. "They're done, more or less. It's not a lie. The whole point was to have them done in time for your wedding. I thought we could get ready up here. You could walk down from the orchard in your dress."

"In the dirt?"

"People could stay here. Car, just look inside one. Gus did such a good job. They're really pretty inside."

"You invited your ex-con boyfriend to work here. This just keeps getting better and better."

"I didn't hire him. Hidalgo did."

"So, Hidalgo is on this?"

"He didn't know about my history with Gus. He still doesn't."

Carmen shook her head. "Lola, who haven't you lied to? How did you hire Hidalgo? Forge my name?"

This was the worst part. Lola covered her eyes. "You signed it. I put it with some invoices and you didn't look at what you were signing."

Carmen stood stock-still, hissing, "You little traitor!"

"You can't even insult me without calling me little."

Carmen's eyes blazed. "Lola, how can you blame me? I'm the one who should have known better. You've always been the spoiled one, and this time, when you didn't get your way, you went behind my back."

"I had to!"

"No, you didn't. There is a way to run a business, and this isn't it." Carmen waved her hands around the clearing. The little cabins glowed in the last streaks of sun crowning the hills. "This is what you like. This is your thing."

"What is so wrong about me"—Lola touched her chest—"making my mark on the vineyard? Your handprint is everywhere." She gestured across the vineyard. "What is wrong with bringing my personality, my strengths?"

"Nothing," Carmen said. "It's the lying, Lola. And if you can't understand that, then I have nothing to say to you."

Lola looked back at the cabins and felt a pride welling inside of her as Carmen headed for the vineyard trail. "I'd do it again, you know."

Carmen stopped, and without turning around, said, "If you were an employee, I'd fire you."

Something split inside of Lola. She was tired of fighting. There had to be an easier way. "Then I quit." Her voice was flat and broken. Although she hadn't planned this, it had been a long time coming, and as soon as she said the words, she realized she meant them completely.

Carmen stayed frozen for such a long time, Lola wondered if she was going to turn around. She hated herself for wanting her sister's approval so badly. Hated her own heart for the desire to be seen, acknowledged. To have a place at the grown-ups' table.

But Carmen started walking, slipping into the vineyard, disappearing quickly from sight, leaving Lola alone in the dark.

Lola was inside her trailer packing her things, determined that she wouldn't spend one more night on the winery. She'd had it with being Carmen's flunky. She wasn't exactly sure what was going into her open duffel, but she didn't care. She called Stella, trying for the fourth time to get a hold of her, but got the same voicemail message. Daisy whined at the door. Lola went to let her out and heard noises outside.

She stepped out of the trailer to see Gus, hauling equipment as fast as he could carry it, tossing it into the back of his truck. She marched over, wondering why he was packing in such a hurry. Surely he would say goodbye, or walk her through, or something? She came up behind him as he shoved a folded table onto the truck bed.

"Where are you going, Gus? They're not done."

"Get out of my way, Lola."

"You know, if they weren't my idea, Carmen would have loved the cabins," Lola said. Gus stalked past her, eyes glimmering in the dark, straight to a tool kit, which he lifted with ease, passing by her again. He really did look devastating without his beard, but now, Lola thought, was hardly the time to be having these thoughts. He tossed the tool kit onto the truck bed, causing it to shake with the weight. He dusted off his hands.

"She actually called me a little traitor. Can you believe it?"

Gus's eyes narrowed as he faced her. "Yes. Actually, I can. I needed this job, Lola. I came back here for a fresh start, and you used me."

"How did I use you?" Lola cried out, astonished.

"To get back at your sister and your father. Who else would be the perfect person to stick it to your family?"

Lola's mouth hung open. "Hidalgo hired you, not me!"

Gus shook his head, his mouth pinched. "You could have told me what was going on at any time. You could have been honest. That is the least of what you could have done."

She bit her lip. How could this be going sideways so fast? "I didn't think it would affect you."

"Oh, right. I'm working on a job that nobody approved, and nobody knows about, for a family who despises me. How could that possibly go wrong?" He pointed down the hill. "I *was* looking for your father's approval. I told you how I felt. And I thought I was the one with issues. Jesus, Lola. I don't need to be around people who use me."

"I didn't use you."

He took a step closer to her. Close enough to smell the pine sawdust mixed with the clean cotton of his T-shirt. "You're twenty-seven years old, Lola. You've had everything handed to you. It's time to grow up." He turned and marched to his truck, opened the door, and then stopped before climbing in. "I used to think I wasn't good enough for this family. But maybe it's the other way around."

CHAPTER NINETEEN

Babies

It was late, past ten thirty, when Lola knocked on Stella's door. Lola studied the piece of driftwood painted with the house name, wishing she had a life as settled as Stella's. That view shifted when Stella opened the door, haggard and wild-haired. Babies wailed in unison in the background.

"Come on in."

Lola saw Stella questioning the bag she carried with her. "Didn't you get my message?"

Stella rolled her eyes. "I have twins, Lola. I don't have time to brush my teeth."

"Carmen and I are officially on the warpath."

"So what's new?"

"You know the tiny cabins I was obsessed with? I built them. Without her knowing."

Stella's mouth went wide. She pretended to lift her jaw with her hand. "That's bold."

"They're really cool, and she hates them."

Stella took a deep breath. "Carmen likes things streamlined."

"Carmen likes to be in control."

Stella nodded, not wanting to step into the middle of a battle nobody was going to win. "I think the timing could have been better. With the wedding."

"I know. I shouldn't have done it now. But when Hidalgo said he was a builder and we started talking about it, I just couldn't stop myself. I felt like if I could just build them, it would change things. I could have my own piece of Blue Hills."

"I understand. I do. Carmen can be very tough. And she's a terrible listener. I can see now that this has been a long time coming. She was used to thinking of you as the irresponsible kid. That doesn't make for good business partners."

"I don't want to wreck her wedding."

Stella raised a finger. "I'll talk to her. If I live through this night."

Lola went into the living room, picking up one of the crying babies. "Where's Paolo?"

"He's still at work. They had an issue with yeast overgrowth in one of the wines. He was trying to tell if it was salvageable." Stella's eyes were blurry with fatigue. "Before you fall in love, ask if twins run in the family."

Lola propped the baby she was holding up on the couch and reached for the one Stella was holding. "Come on…"

"Carlo." Stella handed the baby over. "Or Rosie. No, Carlo."

"I know a sure-fire way to tell, but I don't think it matters at this point." Lola pointed down the hall. "Get some sleep. I'll stay in their room. Do they take formula?"

Stella nodded. "It's in the fridge. Thirty seconds on the stove in hot water."

Lola pushed her down the hallway.

"Do you know anything about babies?"

"No, but Daisy does," Lola said, as her dog jumped up onto the couch, much to the delight of Rosie. Or Carlo.

Paolo came home to the sight of Lola with a baby in a basket on either side and a dog sprawled across her lap. One hand resting on Carlo's basket. Lola woke up as Paolo lifted Carlo, or Rosie, from their basket. She hoped they'd start to look distinct to her soon.

"Hey," Paolo said, leaning down to give Lola a kiss on the cheek. "Nice to see you."

Lola rubbed her eyes, waiting for Paolo to return from the nursery. "I didn't really talk to Stella about it, but can I stay here for a couple days?"

Paolo nodded and went off again to find her a set of sheets. Lola said she'd sleep in the guest room with the babies. "I can get up with them so you guys can sleep."

Paolo's hand went to his heart. "Really? I know I should say no, but my god. They are on the backward schedule."

Lola nodded. "It's fine."

Paolo didn't waste any time. He pointed to the hallway. "I will go sleep now." He put his hands together in thanks, backing down the hallway, bowing.

Lola looked at Daisy. "We're in for it, Dais."

Before she went to bed, Lola checked her phone. There was a text from Hidalgo. *Can you meet me at the building site tomorrow?*

The other shoe had dropped.

*

It felt like an ambush. Lola climbed out of her car and spotted Carmen coming out of one of the cabins with Hidalgo. Her first thought was that the fact that Hidalgo hadn't mentioned speaking with her sister felt like a betrayal. Her second thought was that she wasn't being fair. She had hired Hidalgo under false circumstances, and he had done a terrific job. Lola steeled herself and approached her sister, who seemed to be doing everything she could not to look at her, and Hidalgo, whose face was hard to read. One thing was certain, right now he wasn't the easygoing man she'd come to enjoy hanging out with.

"Lola!" Hidalgo said, with a heartiness that felt forced. Like he was making the best of a bad situation. Or trying to. "Carmen and I have been talking, and given the—ahem—new developments, we're doing the finishing touches without Gus."

Lola should have been expecting this, but her heart fell. She didn't want to live here anymore without seeing Gus. It struck her that Gus wouldn't want to see her ever again, and she felt like crying. Instead, she forced herself to listen.

"Gus has already done most of the work he was hired to do anyway, and the cabins are basically finished. I'm pulling a couple guys off another job for a day or two." Hidalgo looked at Carmen to make sure he'd ticked all the boxes, but she was frowning, looking off in the distance. "Did I cover everything, Carmen?"

Carmen cleared her throat. "Yes. I'm sorry you had to get involved in this. Dragged into what should have been a family matter."

Hidalgo's face was professional, cool. "I wasn't dragged, and I think the cabins came out great. Thanks to Gus."

Carmen rolled her eyes. "Oh yes, thank to Gus. He's done so much for this family. Left you a complete wreck—"

"Carmen, don't," Lola said.

"If you can keep actual buildings"—she waved her hands at the cabins—"a secret from me, why can't I spill a few of yours? I mean, of all the people you could hire, Gus Weaver?"

"I didn't hire him," Lola said, looking at Hidalgo.

"But you didn't fire him either, did you?" Carmen spat, before storming down the hill.

Hidalgo studied Lola's face. "Carmen made me fire him from the cabins job. He offered to quit my business entirely, but I put him on another job."

Lola nodded.

"Do you want to tell me something about Gus? Something that I don't already know?" Hidalgo crossed his arms.

"I should have told you about our history. It was a long time ago."

"That's not what I'm asking, Lola. I don't care about the past."

Lola nodded. "Nothing happened, Hidalgo."

He nodded. "I believe you. Let's just finish this, okay?"

Although she followed him across the dry grass, he didn't kiss her. Just climbed into his truck, lifting his hand in goodbye. Daisy came over to his truck, and Hidalgo got down again to give her a pat on the head that looked like a farewell. Lola watched his truck disappear down the hill, feeling like she was sinking into the earth. Leaving people behind. Carmen. Gus. Hidalgo. The only thing that would keep her going now was what was waiting for her at the bottom of the hill. A kitchen full of people who would help her cook her way back.

The question was, back to what?

*

Gus stared at the shot and beer in front of him. He'd always wanted to try a boilermaker when he was younger. Had seen it in movies and thought it was cool. Drop the shot in the beer and chug it down. All his drinking had been done underage, so he'd never been able to order one before. Now, here he was. Living the dream. A vast menu of drinks before him, waiting to be drunk. He looked at the tattoo on his arm, trying to imagine the taste of the whiskey and beer mixing. He couldn't remember the last time he'd gotten drunk. It was one of the things he and Jeremy had talked about. How Gus had used alcohol to smother his feelings. When the rage about his past, his childhood, had threatened his everyday life, he'd drink. Not in a bar, but at home, methodically, without enjoyment, with the sole purpose of blunting his feelings. It was one of the many things that had been pointed out to him that had rung true.

The fact that he could even think about blunting his emotions meant that he'd learned something. He thought of all the work he'd done in that gray, featureless office with Jeremy. Digging into his past. Talking about the small boy he'd been, waking up on Christmas morning and hoping for something more than a few secondhand toys. Looking at the food other children threw away from their lunches and hoping he could get a hall pass to come back and dig through the garbage before the janitor emptied it. Jeremy had made him go back and love that kid. His grit. His determination to feed himself and survive.

Lola had lied to him from the start, deliberately withholding the truth about this project. Not trusting him enough to be open.

Lola would never see him as anything more than the trashy kid from the kind of family people only tolerated because they were a hornet's nest. The kind of family where social services would show up, knock once, and go away. Teachers would expect every Weaver to do their time and land on welfare, or drift through one low-level job to another. Hidalgo would never really trust him. Juan Alvarez would never welcome him. He hadn't even finished what he'd come here to do. He hadn't talked to his brother, whom he'd left to live alone with an abusive, alcoholic father after their mother died. That was what hurt the most. More, surprisingly, than Lola. Because she'd failed him, not the other way around. Or maybe she'd just shown her true self. Here, he'd always be the boy who'd left in the back of a corrections van and had never come back to the brother who needed him. He'd had to leave Chelan to become someone else.

He was tracing random shapes on the condensation on the side of the beer glass when someone sat beside him. Of course. Because the bar was almost empty.

He was about to move, when the person beside him said, "Where does a waitress with only one leg work?" Of course it was Izzy. She had spies everywhere. He didn't even look over at her as she gave the punchline: "IHOP."

"That's a terrible joke," he said, wishing he'd started drinking before she got here.

She ordered a Diet Coke and then said, "I only know terrible ones."

"Aren't alcoholics supposed to avoid bars?" Gus asked.

"Yes, at first. But it doesn't bother me."

"That's good."

"Yes, it is good, because people spend an awful lot of time in bars. Sometimes I'm going in to drag out one of the people I'm sponsoring."

"Does it work?"

"Sometimes."

"And what do you tell them to get them to stop drinking?"

Izzy nodded. "I say the same thing every time. I ask them where booze got them in the first place. They don't want to go back there."

"Booze got me a few hours' reprieve from my feelings."

"And for some people, that's enough to not want to go back there. Some people want to face their emotions and learn that feeling them isn't as bad as avoiding them. Because the thing about emotions is that they have to have somewhere to go. And if they're not dealt with, they lead to other problems. They leak out and ruin relationships, health, sometimes even careers."

"You sound like my therapist."

Izzy smiled, sipping her Diet Coke. "Thank you."

Gus waited a moment before deciding to tell her what happened at the cabins. The whole tangled mess. She let him get through the whole thing before she spoke. "Wow. And what are you thinking now?"

"I'm mad at Lola, but I'm madder at myself. I thought that if I loved her, it would be enough. But I can't take her away from her family. I know what it feels like to lose your family, and I wouldn't do that to her. She lied to me and that feels bad, but what's worse is knowing that we could never be together. It's like this rollercoaster. I come here and I think I'm over it. I see her and it's like I can't imagine life without her. Now this. I just need to move on."

"I'm sorry, Gus. I really am."

Gus shoved the beer back to the bartender, who swooped in and waved away Gus's money. "Thanks for showing up."

Izzy reached around his shoulder and gave him a one-armed hug. "I will always be here for you. Always."

Gus swiped away a tear as Izzy laid her head on his broad shoulder.

"Always," she said, one more time for good measure.

CHAPTER TWENTY

Rehearsing

"Where is Neil?" Carmen was in the middle of the kitchen, walking from Mike to Ruelle to Felicia, sticking her nose in each one's face, demanding to know where her chef was. Lola stepped into the kitchen from the back patio, glad that she'd been able to leave Daisy at Stella's house. She was going to be here long into the night.

Connie came into the kitchen with some dishes and a dessert order. Carmen turned to her. "Connie, I know you'll be honest with me. He won't answer his phone. He isn't posting on Instagram. Every time I come in here, he's just left or he's running errands. Where is my chef?"

Connie slid the dessert order to Felicia, squinting closely at Carmen's face. "The worst thing you can do at this point is stress. You know what stress does to your skin." Connie wrapped an arm around her friend's shoulder, pushing her towards the patio door. "Come on, I've got a grape skin face mask that I want to try on you. They're super clarifying and brightening."

Connie waved behind her, indicating that someone else would have to take her job while she distracted Carmen with the fruits of her side gig: skin care products based largely on the by-product of a vineyard. She'd just gotten her first order from Barney's in New York.

As soon as Carmen was out the door, Felicia was on Lola. "Where is the food for the wedding? I mean, I don't blame her. There is, like, nothing here. We should at least be making the sauces."

Lola nodded. "Mami's prayer group is coming, and…"

She pointed outside, where a delivery van was turning around. "There's the pig I'm going to roast. And now I have a completely weird question. Who will help me dig a pit to roast the pig?"

Mike, Felicia and Ruelle scattered, suddenly busy with the business of cleaning up and finishing last minute orders.

Rodolfo walked in the door, pouring himself a large glass of water. "Okay, the pizza oven is all shut down." Everyone turned to him with grins on their faces. He shifted, placing his empty water glass down on the counter. "What? What do you want?"

Lola rested on her shovel at the other end of the pit, taking a break while Rodolfo finished digging. It was a shockingly huge endeavor, but Rodolfo, who planned to use the pit himself again, didn't seem to mind helping. Lola, who'd spent more time than she'd care to admit online delving into the mysteries of pit roasting, had explained that the hole in the ground needed to be large enough to fit whatever was cooking as well as a thick cover of coals on all sides. Lola had been surprised by how willing a helper he was, but Rodolfo was one of those people who loved new adventures. He was the perfect foil for Lola tonight as she spoke in rapid-fire Spanish, explaining to him her situation with Gus and Hidalgo as they labored. Sometimes, she thought, it took a relative stranger to sort things out. Someone who had absolutely no skin in the game. The pile of dirt grew as she unburdened herself, breathing heavily with the effort of digging, quietly amused that her side of the pit was shaping up much quicker than Rodolfo's.

"And now, I don't know what to do. Do I try apologizing to Gus again? Let him go? I even called Izzy to see if she'd talked to him. She didn't tell me much. I had to guess most of it but the man has been through hell, and I've made it worse." Lola groaned. "The cabins are so nice. They're beautiful."

Rodolfo took the pitcher of water that she'd brought outside for them and poured himself a large glass, gulping it down. He climbed out of the pit. "There. What's next?"

Lola took his hand to help him up. "The day before the wedding, we can light some coals in the morning and then keep feeding it all day. We put the pig in the night before. I'll stay up with it and keep the coals going."

Rodolfo wiped his face. "I'll do it. I can't have you up all night before your sister's wedding. Also, the smell might bring unwanted visitors." He waved into the dark. "Let me deal with that." As if on cue, a coyote howled, making Rodolfo laugh.

"Are you sure? I can handle it."

Rodolfo finished the last of his water. "No problem. Now, Gus Weaver. You can let him go. You can talk to your papi, or you can talk to him. It doesn't matter. The question is how you feel. Is he someone you can let walk away? If so, then let him go. My mother always said when it came to love there was only one question: does he make you a better person? That's what you need to ask yourself."

*

Ding. Ding. Ding. Ding.

Carmen's fiancé's father, Peter Hollister, a permanently tan, preppy man, stood at the head of the banquet table, clinking his wine glass with a knife. Peter and Estelle, Evan's mother, looked like they belonged in a BMW commercial. According to Evan they moved, like game pieces, from cruise ship to cruise ship, returning home for weddings or Christmas. They said it was wanderlust. Evan said nobody on a cruise ship wandered, and the real reason for their permanent cruising was that they both feared connections. Evan liked to joke that he was marrying Carmen for her family.

The rehearsal dinner was at Wapato Point, overlooking the lake, with candlelight glittering on the tables, elegant with white tablecloths and leafy maiden ferns in shiny gold pots surrounded by flickering tealights. Evan's parents' friends stayed firmly on their side of the room, uniformly bright with a well-moneyed sheen. Evan called them the Rolex set.

Stella, who didn't have local babysitters, had missed most of the speeches as she and Paolo juggled their unhappy babies, standing at the entrance to the restaurant. She'd been around Evan's parents enough to know that this was a speech she didn't want to miss. She'd been there when Estelle had mistaken Carmen for a waitress, when they'd said they had plenty of Mexican friends—their gardeners and cleaning ladies—and when they'd asked why on earth Juan would ever want his children to have Mexican citizenship when they'd achieved the Mexican dream?

"When Evan first told us that he had found someone to marry in Chelan…" Peter's eyes widened comically. "Well, I thought, this will be interesting." He raised his glass to Carmen, who, to her credit, managed a tight grin. Lola noticed Carmen gripping Evan's hand so firmly he winced. "And it has been interesting. Two very different families, from two very different countries, and yet, they have settled." He spread his arms around the room. "On this." He glanced around as if he wasn't exactly sure what "this" was, other than an intrusion on his life. "Welcome to the family, Carmen. We hope your marriage to our son can bridge the cultural differences between us and bring our two families to greater understanding."

Carmen turned to Evan. "Are we countries?"

"I've had it," Evan whispered, standing up.

Lola watched her sister try to pull her fiancé back to his seat. "Evan, not now."

Evan looked down at her. "I should have said something sooner." He tapped his own glass before raising it. "What my dad is trying to say is that sometimes, when you find someone who you think is so different from you, you find yourself. You realize that two people raised oceans apart can find, in each other, home. That no matter where you are from, if you have patience"—he smiled and winked at Carmen—"and Carmen does have a great deal of that, or I wouldn't be here, and at heart, a shared spirit, then you are truly meant to travel this bumpy road together. And thank god for the fact that this lovely woman has consented to put up with me, because I'm quite sure without her, my life would be duller, emptier and undoubtedly more peaceful—but it wouldn't be nearly as happy." He raised his glass. "To the woman who has, shockingly, agreed to become my wife."

*

It was the best time of any party, Lola thought. Most of the guests had left, except the ones that wanted to talk or dance, or had a night away from the children and wanted to make the best of it. Stella, who'd found one of Mami's friends willing to take the kids back to Indigo Bay and sleep in the guest room with the little monsters, was clinging to Paolo like a teenager on the dance floor. Lola waited until Juan was sitting by himself, watching the last few people circulating the party. Most of Evan's guests were staying at Wapato and had moved on to their own houses. The waiters cleared the dishes and blew out the table lanterns.

Juan patted her hand. "Did you have a good time, mi querida?"

"Sí," Lola said, holding her father's hand. "Papi, I know you love me and you want me to be happy."

Her father swirled the wine in his glass, enjoying the red film coating the glass, waiting for his daughter to get to the point. "Sí."

"And I know there was reason to protect me from Gus, when he was young."

Juan waved his hand in front of his face. "We don't need to talk about him."

"Yes, we do, Papi."

"This is your sister's night. A family night."

"Which is why we need to talk about this. Papi, Gus came back to Chelan to start over. He wanted to apologize to you and some other people, and start over. He has worked very hard to become a better man."

"He doesn't need my blessing."

Lola shook her head. "Papi, that's where you're wrong. Working on those cabins was the first job he had back here. And I got him fired. I owe it to him to make it right."

Juan lifted a finger. The candlelight shadowed his handsome face. "But I don't."

"You need to let him apologize."

Juan waved his hand. "I don't owe him anything. He put my child in danger."

"Papi, every family has its patterns, and sometimes we keep them when they are no longer working. I'm the youngest, so I act rashly, and when nobody takes me seriously, I do what I want. I built the cabins to get Carmen's attention. I could have done it differently, but we both fell into those patterns. Carmen will forgive me. But I hurt Gus. I used him to get what I wanted and now I need your help. Papi, please. I want to make this right and break the old patterns. We don't need them anymore."

Lola tried to remember the last time she'd been outside the house with Papi. He found his favorite station on the radio, the one that played Mexican music, and hummed along. He didn't drive anymore because of his memory. Lola thought she ought to make an effort to drive him places more often. He was so happy to be spending time with his daughter. Daisy was in the backseat, happy to be out of Stella's house. She was tired of crying babies. Lola had promised the dog that they'd move back after the wedding.

Lola could ill afford time away from the wedding preparations, but she was afraid Gus would leave town before she'd had chance to make amends. She'd left Mami's prayer group and Rodolfo in charge while she ran this errand. Evan had spirited Carmen away to an all-day spa treatment to give the two of them breathing room. Lola had talked to Hidalgo and confirmed that they were attending the wedding together tomorrow, but he wasn't very forthcoming or warm. Lola thought perhaps she could save things with Hidalgo, but she'd figure it out at the reception, which would be the first time they could see each other. She explained to Hidalgo that she would apologize to Gus because she owed it to him. He seemed to understand.

Lola walked hand in hand with Papi to the Ruiz Construction warehouse in Manson. A cat was sunning itself sleepily on the sidewalk, until it saw Daisy, at which point it hurried across the street and under a fence. Papi turned and put his hand on Lola's shoulder. "Poquita, I'm sorry."

Lola frowned. "Why?"

"The cabins were a good idea. I should have said something to Carmen. Sometimes, with that one, it's easier to listen, but I should remember that I have two daughters."

Lola's eyes filled with tears. "Thank you, Papi."

He nodded. "And now, I talk to Gus alone. Man to man."

This surprised Lola, but she knew Papi's ways. She was just happy that he was willing to talk to Gus at all. "Sure, I'll go down to the beach."

Lola saw Gus coming out from the back of the dark warehouse with a curious look on his face. She clipped a leash on Daisy and headed for the beach, letting the chips fall where they may.

*

Manson Bay Beach was a curved strip of sand on a bay scooped out of the lake. Its shallow depth made it perfect for swimming lessons. Legions of children, including the Alvarez girls, had paddled their way across the beach over the years, eating lunch on the sand while waiting for their parents. Lola walked down to the far side of the park now to let Daisy swim. She chose a piece of driftwood to throw, letting the little dog off the leash, knowing she'd stay fixated on retrieval. There was nobody here to distract her attention from her dog.

Lola had her phone tucked into her back pocket, waiting for Gus to call her and tell her to retrieve her irate father, who Lola knew could very well revert back to his old self, given his Alzheimer's. Lola was just checking her phone when she noticed the stick that she'd thrown was out on the lake, bobbing in the waves. Daisy wasn't on the beach. Lola looked around, wondering if perhaps Daisy had gone off to find some children to play with—but she was nowhere to be seen.

"Daisy!" Lola cried out. Her heart sank when she glimpsed the too familiar sight of Daisy's head bobbing midway out of the bay, her homing instinct in full display once again. She wasn't looking for children. She was looking for home.

Without thinking, Lola dialed Gus's number, hysterically yelling into the phone: "Daisy's swimming across the lake! I can't get her! She'll drown!"

"I'll be right there. Talk to your father."

Gus had apparently handed the phone to Papi, because Papi was now talking to her, using the tone he'd once used when she'd fallen off her bike or had an argument with her best friend. His Spanish reached a spot in Lola that English couldn't. As she listened to him, she saw Gus's truck pulling into the parking lot. Then Gus, sprinting for the Wapato dock. Lola, reading his mind, said goodbye to her father and ran for the dock. Gus was handing a wad of cash to a kid, who shook his head as Lola turned up, and told them to go get the dog. Gus started the engine of the rental speedboat. Lola was untying the lines when the kid told her to get into the boat. Gus reversed the boat and was speeding into the middle of the lake before Lola could say anything to him.

"Hang on."

They couldn't see Daisy until they noticed a kayaker waving their paddle. Lola and Gus approached the kayaker, slowing down until they saw, on the other side, Daisy. She was panting with harsh, rough gasps.

"I can't get her onto the kayak!" the kayaker yelled.

Gus nodded. He tried to approach Daisy, but she swam away. She was exerting herself even more to avoid the two boats.

"Daisy! Daisy! Come on, girl!" Lola called.

"Grab her!" Gus said, making a pass by the dog, who darted away—but not before Lola managed to grab her collar.

Gus put the boat in neutral, scooping the little dog out of the water with one swift move, securing her to the side of his body. Lola grabbed the dog, falling into the back seat, holding on to her.

"Oh my god, Daisy," she said, after they'd thanked the kayaker. "We'll go home today."

"Is that what she wanted?" Gus asked.

Lola nodded. "The only thing my dog wants is to go home. Even if it kills her."

Gus nodded. "I can relate." He turned the boat around, heading back for the dock. "Lola, I made a mistake. I thought that you were my home. That what we had was the only love I'd ever know."

"Did my—"

Gus lifted his hand, kneeling with one leg on the padded seat as he piloted the boat carefully to the dock. "Lola, you're asking your father to accept a man who almost killed his daughter. Enough." He patted his chest. "I can manage my life. I don't need you to make me feel okay about myself. I did that a long time ago. What I need to do is to move on. I think we both need to. Most people don't feel what we did at a young age, but maybe that leaves us stuck in the past."

"Are you saying you regret it? Being together back then?" Lola sounded angrier than she intended.

Gus frowned. "I don't know." He pulled the boat into the dock. The kid at the dock was happy to see the dog. He threw Lola a towel and tied up the boat.

Gus waited until they were on the dock. Lola held the little towel-wrapped dog in her arms, wondering if this was all she was doing—what they were all doing—struggling to cross an impassable lake, trying to make it home.

Gus's voice was rough with emotion. "This is it, Lola. This is our chance to say goodbye."

She gasped involuntarily. "No!"

He kissed her cheek as he passed her and walked up the dock.

As Lola's father walked down the dock, taking the dog from her arms, he took her tears as a sign of relief that her little dog was alive.

CHAPTER TWENTY-ONE

Love Letter

Papi went to his default. Any time one of his daughters wouldn't stop crying, he took them to the Lakeside Drive-thru. A burger and fries in a paper basket, and more importantly, time to talk. He was seated across from Lola, her face swollen from crying. A light breeze blew off the lake. Tomorrow, his middle daughter would be married, and of course, emotions were growing high.

"That night I went to get you from the sheriff's office I was so scared. You looked so small and broken sitting in that chair. I thought you'd never stop crying. I kept thinking, she's in love with a boy who robbed someone. Dios mio. I had a lot of bad nights, and that was one of the worst. Mami was always the one who knew what to do. There was nothing I could say. Nothing I could do."

"I'm sorry." Lola sipped her shake. It hit her head in the wrong way, but she didn't want to feel anything. A headache would be a distraction.

Juan raised his hand. "That's not why I'm telling you. I thought if he got out of prison, you might wait for him. You might get mixed up in some terrible things. Life can hang on the smallest thread. The only thing I knew about Gus's life was that it was on a collision course."

Lola nodded. "I know."

"I hope you can forgive me for this."

Lola was confused as Juan reached into his jacket pocket and handed her a letter. It was on Washington State Department of Corrections stationery. It was dated ten years previously. It was from Gus Weaver.

Dear Lola,

I guess you and the whole town know by now that I'm in jail. It's not really that bad. They have a library and I work in a shop. I'm really sorry that it ended up this way. Maybe you've heard what really happened, but probably not. I was holding the gun but I didn't shoot the guy. I can't believe I wrote that sentence. Me and a gun. I'm not saying what I did was right or that I didn't deserve what I got but I didn't shoot anybody and that's important, I think, for you to know. Nobody in my family has come to see me, but my brother wrote me. You don't have to see me because it's a long, boring drive, but you can write to me at this address. I don't expect you to still love me, but I will always love you. I'm really sorry, Lola. You don't deserve a guy like me. You should have better.

Love always,
Gus.

Tears streamed down Lola's face. Her father had gone to sit in her car while she opened the letter. She faced away from the parking lot, wishing she had read this letter before she'd talked to Gus today. Would it have made any difference? Her heart cracked at the thought of young Gus penning this in his cell or the library. Hoping that she'd read between the lines and be the only person to visit him. Nothing was sadder that this one fact: that Gus had been in jail two hours away, and not one person had gone to see him. Her heart physically ached as she left the drive-thru and opened the door to the car.

"Can you drive?" was the only thing she said to her father.

They drove home in silence, each of them wondering when the pain would finally stop.

CHAPTER TWENTY-TWO

Showdown

When Lola and Papi got out of the car at Orchard House, Mami's prayer group was rushing from the kitchen, spilling out the door as if there was a fire. Papi didn't know what they were doing there, but greeted them all in Spanish with festive waves, assuming it had something to do with the wedding, or quite possibly something he'd forgotten. The ladies hiked up their bulky purses on their shoulders, scurrying to their cars with alacrity. Lola left Daisy in the car, thinking she'd walk Papi in before heading up to the Airstream.

Carmen was in the kitchen, throwing her arms around while the kitchen staff cowered. "There she is! Oh my god, Lola. How could you have done this?"

Papi stared at Carmen, knowing that nothing good could come from his middle daughter when she was like this. "What is it, Carmen?"

Carmen was in tears, she was so furious. "She's ruined my wedding. Ruined it. She fired the chef and they've all been faking it. Pretending he was here." She pointed at Mike, Ruelle and Felicia, who huddled near the ovens. "You're all fired."

"No, you're not," Lola said calmly.

"Do you hear her?" Carmen said to Papi.

Papi looked between his daughters and the staff like a man caught in storm. "Mija. Por favor."

"No. I'm sick of this. She can't get out of this one." Carmen wiped her eyes. "I don't even know if I want you in my wedding."

"Carmen, I love you, but you have no idea what everyone in this kitchen was dealing with. It was abusive. It was sexist, and in the end, it was dangerous. I had a duty to protect all of us. I will cook the best dinner anyone has ever had in this valley. You can't even conceive of the fact that I might be able to do it, but I will, and it will be better than anything that piece of shit Neil could have done."

"He's suing us for breach of contract," Carmen said quietly.

Lola stepped back, shocked by this latest bit. "He wouldn't dare." She pointed up the hill. "He came to my trailer, you know. He grabbed me, and I have a witness."

"Who?" Carmen snapped.

"Gus."

"Oh, great. Gus Weaver's name will go a long way in court."

Lola shook her head. "He protected me, Carmen, which is more than you would do. I'll cook your wedding dinner, but then I'm done here. I'm done with you."

Lola couldn't sleep so she hiked down the hill by the light of her phone flashlight. She'd brought two beers. One for her and one for Rodolfo, who was poking at the coals. A coyote howled long and high in the night sky. Bats flitted low over their heads. Rodolfo didn't seem the least bit surprised to see her. He opened both beers on the edge of the patio, letting the foam drop off before drinking his.

"My sister is getting married today," Lola said, craning her neck to watch a shooting star. Rodolfo nodded. "She's a real bitch, you know."

Rodolfo laughed. "Weddings can get that way."

Lola shook her head. "I don't know. Adella's was a walk in the park compared to this."

Rodolfo exhaled, putting down his beer to stretch his legs. "You weren't in business with her. You know, change is hard. And sometimes people make it harder than it has to be. You want more power, and Carmen doesn't want to give it up. It was never going to be easy."

Lola sipped her beer. "I guess not."

Rodolfo grinned, his teeth white in dark. "Do you think in ten years you're going to be happy that you decided not to go to your sister's wedding?"

Lola took another sip of her beer. "Depends on if she's still a bitch."

The restaurant was closed on a Saturday for the first time since its opening. Lola pushed into the kitchen expecting to find it empty, but Carmen was sitting at the counter, sipping coffee with Adella, who jumped up to hug Lola.

"Wow, you smell like a campfire," Adella said.

"I was up roasting the pig," Lola said, sniffing her hair as she poured herself some coffee. "Which, by the way, is part of the menu, with three kinds of enchiladas, street tacos and a tres leches cake."

Adella studied both sisters. "Sounds amazing."

"Mami's prayer group is cooking a lot of it. Has cooked it," Lola said, staring directly at Carmen. "I'll probably run a food truck—after I leave here, I mean."

"You don't have to leave here," said Carmen in an exhausted voice.

"No, I'm tired of not mattering. But I'll still run the cabins. After you hire Gus back."

Carmen set her coffee cup down so firmly that coffee spilled from the rim. "Oh my god. Today of all days, you've found a way to make it about you."

Lola took a deep breath. She reached over and grabbed her sister's hand. "Car, this is about us. Maybe if I give us some space, we'll do better."

Carmen poured her saucer of coffee back into her cup. Lola was relieved to see a glimmer of a tear in her eyes. She took it as a good sign.

Adella draped her arms around her sisters. "Come on. It's a happy day."

Carmen wiped her cheek with the back of her hand. "It is." She kissed Lola's cheek. "I'm sorry I'm such a bitch sometimes."

Lola sighed. "Come on, now. I wouldn't say that."

CHAPTER TWENTY-THREE

Forever

It was the best part of cooking. Losing herself in the moment, all senses engaged, spices in the air and the feeling that the party was shaping up. The wedding party, in this case. Mami's friends were a hoot. They drank sangria, laughed about the old times, and could taste, gossip and correct spices while not missing a beat. Four tortilla presses were churning out neat tortillas that were quickly fried and stuffed. An entire assembly line, which ended with vast trays of enchiladas being shoved into the oven.

Connie came back with an empty tray. "More mini tacos," she shouted. Outside, people munched on a variety of little filled tacos, ceviche on large tortilla chips, and cups of radishes topped with creamy dressing. Waiters poured a special Hollister Blue Hills sparkling wine. Hidalgo came in to check on his mother, smiling at the activity in the kitchen. He squeezed Lola's hand. "See you outside," he said, as she looked up.

Adella ran down the stairs, grabbing Lola. "Get dressed. We have about ten minutes!"

"I can't," Lola said. "Oh my god. The cake. It has to sit out. Get it out of the fridge!"

"We can carry a cake," said Betty, one of her mother's oldest friends. "Go get dressed."

Walking down the aisle was like coming home. Faces from her past crowded on either side as Lola preceded her sister down the aisle on their back patio. Izzy beamed at her next to Stella. Paolo reached out to squeeze her hand. Mami's prayer group had changed and were fanning themselves under the canopy. Crystal Huttinger, in a flowy dress and Birkenstocks, was wiping her eyes with a well-worn handkerchief.

These were the people who'd lifted them up when Mami had died. The people who had been there to celebrate her quinceañera, her high school graduation, Adella's wedding, and now, Carmen's wedding.

Evan's parents turned when the string quartet began to play the wedding march. Lola moved next to Evan, in front of the seated guests. He leaned down to tell her how nice she looked. Lola wondered if he could smell her hair, scented with delicious roast pig, or see her chipped nail polish, or hear her racing heart. But she was happy. Things were going well.

As Carmen walked down the aisle, Lola noticed Hidalgo respectfully eyeing the bride. He was standing next to Felicia, and Lola saw him nudge her as her sister walked past. Carmen was beaming, surprisingly fragile-looking, with a trembling smile. She reached Evan, and her face relaxed. She looked like the old

Carmen. The one who'd shared bowls of popcorn while they'd watched old movies. Who'd made amazing milkshakes and brought home donuts from the bakery Lola liked in Seattle. Lola felt a stab of tenderness towards her sister. Maybe Carmen needed to be ferocious, because underneath it all she was just as nervous and worried as the rest of them. Lola remembered telling Gus in high school that he wasn't so different from everyone else. Everyone was scared sometimes.

When Carmen turned to hand Lola her bouquet, she squeezed Lola's arm. "Thank you, Lols. For being here."

She hadn't called Lola that in a long, long time.

Plate after plate of food left the kitchen with such precise speed, Lola couldn't believe she'd arranged it. Finally, she left the remaining meal in the hands of the servers and went to join Hidalgo at the head table. When she sat down in her chair, Evan clinked his glass and stood up.

Everyone fell quiet, but it was Carmen who jumped up and made the toast. "To my sister, who made this fabulous feast. Hopefully, I can afford to keep her on as head chef—if she'll stay."

Lola's eyes filled with tears as she raised a glass towards her sister. "Thank you."

"I'm serious," Carmen said. "I love you, sis."

Lola sat down, too tired to eat.

Hidalgo smiled at her. "This is amazing."

"Thank you."

"You did it. You have nothing left to prove."

Lola sighed, thinking of Gus. Thinking of life fitting into grooves. Cooking. Staying here. Having her life settle down, happy, but for the wild love she'd known as a kid. Was it possible to keep some of that going? Or was letting it go just part of growing older? Saying goodbye to those feelings she'd had up in the hollow. Would she always stand at the top of the vineyard and remember the feeling of waiting for Gus, as if the world hung on the moment she could hear his truck, see his smiling face and know that with him, everything was possible?

She turned to Hidalgo. "Hidalgo?"

He squeezed her hand. "Yes. Let's be friends."

Once more, he'd proved the gentleman. She squeezed his hand back.

Lola had completely underestimated how much the cooking would take out of her. She couldn't move an inch. While the rest of the wedding party mingled and danced under the strings of lights hanging from the trees, Lola sipped wine with her feet up on the table. Felicia joined her, gulping down ice water. "Fabulous dinner. You did it."

Lola lifted her glass. "We did. Cheers."

Felicia clinked her water glass. "Cheers. So. I have a completely awkward question that I would never ask you, but I know how you feel, so here goes." She covered her eyes. "Hidalgo."

"What?"

Felicia peered through her fingers. "I think he's cute."

"Oh god."

"Okay, awkward. I just thought that you were, you know…"

"Well, he is cute."

"I'm sorry. I just thought you were…"

Lola wrinkled her nose. "I was what?"

"In love with Gus."

Lola turned to Felicia in a daze. She was dead tired. Melancholy. Happy. Relieved to finally hear the words. She was madly in love with the same boy who had broken her heart ten years earlier. She was in love with Gus Weaver, and always would be. Lola stood up. She couldn't put on her shoes. She hobbled, barefoot, away from the dancing.

"But what about…?" Felicia remained at the table.

Lola turned around, waved her hand. "Oh yeah. I think he likes you, too. Go for it. He is cute. And nice."

She was in love with Gus Weaver. It was as simple and obvious as the blue sky. Why had she fought it so hard? Had she been holding onto old anger? Trying to shape herself into the kind of person who chose the safer route? Afraid of losing herself? Whatever it was, Lola knew the sun could not come up on another day without her saying the words she'd been waiting ten years to speak.

Lola knew that Gus lived above the salon, but there was a security door, and the buzzer was a mess of broken wires that looked as though it had never worked. Lola stood barefoot on the pavement, still warm from the sun. She wore her silver bridesmaid dress as she stood under a pool of light from the streetlight. Gus hadn't answered his phone or responded to her texts. She didn't even know which unit was his. Or if he was home.

"Gus!" she yelled, her face turned up towards the building. "Gus Weaver!" She thought she saw a flicker behind the blinds. "Gus, I'm not living in the past. I've always known you, and I've always loved you. I always will. Always."

"Go to bed!" someone yelled from another window.

"I'm sorry for what happened. It was wrong. And I can't promise I'll never make mistakes, but I'll always be honest. I promise."

The blinds came up. A tall figure pulled open a window. "Who's down there?"

"Do a lot of girls stand on the sidewalk professing their love for you?" Lola asked.

Gus shrugged. "Truthfully, it's getting old."

"Then maybe you should let me inside."

Gus scratched his bare torso. "Maybe I should." He shut the window and Lola wondered what, exactly, was going to happen. This would be life with Gus. Never sure what was going to happen. Full of surprises. Spontaneity. The life she wanted. She was one hundred percent sure. For once in her life Lola knew, without a doubt, exactly what she wanted.

CHAPTER TWENTY-FOUR

Winterfesting

Nothing happened. Lola had just served her heart up on a platter and here she was, alone. She paced up and down the sidewalk, trying not to think of what her bare feet were touching. She rubbed her exposed shoulders, not because she was cold, but because it was late and she was tired. And because she'd just offered to share her life, her heart, her everything with someone who may or may not be coming down the stairs to take her up on the offer. Just when she was thinking about driving home and falling into bed, the glass door beside Twig cracked open.

Gus came outside. He was wearing his Levi's and nothing else. A particularly cruel choice, if he was going to turn her down.

"I'm sorry," he said.

"Oh." It was all she could manage.

He lifted his hand, staying far enough away to convey his answer. "I'm sorry I took so long."

"You were getting dressed?"

"That's not what I meant. I'm sorry I didn't come here sooner."

She sighed. "Maybe we would have messed it up."

He nodded. "Probably."

"I went to the sheriff's station, that night. My dad came and got me and I thought it was the end of the world."

"I'm so sorry."

"That's not why I am telling you. I'm telling you because I want you to know that I was there. I want you to know that someone was there for you that night." She took a deep breath. "And then, when I didn't hear from you, I thought you gave up on me."

"Never." He smiled and her heart just about leaped out her chest. He ran a hand across his chest, grinning down at himself, as if he'd just realized. "I went to talk to my brother today." He scratched his head. "He's fine. All this time, I'm thinking I left him and he's going to be furious and a mess, and he's got a nice little house and a girlfriend. His own business. He's an electrician."

"That's good."

Gus nodded. "Yeah. Jeremy calls it a Jesus complex. When you think people are reliant on you and it turns out, they're perfectly fine on their own and all you're worrying about is just, well, stupid." He looked up at the dark sky, shot through with winking stars. "It made me realize that I'd made amends with everyone and asked for forgiveness, but I hadn't forgiven myself."

"For what?"

Gus sighed. "For leaving you. Deserting my brother. Getting arrested in the first place. My mom always used to say I was supposed to be the man of the family, and then I left and I didn't come back."

"You can't ask a kid to be the man of the family."

Gus wiped away a tear. "I know."

"My dad finally gave me your letter. Yesterday."

"Wait, what? The one I wrote from jail?"

"Yes. He thought it would set me back. So he kept it."

Gus shook his head before nodding. "Bit late."

Lola shook her head. "No. It's not. In some ways, I'm glad I didn't get it at the time. Because if we'd gotten back together, we wouldn't be here now."

"And where's here?"

Lola took a deep breath and crossed the pavement, throwing her arms around Gus and kissing him. His lips felt firm and resistant at first, before he lifted her up and crushed her against him. She felt every muscle in his body respond to her.

A pickup full of teens drove past, honking their horn. "Get a room!" Hysterical laughter from the truck echoed down the street.

Gus laughed. "I have a room right up there. It's nothing fancy, but…"

Before he could finish the thought, Lola was dragging him up the stairs. They entered the room, tossing off their clothes as if they were on fire, and dove into each other, a tangle of limbs that did not unwind for a very long time.

The sisters had matching scissors. Carmen had insisted upon it. Daisy wore a wreath of flowers around her neck, and the first guests to stay in the cabins had their pictures taken with champagne. Gus would be up to his eyeballs in orders and Hidalgo, who was indeed now dating Felicia, was forming a second company with him, dedicated to nothing but tiny cabins.

"One, two, three!" Carmen and Lola said, cutting the ribbon on the middle cabin.

Afterwards, the guests mingled. Gus's brother, Jacob, was there, inspecting the wiring and chatting with Gus about how they'd wire the new cabins. Jacob's girlfriend, who was a veterinarian student, threw sticks for Daisy. She'd heard about Daisy's bolting issue in the lake and had brought a doggie life vest, suggesting that maybe Daisy should have it on when she went to the beach.

Felicia was very excited about bringing baked goods up in the morning from the restaurant via the new golf cart, something Carmen had bought in the hopes that she could also use it to ferry food and wine between the restaurant and her office, which was higher up in the vineyard. The golf cart, festooned with ribbons, was being used right now as a handy serving place for the cake and drinks. The Blue Hills winery staff mingled with friends and family in a congenial group.

After a half hour, Carmen tooted the golf cart horn and raised her glass. "Since we have our first paying guests, thanks to Lola's blog, let's let them enjoy their beautiful cabins. I want to thank my sister, Lola, who managed to get this grand project done, along with Gus Weaver, despite my fear of branching out. I just want to say: thank god for a different perspective, and mostly, for my sister!"

As she passed Lola, she hugged her. "Not my little sister. My sister."

Lola grabbed her sister's arm, picking her way down the path in her sandals, making sure Gus was coming. "But you had to say it, didn't you?"

"Oh yes. I'm still me."

Juan grabbed Gus's arm as they followed the women. "If you want to have a peaceful life, don't have daughters."

"I'll try to remember that, sir."

"Here you go." Lola handed a family a bag of churros, fresh from the deep fryer. The cinnamon-scented pastries filled the frozen air with a festive smell. The food truck, painted with colorful flowers and a brilliant blue lake, was a beautiful addition to Winterfest, Chelan's snow festival, meant to bring in visitors during the slow winter months. Lola enjoyed the break from the restaurant, which only served dinner in the winter season, featuring her Mexican-themed menu which brought locals year-round. She and Carmen had been working on bringing in more winter weddings, but it had proved harder than they'd both thought.

"One churro please, ma'am." Lola looked up from the deep fryer. Gus smiled, blowing into his hands in the cold, his face ruddy over the collar of his down jacket. He'd let a bit of the beard grow back, until he had a rakish stubble that suited him.

"You're going to have to wait for the next batch, sir." The down coat had been her Christmas gift to him. She was happy to see him in it. It came in handy during their winter drives up in the hills in the old truck, looking for a piece of land for him to build a house. Their house. She'd already sketched out a garden. Sometimes she wondered if they'd gotten pickier just to keep the long drives going.

Daisy, curled up on the driver's seat of the food truck, waiting for scraps, whined when she heard Gus's voice. "How about if I take her for a walk?"

"She'd love that."

Lola got Daisy's leash and Gus opened the door, grabbing for the little dog's collar. Daisy slipped out of his hand, darting straight for the park. Lola and Gus exchanged looks before racing after the dog. By the time Lola had reached the beach, the dog was in the water. Gus was still taking off his jacket when Lola dashed into the water. She grabbed the dog before she could make it very far. These days, Daisy didn't seem to try that hard. She was just making a statement. Lola scooped the dog up in her arms. "Daisy, my god. We're together. This is home."

Gus was waiting with a towel when Lola waded out of the water. He had his truck parked nearby and they ran to it. Luckily, he'd had the heater fixed and it warmed up quickly while Lola stripped out of her sopping clothes, wrapping herself in Gus's coat and an old blanket.

Daisy seemed quite pleased to be sitting between the two of them.

"Daisy, girl, you sure know how to get your way," Gus said, patting the dog's head.

Lola grinned, looking between the dog and the man, then beyond, the cracked dashboard and the lake. "You know what? It's okay. This is really everything I want. A crazy dog. A wonderful man." She waved her hand at the lake. "All this. I mean, what more do we want from life?"

"Maybe," Gus said, his hand on the gear shift. "We could wreck it all by having kids. What's life without a little risk?"

Lola looked back at him, eyes brimming with tears. "Gus, I'll take the odds with you. Every time. I pick you."

Gus kissed her back, and it felt like the beginning of forever.

A Letter from Ellyn

Hello and thanks for reading!

I'm thrilled you've read *Long Walk Home*. If you enjoyed it, and want to keep up with my new releases, sign up at the following link. Your email address will never be shared and you can unsubscribe at any time.

www.bookouture.com/ellyn-oaksmith

I really hope you loved *Long Walk Home* and if you did, I would be grateful if you could write a review. It's a great way to help other readers discover my books.

There are two other books featuring the Alvarez family. Lola's sister, Carmen (*Summer at Orchard House*), and their friend, Stella (*Promises at Indigo Bay*), each have their own books set in my beloved Chelan.

Writing book three in this series was rewarding because the world of Blue Hills became very familiar and, to be honest, writing was a lovely escape from 2020. All the little things that I'd unwittingly layered throughout books one and two—friendships, Lola's conflicts with Carmen, and the differences in the sisters' temperaments—could all come into play. I recently heard an author talking about writing a series who said, "Don't leave anything on the table," meaning, don't save things for later books. I have never done that, but it's amazing, as you write more in a world, how many threads you can pick up in subsequent books. If I didn't know better, I'd say it was very clever of me, but it's just the nature of creating a world. As in life, there will be connections and circling back to the past.

It was also fun to write a dog character. I'm looking forward to getting my own rescue dog. Stay tuned to hear more about that adventure.

I'd love to hear from you—a great way to keep in touch is on my Facebook page, through Twitter, Goodreads or my website. I also have a really fun, chatty Readers Group on Facebook.

Thanks and happy reading,
Ellyn Oaksmith

Find me on:

ellynoaksmith

EllynOaksmith

@EllynOaksmith

EllynOaksmith.com

Acknowledgements

A book is the tip of an iceberg. Bookouture is a special little island of cheerleaders and tireless promoters who are the unicorns of publishing. Hannah Bond set this book on its course while Therese Keating gracefully took the hand off. I'm lucky to be edited by them both. Sarah Hardy is the busiest bee in promotion. I'm not sure she sleeps. Kim Nash is the girlfriend in publishing that everyone needs and who I'm lucky to know. Alex Holmes is the person who somehow shepherds I don't even know how many books out into the world with an attention to detail that boggles the mind. Gabrielle Chant's copyedits annoyed the hell out of me because she's so good. She really ups my game. I've grown even closer to my family this year. My sister Liz, brother Jim and mom, Gwen. Dad, we lost you this year but you're never very far. We all miss you so very, very much. Good thing we left nothing unsaid. My writing group has expanded and for that I'm thankful. As always, AMS/CES/SMS, you're everything. Love you so much. Honk.

Made in the USA
Las Vegas, NV
03 September 2021